KING

OF A

SMALL

WORLD

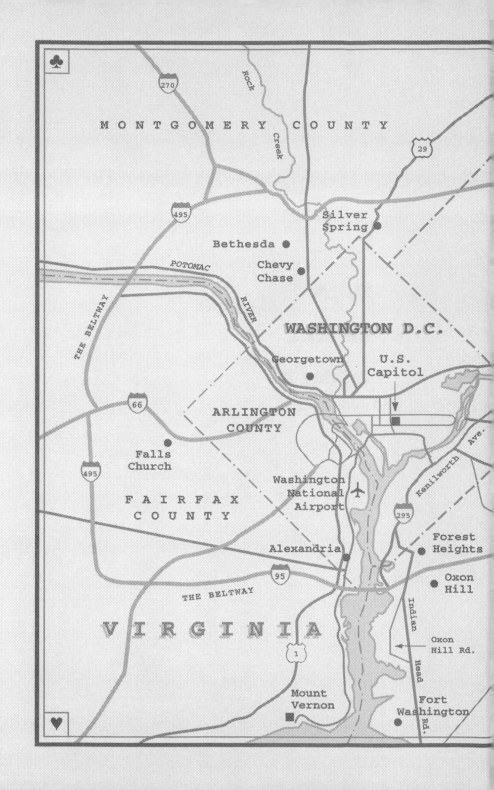

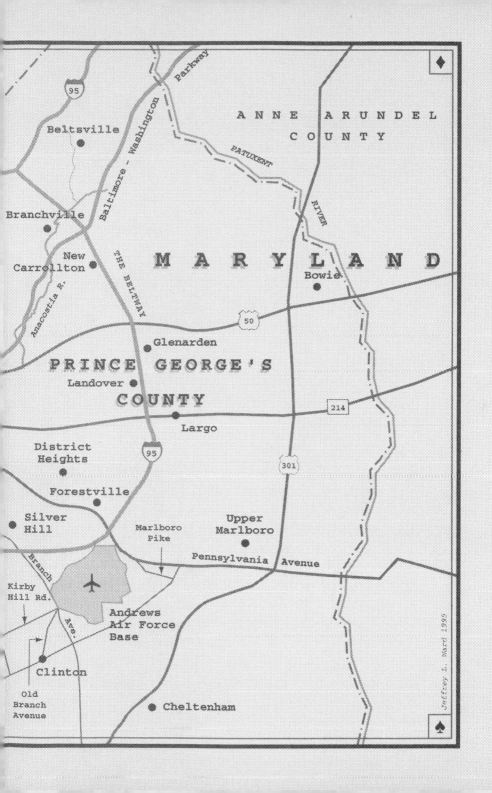

KING
OF A
SMALL
WORLD

RICK BENNET

ARCADE PUBLISHING • NEW YORK

Library of Congress Cataloging-in-Publication Data

Bennet, Rick.
    King of a small world / by Rick Bennet. —1st ed.
       p.   cm.
    ISBN 1-55970-284-2
    I. Title.
    PS3552.E54753K56   1995
    813'.54—dc20   94-42742

Published in the United States by Arcade Publishing, Inc.
Distributed by Little, Brown and Company

10 9 8 7 6 5 4 3 2 1

BP

PRINTED IN THE UNITED STATES OF AMERICA

(2.00)

For my family for their support through the years; for my poker brother, Cong Do, for always believing in me; and of course this, and my life, for my son, Sean Lord Macaulay Bennet.

My thanks also to Frances Jalet-Miller, for perseverance beyond the call of duty.

PART ONE

ONE

I look in the mirror and scare myself. My hair is stringy, my eyes are mapped by red lines, and my skin is the color of newspaper. But I just piss out my ninth or tenth or whatever cup of coffee it is, wash my hands, wash my face, comb my hair, and step back out to the smoke and chip-clicking drone of an all-night card game.

The dealer looks up at me. She's a wrinkle-eyed old Chinese woman wearing a ball cap. She doesn't need to voice the question — do I want a hand? I nod. She knows. Cards come my way as I flip an ante into the pot.

The other players are on auto-pilot. We started at seven in the evening, it's now two in the morning, and they have the intense look of people well settled into a long night. Not rookies, my opponents, but not pros, either. Only a few completely track the exposed cards to know which ones are no longer available. Only I could tell you the odds of hitting a flush draw with two cards coming and three of your suit dead in other hands.

We're in the rec room of a big house in northern Virginia owned by a criminal defense attorney, Bobby "Lotto" Johnson. He got that nickname because whenever you ask what he's doing these days, he'll say he's waiting for his number to come in, which is a joke, because he's already rich. He's a skinny, nervous man with dark, curly hair. Overly friendly and fast talking. Divorced. Three kids living with their mother. He told me his family had owned tobacco farms in Virginia for two hundred years until they sold the land to developers the week he was born. He goes to Harvard but ends up working for drug dealers. For fun, I think. Just like he hosts this poker game for fun. Everyone else holding games takes the standard three dollars per pot for their services, but not Bobby Lotto. He's not in it for the money, he just likes having the game here. Likes having the characters over. Once a month for a few months now. This is the first time I've come.

"Friendly game," I say sarcastically, because it's quiet and everyone's in a bad mood.

"Not to me," says Grizzly with a laugh. Grizzly is a building contractor. Silver-haired and strongly built. Old-time white southern Marylander. He's known me my whole life. Friend of my mom's. Used to date her a bit.

"I like games like this," says another player, an Arab with a British accent. "Fuck that friendly poker."

"Watch your language, man," I say to him. "We got a woman present." I wink at the dealer. She smiles.

An obese middle-aged white woman at the other end of the table, a schoolteacher, says to me, "I'm not a woman too, Joey? We can go in the back room right now and I'll show you all the woman you can handle!" She shakes her big tits into the table and everyone jumps to keep their coffee from spilling. "You like them skeleton girls," she says. "They just breadsticks, honey. I'm a whole loaf."

"You're too much for me," I say.

"You know it, sweet-cheeks," she says, dropping a lipsticked cigarette butt into an empty beer bottle.

Bobby Lotto gets up and puts on a tape. Some jazz thing. He's into jazz. Into nightlife. Into gambling. A rich lawyer who loves to sit here surrounded by this odd-and-end crew. Lets himself get beat

4

for bad loans to every railbird on the circuit because he likes having them around. Likes the scene. Loves any old black-and-white movie with gambling in it. That's something we have in common.

He's wearing a fedora. Has a cigarette dangling from his mouth. Says, "Hey, Joey, Monday at the Art House, downtown, there's a Paul Newman double feature. *The Hustler* and *Cool Hand Luke*. Want to meet me for the matinee?"

"You asking me out?"

"You're prettier than most women I know."

"Okay, stud."

"I'm serious."

"Okay. I'll meet you there. But I didn't know you worker bee types could take an afternoon off."

"Not everyone with a job is a slave."

"Tell yourself that."

The cards get shuffled and dealt and played. Chips go in, pots come back. Hours pass. I take my breaks, every thirty minutes or so. Step outside. Smoke a cigarette. Clear my head. Feel the weather.

Lotto's got a big backyard. A bench under an oak tree on which I can sit on this Indian Summer night and see the stars. The waitress Lotto's hired for the evening keeps me company. Fills me in on the other games she works. I note the info, staying on top of the ever-changing action.

I lie back on the bench, eyes closed, breathing that sweet fresh air. A long moment passes. I'm startled by a touch — the waitress stroking my hair. Like Grizzly, she's known me forever. She smiles. I smile, too, saying, "Leave my hair alone."

"You used to be the nicest boy," she says, still playing with my hair, knowing me too well to fall for the tough act. "I remember one day, you were only seven or eight, and I came over to your mom's just to be with someone because I was sad over something some man did, I don't even remember what, and you took one look at me, and even though I hadn't said anything and was trying not to show anything, you came right over with such a look on your face, and hugged me and made me sit down, and then you went and got your mom, and some cookies, I think. My God, what a precious child you were."

I'm trying, but I can't remember that day.

"Me and your mom," she said, "we used to talk about what you were going to be when you grew up. She loved to think about what you might be. She thought maybe a movie star, who'd take her off to Beverly Hills. I thought you would be a doctor, because you were so smart."

I smile. Nod. "Instead I turned out *baaad.*"

"No."

"Some people think so."

"It is funny how you play cards like you do."

I laugh. Close my eyes. Let her stroke my hair like my mom used to. Try to remember the little boy women say I was.

Back inside, the jazz plays on and on and it's background to the thirty hands an hour a good dealer can get out. Every hand's a story, every card a chapter.

My toes are tapping from caffeine and music and a chocolate-bar sugar rush. Four A.M., then five and six. I know how I stay up this long — I'm a youngster and I slept all day. But there's no one at this table without fifteen years on me, no one here who doesn't have a job getting them out of bed in the morning. What keeps them going? The action.

Picture it:

Mikey the Cop's on a roll. Mikey's a scraggly-haired, broad-bottomed Maryland state trooper. Also called Mikey Too Long, because he always ends up saying "I've played too long, I got to get home, I've played too long." Also too long in making up his mind when he plays. One of those guys who thinks forever about a decision he gets wrong anyway.

He's got more than two thousand dollars in front of him, which is a good hit for a game this size, of fifteen- and thirty-dollar bets. He's a bad player and a real addict whose last win no one can re-

6

member, but the deck has hit him on the head and he's loving life and thinking he's good. Though usually quiet, he's sitting next to me now talking my ear off. Talking about strategy. In a low voice, like we got to keep things secret. Talking about the mistakes people make. But not people like us, he says. Not people like us. People like Grizzly, who's sitting close enough to hear Mikey's comments. Grizzly, who in spite of his easygoing nature is getting numb-eyed over his losses tonight.

Mikey's been talking about "us." How good "we" are. So when he bets out early in a hand and I, with nothing, raise, he nods like a wizened sage and says, "Take it, Joey." He's trying to play good. Thinks he suddenly knows how.

I say, "Thanks," and rake in the pot while flipping over my cards, showing the bluff. Rubbing his face in it because of how he had talked about Grizzly. He gets a bit of a funny look, but says nothing.

Five minutes later he bets at a small pot. I raise. Everyone else folds. He thinks about it, does that sagely nodding thing again, mucks his hand again. I rake in the pot again, flip over my cards showing a bluff again.

I say, "Mikey, what you doing?"

I'm jerking his chain. He was confident and playing well; now he's rattled, which is where I want him.

Ten or fifteen minutes later I've got a king showing, he's got a queen showing, I bet and he calls. I keep betting and he keeps calling as the other cards come, and then I show him exactly what he should have known I had — a pair of kings. He's got what I knew he had — a pair of queens. Why did he pay me off? Fear. The bluffs I made earlier win money for me now.

The Arab asshole says something about Mikey paying off like a slot machine. He says, "Ka-ching, ka-ching." A couple of people laugh. Mikey's fingers shake. The obese woman belches and says to him, "Come here, Mikey. I'll cheer you up."

Mikey says, "Why do we let him"— me —"play? Why?" That's an unusually bitter comment from Mikey. He generally takes his pounding pretty well.

Bobby Lotto says, "I was reading this book, called *Homicide*. It's about detectives in Baltimore. There's a story in there about a guy who was always picking up the cash at dice games and running away with it. He was famous for doing this, and one day the other guys at the dice game got fed up and shot him in the back as he ran, killing him. The cops asked the shooters, if this guy was famous for running away with the pot, why did they let him play? And the shooters, dumbfounded by the question, said, 'This is America.'"

I laugh. It's funny.

The jazz keeps coming, the hands keep playing, the hours keep passing. Seven o'clock in the morning, eight o'clock, nine o'clock.

Mikey is such a mess now he's dusting off his chips as fast as he can. Everyone he beat earlier beats him now. He's slumping in his chair looking ready to cry. Throwing his chips in every pot, start to finish, like he doesn't care anymore, like it doesn't make any difference. That's what you tell yourself when you've lost a lot — that it doesn't matter. That's what you tell yourself.

Mikey goes broke, then begs Lotto to take a second check. Begging so loud we all get uncomfortable. Lotto says no.

Mikey turns to the rest of us. Asks us to take the check.

People avoid eye contact with him. Make up little excuses.

Finally he leaves, slouching on out. On home. Saying as he goes, "I played too long. I should have quit when I was ahead. I always play too long."

I feel sorry for him. "He's like a pregnant woman," I say, shaking my head sadly.

"What's that?" Lotto asks.

"Somebody you don't want to play with because it's bad luck to beat them," Grizzly explains for me.

An hour later the obese woman is nodding off. Says she's done. Grizzly left a few minutes ago. Everyone else? Lotto asks.

We nod. It's been a long enough night.

I stand, stretch way back, and yawn from deep down in my chest. "God*damn!*" I say, shaking my head.

Lotto has cashed out everyone except me and Kenny Jones, saving us, the night's biggest winners, for last, as is poker tradition. Kenny, here all night without saying ten words to me, now asks, "How did you do?"

"Eighteen hundred."

"I won twenty-four," he says proudly.

"I'm happy for you," I say mockingly.

He eyes me. His broad-foreheaded, narrow-mouthed, redneck-looking self eyes me. He won the most tonight and feels good. Loves life. Eyes me.

"What?" I ask him.

"You want to keep playing? Pot-limit?"

"Heads up?"

He nods.

I think half a second. Shrug okay.

"What's going on?" Lotto asks.

"Looks like we're going to play pot-limit," I say.

Lotto nods and sits back down to watch. One-on-one pot-limit challenges are rare items. And there's more to this one than meets the eye.

"Let me piss first," I say, wanting to think about this for a second. Maybe I'm being reckless.

In the bathroom with the door closed, I douse my face with cold water and sit on the toilet and wonder what he's doing. I think of Kenny Jones as the Grey-man. Grey hair, grey eyes, grey skin. Not real tall. Pudgy and sagging. Seems to always be wearing Redskins paraphernalia. He's a longtime gambling operator. He's run sports books, craps tables, closet slots, home games, and charity casinos. Keeps Bobby Lotto on retainer.

Like Grizzly, Kenny's been my mother's friend my whole life; unlike Grizzly, he's never been mine. We've always had an unspoken

9

mutual dislike. And now he's challenging me to heads-up pot-limit? Kenny's no great player. Solid. Tight. But not particularly creative. Not particularly aggressive. Which means his game's not particularly suited to heads-up play, especially pot-limit. Which means maybe I'm not the reckless one. Maybe he is. Maybe he was just feeling so good about having won big tonight that he asked if I wanted to play before considering that maybe I did. Maybe he thought because I'm so much younger, that I'd be scared of a big game. Maybe he asked because he didn't think there was any chance I'd say yes, leaving him to go around padding his rep saying, "Yeah, I challenged Joey heads-up but he wouldn't go for it."

I go back out. Sit down. Say, "Come on."

The betting in pot-limit is simple — you can bet an amount equal to the size of the pot. If the pot is a hundred bucks, that's how much you can bet. Things get big fast. I have a saying about the game, a true one — cards are good, but balls are better.

First hand and the tone is set: he bets ten dollars, and without even looking at my cards — what do they matter?— I raise him. He thinks about it, and folds. Of course. It's a new game. A bigger game. First hand of a dangerous game. In pot-limit, on any given hand you can lose every dollar in front of you. Who wants to mess up on the first hand? Who wants to dive right in? His natural desire is to start out a bit conservative until he feels comfortable. Hell, Kenny's desire is always to be conservative. That's why I didn't need to look at my cards. I knew, just from the situation, that he wasn't prepared to get involved. His instincts were probably screaming that I didn't have anything, but he just wasn't ready to gamble. I'm ready to gamble. Everyone, in life and poker, has good points and bad points. One of my good ones is that I don't give a *fuck* about money when I'm playing. That part of my brain is missing.

Some more hands go this way. I'm pushing every pot. He's afraid to tangle. He's the one who suggested we play pot-limit, maybe thinking I'd be unnerved, but he's the one choking. He wants to chase a little, but I'm not letting him. He keeps hoping I'll relent, but I don't.

Then he gets some good cards, and I can't fight him, so I get out of his way. There's no difference between money you don't lose and money you win. Spends the same.

But when it's my turn for some good cards, and because, his aggressiveness having picked up, he's in the habit of betting, I sit back. Seduce him. Let him bet ten. Let him bet thirty. Let him bet ninety. Then I step out and raise, two-seventy. He calls without thinking. He's not happy about calling, but he's not sad, either. That tells me something. Tells me he's on a draw. A straight draw, it appears, in this case.

The sixth card comes and we both check. If he's on a draw, he isn't going to fold now, so if I bet, I'd just be risking more money on a hand decided now by pure luck. I've only got the one big pair I started with. If he's got a small pair with that straight draw, then he has even more outs. I'm a favorite, but not as big as I want to be. This isn't the hand I'm looking to finish him off with.

The last card comes face down. I don't look at mine. It isn't too relevant, and I don't want to take my eyes off him. I can't afford to miss his reaction to his own last card.

He looks at that card. Considers. And bets, eight hundred.

I close my eyes a moment. Think. Feel.

Good poker is hard work. Technical skills, you might say. Learning the odds, remembering exposed cards, having the discipline to fold, maintaining attentiveness to your opponent's appearance.

Great poker is courage. Technical skills will get you through most poker situations because most poker situations don't give rise to your emotions. But the big decisions do. By definition, you might even say. You certainly want to keep your emotions down, but if they do come up, as they will at key moments, you have to deal with them. And the secret to finding the truth in emotional moments is this: your conscious fear will mirror your subconscious knowledge. If your subconscious knows your opponent is bluffing, your conscious will fear that he isn't. And then, if you have strength, pride, character, or whatever you want to call it, you'll conquer that fear, and act on what you *know* to be the truth.

Here, now, I clear my mind. With Kenny Jones betting eight hundred at me in a heads-up pot-limit game — a man and an amount and a situation any of which alone would bring forth my emotions, all of which together unbelievably pressure me — what do I fear?

The shame sure to follow his turning over nothing after I fold, showing that he outplayed me, that I choked under the pressure, as he must have been thinking I would when he first challenged me to this match. It wouldn't matter if no one else knew I'd choked. He, a man who hates and despises me, would know it. That's my truest fear on this hand — the humiliation of being bluffed. That's the fear I need to conquer.

I say, "Good hand, Kenny," and throw my cards away.

He doesn't show what he had. Just stacks the chips when the pot goes his way. But the fact that he isn't real happy as he stacks them tells me I made the right decision. Though he won the pot, he's not real happy. He wanted to win more. Plus, if he had been bluffing, he would have loved to show it.

Kenny gets a bit of a run of cards after that, but I don't bite for anything, and don't lose much. He's feeling a little better about things, but I'm actually still ahead since we started. About five hundred ahead. But he does have some momentum, so I slow the game down. Fake longer decisions. Eat an omelette the waitress brings. Drink my juice.

Then I get a series of better hands, and he pays off with some losing hands, and suddenly the momentum switches, and suddenly I'm betting every time, boom boom boom, good cards or not, and he's one step behind me. These aren't big pots, but they add up. Thirty bucks many times; a hundred-and-twenty bucks a couple of times; four hundred once.

And then, as the dealer shuffles, I see something very important — Kenny counting his chips. He has them in hundred-dollar stacks, and he's got nineteen stacks left. Counting chips usually just means a player is bored. I do it a lot myself. But this isn't a boredom count. And just that fast do I know I have him.

If you had just won a lot of money, what is the one thing you would least want to do?

Lose it back.

And what fear is going to enter your head if you lose *some* of it back?

That you'll lose *all* of it back.

And who would you most fear losing it back to?

Someone you hate, like he hates me. That emotion weighs on him. The emotional desire to beat me. It's what gave rise to this game to begin with.

Kenny Jones feels stupid. I know he does. He played all night, had great luck, hit big, and then after the game was over, when he could have just gone home, he challenged the best player he knows. By counting his chips he tells me he knows he's losing, and is worried about it. He's no longer playing to win, he's playing to not lose. To not lose to a kid half his age. To not lose to a kid he used to smugly say would never catch on to the game. To not lose to a kid who's had more and better-looking women than he could ever dream about.

My killer instinct rises. I slip into The Zone. It's a feeling of speed and power and control. A feeling that I'm going to hammer somebody. I'm all knowing, all seeing, all hitting.

I keep up the pressure, betting him quickly. Giving him no chance to think. Dazing him into not realizing how fast the hands are going. Putting on him the burden of deciding whether there will be a confrontation. And because he's now playing to not lose, he plays backward. Calls when he fears I'm bluffing, folds when he fears I'm not. And he's wrong every time. That's human nature. Your fears will always lead you down the wrong path. There's a slender difference between fearing to lose and wanting to win. There's a huge difference.

I whittle him down. He's got eighteen hundred, then seventeen, sixteen, fifteen, fourteen. He's rubbing his face, putting his hands over his eyes to block everything out. Lighting cigarettes but forgetting to smoke them. Shaking his head in frustration at his "bad luck." And when he enters the next stage, a pathetic combination of it-doesn't-matter and maybe-I'll-get-lucky, I'm waiting for him. The weight of his loss is crushing him. Not just the money loss. Not just the rep loss, either, though he knows how quickly word of this game will spread. But also the emotional loss. To me. His character lost to mine. This longtime gambling operator is losing to a kid he taught how to play.

The main thing now, for me, is to keep the luck out of it. That's what he wants. To hide in the game's luck. To avoid making decisions for himself, and have the deck make them for him. He doesn't want to admit he got outplayed. He wants to blame luck.

We play a few hands. He makes some loose bets and raises. I back down, though I might have marginally better hands, because I'm looking for a killer hand. He's looking for a chance to put all his chips in. I don't want that to happen until I've got him locked up.

By the fifth card of the next hand, I have aces and jacks, and bet two-seventy, which he calls. He has a nine, seven, and four showing. I'm not sure where he's at, but the only way he could have me beat is with nines, sevens, or fours in the hole, to make three-of-a-kind, and I don't put him on a hand that big played this slow.

But his next card is a nine. Pairs his door card. The last thing I want to see in this spot.

His face-up pair of nines makes him first to act and he quickly bets eight hundred dollars. And now I've really got to bear down. This is the whole thing. The whole game. If he's bluffing and I fold, his confidence is restored. If he isn't bluffing and I call, his bankroll is restored. He only has four hundred more dollars in front of him. He'll bet that on the last card regardless.

I stretch, yawn, and try to relax. I think it out. But this is an easier decision. For whatever reason, I'm feeling little emotion, and so can focus on his emotions. That fold I made when he hit his straight boosted my confidence so high that now I don't have to conquer any fears because I don't have any. And I *know* he's bluffing. He was happy to bet when that nine hit only because he knew it was the scariest card he could get. He's been looking for a chance to get his chips in the pot. To get back in the game, or get it over with.

I'm so confident that second nine didn't beat me, I don't just call, I raise. I put twelve hundred out there, to get his last four hundred in the pot. To turn him out.

He nods, puts out that four hundred, and sits up. The dealer gives us our last cards, which we both turn face up because there can be no more betting.

He was drawing to an inside straight, or the third nine, neither of which he got. He loses.

He acts cool. Says, "Good game, Joey." I just nod a thanks. Voicing it would sound unsportsmanlike.

He leaves, hiding his dejection. When he gets alone it'll hit him. Real hard. I know. I've been there. Never on this scale, of course. At the small games where I first started playing. But the feeling is the same. He didn't go through anything tonight I haven't been through before. The only difference being that I learned when I suffered. I didn't long blame luck. Poker is all about having the courage to confront the truth. To admit to yourself what you know to be true, no matter how much you wish it weren't. Kenny Jones lacked that courage. He faded. He folded his money instead of his cards. Poker fatal.

I let out a deep breath. Throw a fist in the air.

I have fifty-four hundred dollars in chips in front of me. Lotto takes a few minutes to count it, then pulls out a wad of cash. A lot of private games have checks get passed around. I expect to get a few now, the deal being that I'll accept them as payment, but that Lotto is still ultimately responsible for them.

"Who'd you get paper from?" I ask.

"Grizzly, and Mikey the Cop."

"I'll take Grizzly's."

"Not Mikey's?"

"Sweat it, sucker. His check hasn't been good for months." Lotto shakes his head sadly. Gives me Grizzly's check for eight hundred, and four thousand cash. The other six hundred, my buy-in tonight, I owe him back. I don't bring cash to private games, even ones in rich neighborhoods like this. I just play, and if I lose, pay up later. Lotto knows I'm good for it. Everybody does.

"Joey, you ever win this much before?" he asks me.

I can't help but smile and say, "No. This is the best."

The waitress and the dealer are smiling, too. They know what's coming. "Here guys," I say, giving them each a hundred-dollar bill.

I stretch out the ache settling in my back, and pop some Rolaids to settle my stomach. I piss one more time, douse my face with cold water one more time, slip on my sunglasses, and leave.

Outside in the fresh air I smell my own stink and think how nice it's going to be to shower off that odor and sleep and then wake up knowing I won almost five thousand dollars the night before. Except that, already — *already* — I have the uneasy feeling that I've forgotten something.

In my car I take a moment and try to shake that feeling. I even check my pockets, make sure my wallet and the money Bobby Lotto just gave me are still there. I check under the floor carpet where I always keep a bankroll hidden — that's there, too. When I get home I know I'm going to have to check behind the dresser where I keep yet another stash of cash. I'm forgetting something. Missing something. Did something. I never worry about losing money gambling. I always worry about losing it in life. Having it fall out of my pocket. Having it stolen. Something. It's a compulsion. The more I win, the more I feel it. And I just won the most ever.

I light a cigarette. Turn on the radio. Sit a moment.

TWO

When I stay up too long, I sleep too long, and when I sleep too long, I don't sleep well. I wake up, piss, drink water, go back to bed, and get up later and do it again, all without ever really waking. Yet, though I don't wake, my brain doesn't seem to sleep. I dream wild stuff.

This night I dream a feeling. A sensation of speed. Streets and angles and corners and alleys. Shadowed and slick. Rushing through them. Taking the turns too fast and hitting the walls. I don't remember where I'm supposed to be going, or what I'm supposed to be doing. Just rushing. Keeping up some relentless, pointless pace. *Action* — that's what it's all about — action. The way I crave action. Got to have the action. Momentum for its own sake.

And then I hear knocking on my bedroom door, and Old Charlie yelling, "Wake the fuck up, boy."

"I am up," I moan out.

"Wake the fuck up," he yells again.

"I am up. Been up. Shut the fuck up."

"I got an appointment," he says, and then goes back down the hall.

I rise, pull on some jeans, and go out to the living room.

I live in the back bedroom of a little house with aluminum siding in Forestville, Maryland. It's a depressed, working-class suburb of Washington, D.C. Working class, but more than a few poor people live here, too, in the low-rise apartment complexes. More than a few welfare checks pass around.

I grew up just down Marlboro Pike a ways, in District Heights. Last of the white kids. When my mom moved here, when I was a baby, this area was almost entirely white. By the time I went to high school, six or seven years ago, it was fifty-fifty. Now I think the area is about seventy percent black, and the school is ninety percent. I'm estimating, but I'm close to right.

It's Old Charlie's place I live in. I rent from him. Old Man Charlie. Charlie Bad Back. Charlie Perv. He's a shriveled, toothless, bald, dirty-T-shirt-wearing alcoholic geezer my mother suggested I move in with when I first moved out of her house. Another man I've known my whole life. Part of my deal on the room is I drive him to the doctor once in a while.

When I make my appearance in the living room I squint into the brightness. "Close the drapes," I say.

"Listen to the vampire," the old man says. He's on the couch. He looks at me and laughs.

I look bad. Dark, dark hair going in twenty directions because I went to sleep right after showering. White, white skin. Eyes so scrunched their blue must seem black. An itching four-day no-shave. Tall, big-armed, skinny body with the start of a belly hanging out. Fly unzipped.

I fall into the couch beside him, keeping my eyes closed. My brain hurts. Nothing to see in this room anyway. Dismal, worn, dirty furniture. Expensive TV.

"That lawyer called you," Charlie says. "Lotto. Said to tell you he can't make it to the movie today, but said he needs to talk to you about something else, so call him."

"Put it on my list of things to do."

He whacks me in the arm. "Come on, boy."

18

I reach into his jacket pocket for cigarettes, pull one out and light it.

"Do I look dressed?" I ask.

He gets up, goes to my room, and comes out with a white silk shirt, my fine brown leather jacket, black leather shoes, and white socks.

"Here," he says, tossing the pile at me.

I give him a dirty look, but put the clothes on.

"Put your teeth in," I say when I'm ready.

I make the fog-headed, bleary-eyed drive to his doctor, where I wait for two hours to take him back. After which he tells me I'm lucky he woke me up because I was talking some wild shit in my sleep, so loud he could hear it in the living room.

"What I say?"

"Just the usual. Somebody in your room. Under your bed. In the closet. You know."

"I won forty-eight hundred yesterday," I say, smiling as I think about it.

"I could have guessed," Old C. says. "Good game?"

"Good action. Mean game."

"That happens sometimes."

"I was mean."

"That's good sometimes."

I drop Charlie back home and head out alone to play cards at the Elks Lodge.

"Pinocchio Joe, what you doing?" I hear as I walk in the entrance.

That's Larry Red asking. There's another Larry that plays down here, a white guy. This Larry is black, but he's called Red because he's reddish black. That's how nicknames happen. Nobody knows last names; too many people share the same first name. One guy starts talking to a second guy about a third guy, named Larry. The second guy asks which Larry. The first guy says, The black one. The second guy asks, The black one dealing blackjack at Bladensburg? No, no. The tall one. Reddish-looking one. Oh, yeah, yeah. I know him. Red Larry. Larry Red.

Supposedly, when I was a boy, I loved the movie *Pinocchio* so much that for a while I insisted my mom call me that. What I didn't know was that what my mom called me, the poker world would call me. It's an all right nickname, though. I kind of like it.

The Elks Lodge is on Kenilworth Avenue. It's a broad, single-story faded redbrick building, deep in a city-tough suburb. They got a charity casino here two days a week. Charity casinos are legal here in Prince George's County. Sort of.

Larry's there at the door. Just hanging. He's an old guy. Real tall, real skinny. Reddish black, like I said. We shake hands.

"I'm getting by," I say.

"I hear Kenny Jones tried to big-time you. Hear you spanked him."

"Heads-up pot-limit."

"How much you win?"

"Three dimes."

"Damn! That's righteous. I hate that old cracker."

"He's old line."

Larry nods. Then says, "When you coming up to see me, anyway? You know I got a game again?"

He's talking about a home game. Private poker game. After hours. After the charity casino hours. Like what Bobby Lotto has, only for profit.

"I might give you some action. What are you playing? Two-five-ten?"

"Yeah, yeah," he says. He's an animated talker. Hands moving, eyes darting. Always on the lookout. "Two-five-ten. A little lower than you like, I know. But we played last week and you would not believe the pots. Action like crazy."

He's selling. Knows I'm a big favorite to beat the game, but probably figures if I go and like it, others will follow. I've been around so long, if I say a game's okay, people feel more comfortable about going. Especially whites and Asians who might otherwise think of it as a black game. Larry's no bigot. He'll take anyone's money.

He hands me a business card with a phone number, and on the back a map.

"We're getting started around eleven every night," he says. "Call early if you want to save a seat."

I nod. Pocket the card.

You kick around as long as I have down here and you know everybody. You know everybody and you can find a game seven days a week, twenty-four hours a day. I can wake up at three in the morning and know four different places to play. Games of mostly black players, or mostly yuppie players, or mostly redneck players, or mostly Filipino players, or mostly Asian players. And lots of games with all kinds all mixed up. Everybody gambles. Every kind of person.

"I gave that Spanish boy a job," Red says. "That Essay boy."

"Essay's back from L.A.?" Essay's an old friend of mine.

"Yeah. He's inside. He'll be dealing for me."

"Then I'll be there," I say. "Save me a seat."

"All right. You know, also, it's good you show anyway, Jocy. There's going to be some business talked about that you might want to get a piece of."

"What kind of business?"

"That ain't my place to say yet. But some of the brothers are putting something together and there was talk about bringing you on board. You might be doing yourself a favor coming by."

He won't give up anything more, so I let it go. Larry's one of those people who likes being secretive just for its own sake. To make themselves seem or feel more important. A lot of people are like that. And then you find out their big secret is something goofy. That's why I don't press people about stuff. I figure Larry must be talking about a football pool, maybe, or another home game, or a Vegas trip.

I go on inside. The place has six poker tables going. Twenty or so blackjack tables and three or four roulette games, but those don't interest me now. That's gambling, and gambling's for suckers. I'm a sucker for gambling sometimes, sure. But not now. I'm here to work. To play. Poker.

The games I want are full and it'll be at least a half-hour before I get a seat, so I walk around the room to pass the time.

I see fifty people I know. Must be ten that ask me about the Kenny Jones game, which I downplay.

Over at the bar I see big-shouldered Grizzly, slumping like he's got the weight of the world on his back.

"How you doing, Pinocchio?" he says, faking a perk-up.

"Hey, Griz."

He, too, asks me, "What happened at Lotto's after I left? Heard you played Kenny Jones head up and did all right."

"Pretty much," I say.

"Eight thousand is what I heard."

Grizzly's not quick, so I use no sarcasm with him. I just say, "No, Griz, only about three thousand."

"Plus you made about three in the game."

"Two. Eighteen hundred, actually. Where'd you hear eight?"

"Cambo Sam's."

"You coming from her place?"

He nods. He played all night and he's still out.

"Kenny's going to hate you more than ever," he says.

"Fuck him. It's probably because he hates me that he lost in the first place."

Grizzly smiles.

"By the way," I say, "I've got your check."

"Eight hundred?"

"Yeah. Want me to bank it?"

"I'll give you cash next week."

"Give it to my mom. I ain't sent her nothing for a while."

"And when she hears how much you won at Lotto's she'll want a slice."

I nod. It's true, she will. Grizzly knows well as me.

22

Then, remembering something, remembering, maybe, whatever it was he'd been thinking about when I'd come up to him, he stops smiling.

"What's wrong?" I ask.

He says, voice dropping, "Joey, did you hear — Mikey the Cop killed himself."

"What?" I say, stunned.

He nods.

"No!" I say. "After playing at Lotto's?"

He nods again. He's got some kind of fear on his face. I can't place it.

"I didn't know he was that hurting," I say. "I mean, I didn't know he was all *that* hurting."

"They found his body on the Maryland side of the Potomac."

I shake my head. The magnitude of such depression. The magnitude of such an act.

"That man grew up around there," Griz says. "Apparently he waded out into the water and shot himself."

He pauses. He suddenly is even more tired and upset. It shows in the way his body slumps and his voice cracks. "I knew him twenty years," he says. "He grew up playing and fishing on that river."

A moment passes. I've never known anyone who killed themself. That's what I think about.

"I'm going to go, Griz," I say, losing my appetite to play. My hands are trembling. "Ain't no one getting off those games for a while, anyway."

"No, not at this time of day. They all just started."

"You should go, too. Get some sleep."

"Maybe," he says. But he won't. He'll play until he drops.

I walk off. A Korean woman I dated once comes up and says she heard I won ten thousand from Kenny Jones.

I'm heading out, walking by a table, and someone grabs me. Essay. He stands, hugs me. He didn't move to America from Mexico until he was fifteen, but speaks English with no accent. He's lived here in Maryland for twenty-some years. Thick black hair. Usually a mustache, but not now. Medium height, medium build, some belly. Dresses kind of colorfully, but maybe it's just his own sense of style. He's been in California, dealing at a small card club there for about six months. Usually owes me money, but never too much. Pays me back eventually, but then borrows it again, which doesn't bother me. I got people I like less owing me more.

"How you doing?" he says.

"Getting by."

"Where you living?"

"Charlie's. Your old room's empty."

"I might take it. Ask Charlie for me."

"Sure, man." Essay had lived with us for a year before heading out west. Good gambler's roommate. Day-sleeping, beer-drinking, ball-game-watching, no-nagging, no-stealing mug.

He pulls a business card out of his pocket. "I talked to Larry Red last night. Got a job. Come by and give me some action, man."

I nod, and give him back the card.

"I saw him at the door," I say.

"I'm trying to get some people over, you know?"

I'm guessing Larry gave Essay the job because he needs more players. He's hoping Essay will bring in some new faces. That means Essay has to deliver. That's the business.

"I already told him I'd be there," I say.

"Take the card, man. Give it to someone else. And tell Larry you're coming because of me, so I get credit for you being there."

"I already told him I was coming because of you."

"Thanks, man. Plus there's going to be some people there who want to talk to you, I think."

"Larry said that. What's up?"

"I can't say. I know what it is, but it's not my place to tell you. I don't mean to blow you off, Joey, you know that. And there might not be nothing, anyway. But the brothers are putting something together. I was with them last night, and your name came up. Just trust me, man. There could be something for you."

"Whatever." Like I said, I hate mystery-type shit.

"I'll see you at Larry's, then," Essay says.

"Sure."

"Oh, hey — you hear about Mikey the Cop?"

"Yeah."

"That's fucking sad, man."

"Yeah, it is."

He sits back down and gets dealt in.

I go outside. The sun is bright and the day strikes me. I feel like doing something with it.

The track? They're running at Laurel, but first post was forty-five minutes ago. By the time I get there the third race will have gone off, so I'll have missed the double-triple. I could go over to the Knights of Columbus on Route 1. They'll have five or six tables going. I could call my off-and-on girlfriend, but she'll be sleeping. She dealt at Cambo Sam's game last night, which means she's only been in bed a few hours yet.

I decide instead to go to the movies, despite Bobby's backing out. *The Hustler.* It must seem like a cliché, but it is my favorite film. And I've never seen it in a theater before. I got nothing much else to do. Go to a movie. Hang out somewhere. Drive with the windows down for maybe the last time this year.

It doesn't bother me in the least that Lotto can't make it. I love movies, and I love to go alone. In the work week, midday, when the theaters are least crowded. When the suckers are at their jobs, and I have the place to myself.

I take the Parkway into town. I pass a spot where a woman was gunned down by this guy who said he just felt like "busting" some-one, which gets me thinking about Mikey the Cop.

I'd played with him a hundred times, and never seen him win. He was easy to beat. He made no confusing moves. Never check raised. Almost never bluffed.

25

Kept quiet, too, usually. Wasn't quick enough to join in the wisecracking, but wasn't being quiet from studying us, like some good players might be. Just quiet from slowness. Except, of course, for last night at Lotto's, when his run of cards had gotten him talking about how good *we* were.

THREE

"Bobby Lotto!" I call out across the theater's lobby, surprise in my voice.

He turns. His eyes get big.

"Joey! Wow, hey — I guess I should have called you back."

He's really nervous.

"No big deal, man," I say.

"You, uh, so, you came on your own?"

"Quicker and quicker and quicker you get."

"Just surprised to see you."

Embarrassed to see me, too. I know the signs. Don't know the cause yet, though.

A young woman gets off a pay phone and joins us.

Lotto makes an effort to calm down. He's in a suit. Tries to act like it.

"Joey, this is my daughter, Katrina."

She says hello. I nod hi back to her.

"Lotto," I say, "if you wanted to pass me up to see your daughter, I would have understood."

"Lotto?" she asks. "Where'd you get that name, Daddy?"

He gives up a sick smile. "Joey, I'm sorry. I just don't get to spend much time with her."

"That's cool, brother."

"You guys made plans to come here?" Katrina asks.

"Yeah, yeah," Lotto says quickly. "But when you called this morning and said you wanted to go, I thought we'd do it just us."

Katrina shakes her head.

"You like these old movies?" I ask. She's a slight girl, skinny, like her father. Almost his height, five-six or so. Wearing oversized clothes. Jeans, black T-shirt, black windbreaker, black shoes, black socks. A long purplish scarf and purple earrings. Downtown look.

Her features are considerably different from his, like she has some other kind of blood in her. A little something nonwhite. It makes for beautiful coloring, in hair and complexion. Her nose and mouth are small and round. But not her eyes. They are strangely, intriguingly, sharply defined. Intense in a gentle face. Not pretty, her package, so much as interesting.

"I'm a film student," she says. "American University. I have to do a paper on one of these movies."

She looks me in the eye. Likes what she sees. But then can't look me in the eye.

"Yeah, yeah," Lotto says. "She's a film student, and has to see these things for her class. Listen, Joey, could you do me a favor and come back tomorrow, maybe?"

"What?" Katrina says, incredulous.

I look at him. Laugh. Raise my eyebrows in mockery, trying to put some humor into the situation.

He's not amused. He gives me a look like I should leave. That pisses me off. Nothing I hate more than an older man acting like I'm supposed to do what I'm told.

We go on in. Take seats. Lotto is careful to sit between Katrina and me. I guess he's just a typical dad. Doesn't like any guy looking at his daughter. Doesn't like his daughter looking at any guy. Doesn't even like, and does notice when, in the middle of the film, she goes to use the restroom and puts her hand on my shoulder to climb past.

28

"Makes me want to wear a suit, and cock a hat back on my head and order whiskey straight up," I say as the three of us step out to the lobby after the first feature.

Katrina laughs. "What do you do?" she asks.

"You don't know?" I ask back. "Lotto, you haven't told her?"

"I know Joey from poker," he says.

"You're the Pinocchio!" she says, like she's caught on to something.

"Actually there's this cartoon guy who's *the* Pinocchio."

"No, no. I mean, yes, he has told me about you. You're supposed to be this great card player."

"That's him, that's him," Lotto says quickly. "Listen, Joey, we're not staying for the second movie. We're taking off."

"Yeah, me too. I'm not sitting through the whole thing just to hear Newman say 'Sometimes nothing can be a real cool hand.'"

"Right," Lotto says, trying to laugh. "Well, we'll be seeing you."

"Come eat with us," Katrina says. "Maybe you can give me some perspective on a hustler's life."

"I don't hustle, hon. I just play good cards."

"Do you live like that, though?"

"Living in one hotel after another? One city after another? I wish. But running cons on people — that's not for me."

"You run cons every hand you play," Lotto says, derisively.

"What, you don't, every time you try a case?" I say back.

Katrina laughs. "Come on, Joey. Come eat with us."

"He might not feel comfortable where we're going," Lotto says, derisively again.

I quell a *fuck you* because the man's daughter is here.

"I just mean," Lotto adds, catching my eye, "that he's not dressed for a nice place."

Katrina steps back and pinches her jeans. Gives her dad a look that says he's being stupid.

We go to a nearby cafe. Katrina ducks away to the restroom as soon as we get a table.

Lotto takes my arm and pulls me down as he leans closer and says, mile a minute, "Joey, let me explain. This was supposed to be me and her, you understand?"

"What do you want me to do?"

"I just . . . she's coming off some bad relationships."

"*Some* bad relationships? More than one?"

"Hers are all bad. She's really messed up. She's in therapy, and a treatment program, and there's just no room in her life right now for any more trouble."

I laugh.

"Not that you're trouble," he adds, to soften the insult.

I laugh again. He's funny. "Lotto —"

"And don't call me Lotto," he interrupts. "Call me Mr. Johnson."

I laugh even louder. "Mr. Robert Johnson?" I ask.

"No, no. Just Mr. Johnson."

"I'll call you Bobby, okay? But none of that 'Mister' shit."

"Okay, okay. Bobby, then. Bobby." He throws his hands up, like he just made some big concession.

"Bobby," I say, "why are you telling me all this about her relationships? You think I care?"

"No, I don't!" he says angrily. "I know how you treat women."

"What do you know?" I say, amused.

"I just mean, you know, that you're a young guy, and you like your fun. And I hear how the other guys talk about you."

"Yeah, well, like a bookie friend once said about him and money, I wish I had what people put me on." Bobby doesn't get it. "I don't sleep with nearly as many women as people say," I explain. "I sure haven't thought about your daughter that way. I just met her, and you're talking about relationships. Christ, Bobby."

His posture turns defensive. "I just don't need a phone call from her mother about how I'm introducing her to —"

"What?"

"You know."

"Fuck you. What are you? A fucking sleazeball lawyer. Take

twenty thousand dollars to handle my brother's case, and plea-bargain a bad sentence in a lunch hour."

"That's not what happened."

"Bullshit, it's not what happened. You didn't do him no better than any TV attorney would have done. We could have gotten a lawyer at a shopping center if we'd been looking for five to twenty."

"It wasn't that simple!" he says.

"Don't use that tone of voice with me, man," I say sternly. "Remember how I know you."

The waiter comes by. Bobby orders three Perriers for us. I start to order a beer, but he asks me not to drink in front of Katrina.

"I have to talk to you about something else," he says, like he's the only one in the world with problems. "You hear about Mikey?"

"Yeah."

"Yes? When?"

"Today."

"You really heard about it?"

"What is wrong with you?"

"I'm sorry. How did you hear?"

"Grizzly told me. At the Elks."

He bangs his hand on the table.

"Why do you care?" I ask.

"How many people you think know he played at my house the night before?"

I nod, understanding his interest.

"Nine or ten million," I say.

He shakes his head. Thinks. "Okay," he says. "I'll take care of it."

He thinks some more. Says, "Joey, if they ask, I'm going to give them your name, and Kenny Jones's. I'm going to say there were a few others there, but I didn't catch their names. I got to give them at least one more name . . . Grizzly. He's a contractor. He'll know how to talk to them."

"Talk to who?"

"The police. Internal Affairs."

31

"Prince George's County?"

"Automatic investigation, already under way."

"Why not give them everyone's name?"

"They aren't sharp enough to say only the right things."

"Why do we have to worry?"

"Well, technically, playing cards is against the law. I live in Virginia, though"— thinking —"they won't care." Talking to himself, says, "I'll call them tomorrow. Shouldn't be a problem."

I shake my head. "It's not like it's our fault," I say.

"If they think he killed himself over gambling losses, and the last place he gambled was at my house, they might get pissy."

"Don't deposit his check."

"Yeah," he says, tapping the table in acknowledgment.

"Other than the fact that I won't lie," I say, "what do you want me to say to the police?"

"Tell them, if they even ask you anything, and I doubt they will, that I didn't cut the pot."

"You didn't."

"I know. That's why I never cut the pot. It's running a game for profit that makes it illegal. And having a table specifically designed for gaming purposes. That's a little vague, but I'll have my table taken out, and replace it with a regular dining table. They couldn't convict me for anything, but even being associated with this shit would make me look bad, and could get me in trouble with the bar."

"I doubt it."

"How would you know?"

"I long ago lost track of how many lawyers I've played cards with. And more than a few politicians, too. Congressmen. A senator once. None of them worried about it."

"Yes, I know. It's just that I had such a professional setup. If anybody says I cut the pot, then I'm in trouble."

"Look at this — *I'm* advising *you* on legal matters. Bobby, forget about it."

"Easy for you to say. And it's your fault, too."

"What's my fault?"

"That he killed himself."

"Get the fuck out of here!" My hands tremble again.

"I don't mean that he killed himself," he says quickly. "But that he did it last night."

"You are such an asshole, Bobby. How do you figure it's my fault?"

"Because when he was flying so high for the first time I can remember, you busted him up. Showed him how easily you could bluff him and all. Believe me, I could tell it hurt him."

Some kind of fearful, hollow feeling grows in me. I stop breathing. "Man, I just played the game the way you're supposed to," I say quietly, hurt. "I'm not the one who took his paper so he lost more than he could afford."

Lotto shakes his head.

"Blaming me about this," I say, "is like blaming a bad beat on the dealer."

"You're right, you're right," he says. "Nobody kills themselves over something who wasn't going to anyway. Forget I said anything."

"I'll try."

"I'm upset, okay? You know how I felt when the suicide scene came in the movie today?"

I did know. The girl in *The Hustler* commits suicide. I'd gotten that fearful, hollow feeling then, too.

Bobby and I sit silently. Understanding each other.

Katrina returns. She's put on lipstick. Maybe some powder. I don't think she'd been wearing any before.

Bobby and I act like everything's fine. That kind of acting comes in handy in both our professions, I suppose.

The three of us order dinner. Talk about old movies. Classics. *Film noir,* Katrina calls them.

The food comes. We eat. Bobby's more and more nervous all the time, and then I realize what it probably is — he's got to take a piss, but he doesn't want to leave me alone with Katrina. The more his knee bobs, the harder I have to work not to laugh. I'm thinking about asking her out, with him right here, just to see his face when I do it. But I suppress that urge. Wouldn't be real fair to her.

Finally, though, he can't take it any longer, and without saying anything runs off.

Katrina and I laugh together.

"I think he held out as long as he could," I say.

"You caught that? He is so silly sometimes," she says.

"He sure is tonight."

"What did you talk about while I was gone?"

"He told me you were in therapy and treatment."

"Wonderful," she says.

"Said you'd had a lot of bad relationships."

"That's true."

"Why?"

"I'm attracted to bad men," she says, melodramatically. Just after saying it, though, she gives me a little look to see if I believe it's that simple.

"Your father said he didn't want to get a call from your mother about your having met me."

"A professional poker player? She'd die. My mother hates anything the least bit risqué. That's why she and my father split. He's a jerk, but I give him credit — he's not afraid of life. I guess because he grew up so privileged, he isn't afraid of seedy."

This last word she says with a mocking shudder.

"What's 'seedy' about poker?" I ask.

"Oh. Well, I guess nothing, really."

"I don't lie, cheat, or steal. How many businessmen can say that? How many lawyers?"

"How many of anybody? Believe me, I'm not naive about my mom's phony friends. And believe me also when I say I don't mind what you do. I think it's great. Really. I mean, what could be cooler, you know?"

I shrug. Ask, "What are you taking treatment for?"

34

"Coke," she says, like it's a badge of honor. But again quickly, subtly checks out whether I'll let her sum things up that easily.

The waiter comes by and clears the table. We order coffee, for her father, too. I pull out a pack of cigarettes, and offer her one. She takes it. I light them both.

"Another bad habit of mine," she says quietly. "My shrink says I'm compulsive."

I nod. Smoke.

"There's your father," I say, pointing him out on the phone in the back of the room.

She turns. "Always calling somebody, always busy. Loves being important."

"I thought he'd rush back to protect you from me."

"Probably figures I've got your phone number by now."

"That *you've* got *mine?*"

"What is it?"

She's taking out a pen and paper.

"Why do you want my number?"

"So I can call you?"

"Why would you want to do that?"

"Because you're the first guy my age I've ever seen stand up to my father like you do."

"He asked me to call him 'mister' when you're around."

"All the other guys do that without being asked. What did you say?"

"I think I told him to fuck himself."

"Hah! I love it. Really, give me your number."

I give it to her.

"What's up with your habit?" I ask gently.

When her father had been with us, and initially after he'd left, our speech had been quicker and louder. Now it's softened. Our faces, too, maybe.

"The treatment is working, I guess," she says. "No, why am I giving those assholes credit? I just got tired of the scene. Hanging around druggies gets boring. Especially rich-kid druggies. I'm not an addict. I think my therapist mistakes love of fun as a psychological problem. What about you? Any vices besides poker?"

"Poker's not a vice. And you'd better quit knocking what I do."

"Whoa. I don't mean to," she says, smiling.

"If I played bridge or chess or golf for a living, would you put me down?"

"I'm not putting you down."

"Poker is a game of skill played for money. I have the skill, so I make the money."

"Daddy says you're a mind reader."

"No."

"If I were to think about what I had for breakfast this morning, you couldn't tell me what it was?"

"No."

"What if I said what I had. Could you tell if I was lying?"

"Only if it mattered to you. Only if the lie brought out emotions in you."

"So, like, if we were in love, and I swore I'd eaten alone, but really had eaten with a rival lover, you'd know I was lying?"

She's leaning forward, smiling slyly. Coyly.

"Yeah. That I'd know," I say. "That I'd know real easy. Because you'd want me to."

Her smile broadens.

"You want a drink?" she asks.

"Your father asked me not to."

"Now you're going to do what he asks?"

"About not encouraging someone to drink, yes. I've been in his spot."

I tell her about how at a barbecue once when I was a kid, we finished off the iced tea and my mom said that's okay, we've got beer, and I said no, I'll get more tea, and I ran to the store, only to come back and find somebody had already opened the brew.

"Not that my mom was an alcoholic," I say. "Just that she wasn't the most controlled person in the world even when she was sober. Get her drunk and she'd start dancing around and embarrassing me."

Katrina nods. "Okay, that's cool," she says. "Especially the part about the embarrassing parent."

"You like that, huh? Good. Because here comes yours."

Bobby rejoins us. The coffee arrives and he asks for the check. But I grab it, pull out a wad of hundreds and drop one on the tray. I don't let people buy me things.

FOUR

The radio's on and Snap is rapping.

This is the game Larry Red told me about at the Elks'. I show at ten-thirty, and it's me and the waitress playing Tonk for a half-hour before the rest of the players arrive. As far as I know, Tonk is a black thing. That's who I learned it from. Simple enough game; good for two people to play while waiting around. White people in the same spot tend to play gin. Asians in the same spot play Pai Gow. Filipinos play Pusoy, which the Chinese call Russian poker, and which a New Yorker I know calls Chinese poker. I play anything. Learned Tonk when I was eight.

This game is in the low-ceilinged, unfinished basement of a small, redbrick detached house with a tiny fenced yard. It belongs to an old man, a retired hair-cutter, who keeps a barber's chair down here with the ragged old poker table, ragged old couches, and cheap aluminum folding chairs. Dressers and other furniture crowd the already limited space. A washer and dryer take up one corner. The waitress has the radio on.

Keys jingle and locks pop and Larry Red comes in. He says to the waitress, "Shut that shit off." She won't turn it off, but does turn it down.

"How you doing, Pinocchio?" he asks, locking the door back up.

"What's up, old man?" I ask.

"Old and getting older," the waitress says.

"Young folks with a smart line," Larry says. "Dime a dozen, dime a dozen."

We shake hands.

"I'm glad you're here," he says. "Kevin talk to you?"

Kevin's a rich black kid, my age or so. From a rich family, I mean. Doesn't get much from them, I don't think. He's a C.P.A. Plays cards all the time. Decent player. Steady guy.

"Nah, I ain't seen him."

"He'll be here tonight," Larry says. He rubs his hands, smiles, keeps moving. Fixes coffee, lights a cigarette, sets up the chips. Uncontainably energetic. "You the snow in a mud bowl tonight," he says. "The salt in a pepper shaker, the whipped cream on the hot fudge sundae."

I widen my eyes in mock horror.

We hear a soft knock. The waitress pulls back the window curtain, looks out, undoes the three deadbolt locks, and opens the door. Two middle-aged women come in. I know them and say hello. They both have jobs downtown, working for the federal government. Terrible players. No shot at winning. Fish to be fried. But very nice women. Churchgoers. And they love to play.

Right behind them is a huge guy, drug dealer. I've played with him twenty times before. Nice as can be. I suppose he'd do what he had to, if it ever came to it, but at least he doesn't reek of paranoia or quick temper, like most men in his business. I generally like playing with drug dealers. They usually have too much gamble in them to play well, and cash they don't know what to do with.

Next in are five or six people coming together from the same charity casino, where they all work. Home games get a lot of business from casino employees.

Kevin comes in right behind them. He's average height, slender build. Light complexioned. Wears glasses. Sensitive sometimes about race. Probably comes from growing up in a nice white suburb. Went to nice, white prep schools, and a nice, white college. Got upset when Bird's Celtics beat Magic's Lakers.

"Joey," he says, in a voice whiter than mine. "How are you?"

"Same old shit."

He sees Larry. Nods to him. Says, "Red, good to see you."

"Yeah," Larry says back.

There's something funny about that exchange. They are both so excited it's scary. Can't stop smiling, either one of them.

"I need to speak with you," Kevin says to me.

I stand. Larry does, too. The three of us walk to a backroom.

"What's going on?" I ask.

"Our ship has come in," Larry says, beaming. He's actually snapping his fingers.

Now, Larry is the type to be thinking his ship has come in several times a year. He's always got things scheming, and failing. Eternal optimist, eternal loser, as long as I've known him. I'm waiting for the pitch here, and then the hit for a loan. In the past he's wanted me to go in with him on two-year-old thoroughbreds, porn-oriented newsstands, a dice game that was to really float (on a houseboat on the Potomac, supposedly protected from raids by local jurisdictional problems), and some minor league loan-sharking. I've always said no. He's always come back six months or so later with another idea.

But he's never had Kevin involved with him before.

"Keep this quiet, okay?" Kevin says.

I nod.

"We got a license."

"Wow!" I yell, happy for them. I shake their hands; they beam with pride. They're talking about a charity casino license. A steal-money-fast-as-you-can-count-it license.

"That is great, guys," I say. "Especially for you, Red. About time, huh, you old fart?"

Larry laughs. He's so overjoyed I think he might cry. He's al-

40

ways wanted to be bigtime. Always tried to act the part. Now he could really be there.

"Told you he'd be cool," he says, of me.

"Yeah, you're all right, Joey," Kevin says.

"Hey, man, it's good to see friends of mine get a piece of this racket."

"Well," Kevin says, "it's not just us." He's smiling like a man giving out a present he knows the receiver will love.

"We want you to run the poker room," Larry says, with the same kind of smile.

"Get the fuck out of here," I say, with a smile to match theirs. "You serious?"

"Need your white ass," Kevin says. "You're tight with all the Orientals, and the yuppies. You know all the higher stakes players. You'd be perfect. Help balance our appeal."

"Sign me up," I say.

"How much you want?" Larry asks.

I mention that a mutual friend of ours, Nug, is getting five hundred a day (for each of the two days a week the casinos are allowed to operate) from the Filipinos. I know that to be true, and it's my only point of reference.

"We were thinking about an incentive system," Kevin says. "No salary, but twenty percent of the drop."

"That'll work," I say.

"If you can deliver the players, you'll make good money," Larry says.

"I got a free hand on hiring and firing?"

"You got a free hand on everything to do with poker," Kevin says.

"Then I'll deliver. Who's banking this place?"

I don't think Kevin and Larry have a whole lot of money. It doesn't take a ton, but you've pretty much got to have at least fifty thousand, and a hundred thousand is more than twice as good.

"I mean, if you need someone," I say, "I know people who'd

41

love to get in." Lots of people. I wouldn't mind getting a piece myself. My bankroll is up to about twenty-two thousand.

"We're cool about that," Larry says. "There won't be no trouble with the cash."

"We can't talk about it, though," Kevin says.

"You don't have to," I say.

Larry puts his hand out. "So you're in?"

"No, man," I say sarcastically, "I hate life and don't want it to get better."

They laugh.

We shake all around.

We go back to the game, and more players have arrived. Essay's here now. To deal. Says, in front of everybody, he's glad I showed so he isn't the palest man in the house.

I stay all night. The game has good action, but it's messy. The players are slow, the etiquette is poor. Too many people having too much fun for the game to progress quickly. The ventilation is bad, so the smoke goes nowhere, even with the windows open. There's a lot of railbirds. Twenty people in the room, nine of whom play.

I quit at six in the morning, two hundred loser, but not caring about it. If this poker boss spot works out, two hundred won't be nothing.

Kevin and Larry ask me into the backroom again before I go.

"Joey, we been thinking," Larry says. "You know everybody around here. Where can we get the equipment?"

"Freddy Sorenson rents out to a lot of people."

"You think Sorenson is right for us?" Larry asks.

"Sure. He rents out to the Filipinos in Oxon Hill. He's been doing this shit a long time. He's the one to go with. Helps out in a lot of little ways, too."

"I guess he figures it's in his best interest," Kevin says.

"Sure it is. The casino's got to work for him to make money. Part of the deal he had with the Filipinos was that he would provide consulting services. He'll bring in some people to help train the deal-

42

ers. He'll explain the bookkeeping to you, and set up cashier proce-
dures. The works. He'll also explain how to get by with the county.
Like I said, he's been doing this shit a long time. Supposedly used to
be mob-connected."

Kevin and Larry are both nodding. Larry was a pit boss in
Atlantic City for a few years before getting into the bingo halls downtown, and was born into a numbers family. And Kevin, like I said,
has been playing cards and hanging around gambling a long time.
But neither has ever run an operation like this.

"Can we trust him?" Kevin asks.

"I can't know something like that for sure," I say. "But he's always been square with me."

"You dealt money with him?" Larry asks.

"Christ, man — he's my main bookie! Got a real deep pocket."

"The reason we ask," Kevin says, "is because we *are* working
with him. We didn't tell you right away, to get your real opinion of
him."

"Freddy's cool, man. Knows everything. *Every* thing."

They nod. Satisfied.

We spend the next hour talking. They fill me in on the charity
scoop, and the hall rental. I suggest some people to bring aboard. We
talk about advertising, specials, food. We're excited, and don't want
to stop talking about the casino because talking about it is thinking
about it and thinking about it is fun.

When I finally do get outside, I sit a moment on the hood of
my car, run my hand through my long hair, puff on a cigarette, narrow my eyes against the rising sun, feel the fresh air, and try to appreciate what has just happened.

Poker boss at a charity casino — what a freeroll that is. What a
break. It's something I've been wanting for several years. Ever since
Nug went to work for the Filipinos' organization, and I found out just
how sweet the spot could be. And I've been feeling tired of poker lately.
Of the constant grind. The hours of smoke and coffee and old stories.
It just hasn't seemed enough anymore. Hasn't seemed challenging
enough. My concentration's been slipping. My play getting routine.

And I'm all the more aware of this slip in my effort and lessening of enthusiasm because of the pot-limit win over Kenny Jones. *That* was poker. Real poker. Poker the way it's supposed to be. Frightening and heroic and exhilarating. But, unfortunately, rare. Far more typical of the poker I play was the game tonight. Against players who don't fold, so against whom there is no bluffing, and from whom therefore money is made by playing the percentages. A game requiring scientific play, not artistic. A game that is now very boring to me.

And what better ticket out of such games than becoming a poker boss?

Three young black guys come down the street, wearing low-slung jeans and oversized sports team jackets; ball caps pulled down. I'm so deep in my thoughts I don't see them until they're right on me.

I look up. Nod. Say, calmly, "What's up?"

They nod back. Say, "How you doing?"

I go back to my thoughts.

They go on, to school probably.

FIVE

I sleep all day and at four that afternoon Old Charlie's knocking on my door. I'm dreaming of my girlfriend, Laura, nude, on her stomach, on my bed, and I'm kissing her toes and ankles and calves and thighs, and then Old Charlie's knocking on my door.

"Phone!" he yells.

I get up, poke my head into the hallway. "What?" I ask, giving him a look. He knows I don't wake up for calls.

"It's Laura."

I reach over beside my bed and plug in my extension.

"What, baby?" I say, grumpy.

"Hi, hon. I'm sorry to wake you," she says, sweetly.

"Anything wrong?" I ask.

"No. What are you doing?"

"I *was* dreaming about you. *Now* I'm waking up. What do you want?"

"K.C. and Sam want to go out tonight. Dancing at Nipa Hut. Sing-along."

K.C. is Korean Charlie; Sam is the Cambodian woman Laura deals for. Nipa Hut is a Filipino bar in Fort Washington. They have a karaoke machine there. Sing-along. Laura loves it. She's a Filipina. Sings nice.

"All right," I say. "Why are you calling me so early?"

"We were going to Thai Am first to eat."

"Now?" I ask. Gamblers have no time frame. If we can eat breakfast at night and dinner in the morning, why not dancing and drinking in the afternoon? "What time are we supposed to meet them?"

"I'm calling you from the restaurant."

"So I'm just supposed to come over?"

"We'll have a good time. We haven't seen each other for a while."

"Yeah. Okay. I'll see you in an hour."

"No, just come on now."

"Baby, I played last night. I need to shower."

"You didn't before going to bed?"

She knows I almost always do. I hate waking up to that gambling smell. That sweaty, smoky stink of an overnight poker shot.

"I was too tired. You guys eat, all right? I'll just meet you at the bar."

"You promise?"

"I'll be there. I just don't want to rush."

"Hon?"

"Yeah."

"I have to talk to you about something important."

"What?"

"I'll tell you later."

"Baby, don't do that. Don't say you have to tell me something important and then say you'll do it later." It's just like Larry Red and Essay at the Elks'. People love to dramatize their secrets.

"I don't want to talk about it over the phone," Laura says.

I lose. "Okay, okay, okay," I say.

"But tell me about your dream. It was of me?"

"Maybe not. I couldn't see your face."

"Joey!"

"I don't want to talk about it over the phone."

♣   ♣   ♣

46

I take a long shower. Steam off the stink. Get out, dry myself, fish a cigarette out of my jacket, and light up. Wearing a T-shirt and underwear, I go to the kitchen. Coffee's on. Old C. is sitting at the dining room table, smoking, reading the paper.

"How old's this shit?" I ask.

"What shit?"

"The coffee."

"Just drink it."

I do.

I sit with him.

"How you feeling?" I ask. He's always sick. He's on permanent disability. Got injured in an accident at the factory he was working in. That was twenty years ago. He got a decent settlement. That and the social security keep him going. But he looks a lot older than he is. Looks seventy, is fifty-five.

Getting smaller. Bad back from the accident. Some bone disease, too, I think. Heart problems. Lung problems. Chain smokes, chain drinks.

"I'm not bad," he says.

I tell him about Essay being back from L.A. and wanting to move in again. He says, "Fine."

I nod.

The phone rings. Charlie answers it, then hands it over.

"Hello?" I say.

"Joe?"

"Yeah."

"Freddy Sorenson. Larry Red called me today. Told me they talked to you."

Freddy talks in an emotionless monotone that's always impressed me. If he's telling you the time of day or how much money you owe him, he does it matter-of-factly.

The man knows more about gambling than anyone I've ever met. He used to have a poker game at his house. Me and the guys used to sit around for hours listening to him talk, after the game broke.

Freddy's real old. New Yorker. Jewish. As a kid he worked for Meyer Lansky, first in Saratoga, then Miami. He was working in Las Vegas back when it was a mob-run town. He had a piece of the casinos that used to be on the piers on the Potomac. He used to have slot machines in rural southern Maryland when they were legal. He owned a Las Vegas Night charity casino in Baltimore before they all got closed and one around here before it got closed. My mom worked for him there. Among other things she might have done for him. They dated for a while.

He's an old school kind of guy. Told me once always to remember: anything you say can and will be used against you. *Anything* you say. To *anyone.*

He's too hot now to run joints himself. So he rents out equipment. For which, because he provides other services, he is very well paid.

And he's Washington, D.C.'s biggest non-Greek bookie, working now with only a select few high-rolling customers he's known a long time. Them, and us — me and Nug and K.C. and Fat Boy. He certainly doesn't need our money. He just likes us. I think it's because we're young. We give him an audience. Especially me. He knows I have an interest in the history of gambling. He knows how I romanticize the old days.

"You busy?" he asks.

"I got to meet Laura in a while." I tend to emulate his monotone when I'm with him.

"Come on over," he says.

I agree.

I shave, dress in some new light-brown pants and a fresh-pressed black cotton shirt, and drive the short distance to his house in Clinton.

He's got a big, white brick place, with a small parking lot in the back, surrounded by trees, so that when he's got a game the front isn't crowded with cars. Parking is the biggest giveaway of a home game, and the leading cause of police problems. Neighbors complain and the cops have to do something. Freddy's got no parking problem.

I park my old van between a Lincoln and a Cadillac.

I ring the bell. A well-shaped middle-aged blonde answers. Freddy's seventy something. He always has a large-breasted, younger (for him) blonde around. He hasn't been married and has no kids that I know of. But I might not know.

The blonde says hi and leads me downstairs.

Upstairs is expensively furnished. Downstairs is appropriately furnished. There's a bar, a kitchen, a pool table, a full-size eleven-seat poker table, a dining table, a large-screen television, two smaller televisions (for watching two or three games at once), and a little partitioned-off computer room. The computer is hooked up to a modem, so Freddy can pull up twenty-four-hour sports news from papers and wire services across the country.

I spent an NFL Sunday with him here once, watching him book. His setup is to have his girlfriend — out on the road — take the bets on a car phone. With a portable computer and modem, she uses a pay phone to send the bets, in code, to the home computer. If he ever gets raided, he only has to turn off his terminal to erase the evidence.

Freddy's sitting at the dining table, eating a sandwich.

Boulder's with him. Boulder is a wide man. Two inches shorter than me; hundred or so pounds heavier. Greased-back dark hair. Forty something. Heavy-jowled. Freddy's friend, assistant, and, I guess, bodyguard. Carries money for Freddy. Picks it up, too. I'm not sure you could call the guy Freddy's "muscle." Leg-breaking is a movie thing, and not often a real life one. But Freddy says there was a time when Boulder's size was good to have around. Now Boulder mostly just sits around bulging out of designer sweat suits, stuffing his face with whatever's available, and drinking diet sodas.

Freddy stands when I enter, reaches out and shakes my hand. He's a tall, skinny man. Soft-bellied, of course, because of his age. A few strands of white hair left. Seriously wrinkled, spotted skin. Too much sunbathing in Miami, he'd said once. He's wearing golfer's clothes. Plaid stuff.

"Sit down," he says in his monotone. "You want a beer?

49

Something to eat? Have something to eat." He waves over to the blonde.

"What do you want, Joe?" he asks.

I'm not hungry, but I order a hamburger. The blonde, who cooks and waitresses when we play poker there, leaves.

"Bring me a Coke with it, please," I call out after her.

Boulder, who hasn't acknowledged my presence, also calls out after her.

"Hamburger here, too," he says. "Diet Coke." He's got a sandwich in front of him already. What's left of one.

A moment passes. Freddy says nothing.

I don't really know what I'm doing here, and for some reason I'm nervous. If you're calling a girl to ask her out, you know you'll be nervous, so you're careful not to appear so. But if you aren't expecting to be nervous, if you aren't even thinking a situation might have pressure, you can be ambushed by it. I never get nervous when I play cards. I'm the most relaxed, attentive player in any game I'm in. But here? Now? This game? If it even is a game. Feels like one, but I don't know what kind.

"I talked to Larry earlier today," Freddy says. "He told me you were coming on board. He also said you spoke highly of me. Thank you. But apparently they played you along a bit. I've been talking to them for quite a while now. Long before yesterday."

I sit quietly.

"They're going to be at Churchville, Thursday and Friday nights," he says.

"Right," I say.

"Who's backing them?"

"I don't know."

Freddy nods, like I gave the right answer. He looks at me closely. "You sure you want to get involved with these people?" he asks.

"Are you?"

He smiles. "Okay," he says, "but let's remember some things. Some problems."

"Like what?"

"How many black people live in this county? What percentage?" he asks.

"Sixty, I guess."

"And of the twenty-six Las Vegas Night charity casinos open now, how many are run by blacks?"

I think a moment. Answer, "None."

"Three are run by the Filipinos. The rest are white. Why do you think that is?"

I shrug.

"You know, there have been black casinos before. Two. Both got closed down."

"I know."

"And Kevin and Larry's charity is just as fake as the others were."

"Then how'd they get the license?" I ask.

"It's all paper. All the county can require is that the organization meet the filing requirements. You know what the charity is called?"

"HOME," I say. "H-O-M-E. Help Our Mothers Escape. Supposed to raise money to help teenage mothers get off welfare."

"Sounds as good as the Jaycees or the fire departments or the other excuses people use to run these operations, doesn't it? I know. I came up with the idea. But you know why some casinos get shut down and others don't?"

I'm listening.

"Joe," he says, "a well-run charity casino can clear a million dollars a year. They can skim eight-hundred thousand for a long time, giving two-hundred thousand to the charity. Or they can steal the whole million and get raided. This county is not completely corrupt. The police are not on the take. There are politicians getting all the campaign funds they need, but the police are not paid for. And they will shut you down. It isn't racial. Plenty of white organizations have been closed. But the ones open now have learned. And you guys have to learn — don't steal it all. Most of it, fine. But not all."

"I think we'll be all right."

"Why?"

"Well, for one thing, I'm sure you've given Kevin and Larry this speech more than a few times."

He smiles.

"Plus, these guys aren't stupid. Kevin isn't, anyway. You must think that yourself, or you wouldn't be getting involved with them. You know Larry worked in Atlantic City. He'll keep the blackjack pit running smoothly. Roulette is pretty simple. Kevin will be handling the money, and he has an accounting degree. He's smart, and he's pretty dependable. And I've got the poker room. I think I'll do all right with it."

"You'll do great with it. That's part of why I'm glad they brought you on board. It's a good sign that they chose you. They are smart. By bringing you on board, instead of a black, I also know they're after the money. Which makes them a lot more dependable. Which is why I suggested you to them. You're a white they know and trust. And one I know and trust. I used to change your diapers, you know."

I'd heard that before. My mom had confirmed it. Freddy has known me my whole life.

"I changed your diapers once, too," Boulder says, and then adds with a laugh, "Your dick still that small?"

I give a mocking chuckle. He, too, had changed my diapers.

My hamburger and Coke arrive. I take a small bite. It's a big, juicy, messy-to-eat burger. And I don't want to be messy right now. I take a small bite and chew slowly. Boulder gets his hamburger at the same time. He doesn't worry about being messy.

"How's your mother?" Freddy asks.

"She's okay," I say, caught with my mouth full. Freddy might have timed it that way.

"When's the last time you saw her?"

I swallow quickly. "I guess it's been a few weeks."

"She playing much?"

"Nah. Broke."

A moment passes.

He reaches in his pocket and pulls out a piece of paper. A list of names and numbers.

"You'd do well to hire these poker dealers," he says.

I look at the list. I know the names, and don't like them much. But I keep quiet.

"As you know," he says, "legally, no one working at any of these casinos is allowed to be paid anything. And they have to have been members of the charity for one year. The county knows that's bullshit. But they're happy as long as they're protected. So everyone who comes to work for you has to sign an affidavit saying they receive no compensation for their twenty-five hours of work every week, and that they've been a member for one year of an organization which hasn't ever done anything before." He pulls out another slip of paper and gives it to me. "This is the name of a woman who will notarize the affidavits for the people you hire. Larry and Kevin will be using other notaries."

I nod. There are a thousand people working in this county's casinos. All with affidavits on file swearing they don't get paid.

"How much are you going to get?" Freddy asks me.

"No salary. Twenty percent of the poker drop."

"Whose idea was that?"

"Theirs?"

"Mine. I know you, Joe. You're not a worker. You're a player. You need incentive to do your best. This way you have it. You could make a lot of money."

"I wouldn't mind it."

"Just don't get flashy. And try to keep the others from getting flashy. It won't last forever."

I nod. I've known Freddy my whole life. When he talks, I listen.

"Okay. That's all, Joe. Finish eating if you want, but I'm going to take a nap."

"Actually, I'm supposed to meet Laura for dinner. I shouldn't fill up here."

"Well then, you'd better get going. You should never keep a girl as pretty as Laura waiting. Unless, of course, business calls. Don't ever put the cart before the horse, Joe. Women are easy. It's money that's hard to come by."

I nod. Okay.

SIX

I step outside of Freddy's house and zip up my beautiful, dependable leather jacket. The day is overcast, and the sun won't be up much longer. A dismal, grey day. Normally the kind I like. But right now I'm troubled.

I drive. Think about it. Figure out what's bothering me: I didn't stand up to him when he suggested those poker dealers.

I have the same feeling now I sometimes have when I find myself with good starting cards but know the hand will turn out bad. I shake it off.

I hit the Beltway and the evening rush hour is ending. I put on a jazz tape and pump up the volume. I don't know anyone my age who listens to jazz, but I pump up the volume.

The traffic's not bad, and fifteen minutes later I'm at Nipa Hut. It's in a shopping center that looks like it could just as easily be a warehouse. A shopping center thrown up real fast.

From outside I hear a woman's amplified singing and know it's Laura. Inside, in the dark, completely ordinary cocktail lounge, she's up on the little bit of a stage. There are only twelve or so people in the place, but they're all paying attention to her.

The karaoke machine plays the music for "The Way We Were." Laura sings the words. Her eyes are closed. She doesn't see me. She's into her fantasy.

I see K.C. and Cambo Sam, and join them.

K.C. and I shake hands. He's a brother pro. Runs an after-hours home game once a week, but it's a short game and he mostly lives on what he makes playing. He came to America sixteen years ago, when he was eight. He's very intelligent and sensitive, and I think that prevented him from fitting in with the American kids. He did well in school, and went to three years of college, but for social reasons didn't enjoy himself. He started gambling at the charity casinos because it was something he could do alone, and found poker. I gave him his nickname. The initials, I mean. His parents, in poor judgment maybe, started him using the American name Charlie. Around the Maryland poker world, with its five-or-so other Charlies, he became Korean Charlie. I didn't like the sound of that. K.C. though — that works. He told me there were two things about the game he loved — the camaraderie with friends like me and Nug and Fat Boy, and success that did not depend on being good-looking (he's fairly unattractive) or well built (he's skinny) or witty (he's very shy). At first, at poker, he lost. But he studied the game. After we became friends, he spent three months going around the county with me, and I taught him what I could. I liked his intelligence. I liked having one friend who was quiet. We went on road trips. Spent hours and hours in silence, when we weren't spending hours and hours talking about poker. It was good for me, too, those hours analyzing hands. Made me think about the game. Made me articulate things. Made me share things with him. Made us close.

His girlfriend Sam, however — well, I probably don't like her only half as much as she hates me.

"Hi, Pinocchio," she says brightly when I come up.

"Hey," I answer.

"God, Laura sings so good, you know?" she says.

This woman has told me that Laura gives blowjobs for money

in parking lots. She's told Laura that I mark cards. Says now, with K.C. here, "She really has so much talent, Joey."

I sit and watch Laura. She loves to come here and perform. And the local Filipino community loves seeing her. She should get paid.

I look at her on stage. A silken-haired, creamy-skinned, big-eyed girl with legs so long you can't start at one end and get to the other. An absolutely beautiful girl. And I don't say that about many women.

She finishes her song and comes down off the stage, beaming, happy. She's wearing black heels, tight jeans, and a high-collared red blouse. Her hair flows long and dark and free. A little eye shadow, nothing more for makeup.

She kisses me.

"Hi, hon," she says.

"Hey, baby."

"Hon, K.C. and Sam are going to go home."

"I'm sleepy, brother," K.C. says. "I played all night last night."

I nod, understanding his tiredness. Card players can be up a long time, catching a second and third and fourth wind, and then suddenly find themselves exhausted.

I look at him more closely, though. Checking. Something else. He can't fool me.

"You look down, man," I say. "What's wrong?"

He shakes his head.

"He sad," Sam says in her heavy accent. "He hear about Mikey the Cop."

"I don't understand it," K.C. says. "Some people are saying it was the gambling losses, but I don't know."

"Nobody okay kills themselves over money," I say. "I think the way he gambled was the symptom, not the disease."

"But I always lent him money I knew he couldn't pay back," K.C. says. "Like I was giving him rope to hang himself."

"You no get paid, too," Sam says to him, harshly. "I get my money. But you too easy."

K.C. shrugs. He's a first-rate player, but no business-man. Completely unable to ask anyone who owes him money to pay up.

K.C. and Sam leave. "God, I hate her," I say after they do. "Why do you ever ask us all out together?"

"She's not so bad, Joey. She just doesn't know how to be herself around you all. I mean, really, what crime did she ever commit to make you guys hate her so much?"

"She's a gremlin-faced sag-assed forty-two-year-old two-time divorcée back-stabbing midget."

"Joey!"

I shrug.

"You guys just resent her for taking K.C. away. For helping him to grow up."

She took K.C. away from us, all right. Us being me and Nug and Fat Boy. Twenty-four-year-old, probable prior virgin, true poker brother Korean Charlie dumped us all because she gave him his first taste of the woman thing. She spotted him, worked on him, and gave it to him. And because he's a shy, sensitive, unattractive immigrant kid, he thought what she gave him was worth something. Been blind about it all ever since.

"I just think he deserves a woman who doesn't need a girdle to keep her belly from sticking out more than her tits," I say.

"That's disgusting," Laura said. "If he's happy, why can't you all just be happy for him?"

"Why is she scared of him being with us?"

"Because you all hate her!"

"She takes his money, Laura."

"If a man loves a woman he should want to give her money. K.C.'s very generous. I think he's nice."

I look at Laura. I know better than to argue with her that money might not be a man's truest expression of love. And I remind myself that I don't know what Sam might have suffered before getting out of Cambodia.

"So what are we going to do?" I ask. "Did you guys eat?"

"Yes. I have some takeout for you in the car. Pad Thai."

"Cool."

She takes my hand. Looks me in the eyes.

"What's wrong?" I ask.

The lights are low, the music soft. The girl beautiful.

"I'm pregnant," she says.

Fuck.

"Remember that night we went to the Red Roof Inn? Fourth of July?"

"Yeah."

"And we didn't use any protection?"

"Uh-huh."

She looks at me.

I take a deep breath. It's possible.

"Wait a minute," I say, remembering. "That was three months ago!"

"Three and a half."

"Laura — you're just now telling me?"

"I wanted to think about what to do."

"I can't believe you waited this long!"

"I didn't know for sure until last month. And I haven't seen you that much. And I didn't know how to bring it up."

I shake my head. I take her hand, study her face, look for clues.

She looks down, away.

I'm still in shock that she waited this long to tell me, but I ask, "What do you want to do?"

"You know I can't have an abortion."

"You have to have an abortion."

"I can't! I've been thinking about it. I even thought about doing it, and never bothering you at all. But I couldn't."

She's seriously Catholic. And yet American. Caught in two worlds. Confused. Pulled. I know a lot of immigrants. Some love being of two cultures. Some, however, need more direction.

I take a deep breath. I look around. Suddenly I don't like the atmosphere. Dark, cheap, plastic place.

59

The waitress comes by. I ask for the bill. She says K.C. paid it on his way out.

We get up. I help Laura on with her coat. It's full-length, black cashmere I bought for her last Christmas when we were first going out. I hadn't seen her wear it yet this year.

"You bought this for me, remember?" she asks.

We leave. Outside, by her car, she says, "That's when you were crazy about me. Bought me anything I wanted."

"That's when you were crazy about me, and didn't ask me to buy you anything."

She's not happy I said that, but can't argue with it. I'm not too happy I said it, either.

"What do you want to do?" she asks.

I shrug. I don't know.

"You want your Pad Thai?"

"Where? I know you don't want to come to my place. And I don't want to go to yours."

She lives with her parents. I don't want to see her family right now. And we'd have no privacy. And she won't come to my place because Old Charlie Perv leers at her. The morning after the one night she spent over, he told her she must have enjoyed it because she made so much noise. She hasn't been back since.

Night has fallen. The temperature's dropped. She looks at me, her eyes all big and sad.

"You want to get a place?" she asks. "Just to talk?"

"Fifty bucks just to talk?" I ask, and then regret it. I hadn't been thinking. "Getting a place" was her way of asking to spend some time with me. She was brought up far too straight to ever just ask for sex. We always have to get a place "just to talk," or "just to sleep." And then I have to seduce her, so that none of it is her fault.

"Yeah, come on," I say, and add with a laugh, "Red Roof again?"

She smiles. She's sad, but she smiles.

We take her car. A BMW her dad pays for.

I know her father. I play cards with him sometimes. He's got a piece of one of the casinos. Works as a civilian at Andrews Air Force Base, but leases a BMW for his daughter with the money he skims from the charity.

She stays in the car while I get the room. She never comes to check-in. Too embarrassed.

In the room, I turn on the lights. She opens the box of take-out food on a little table, sets up a napkin and plastic knife and fork.

I look at it.

"Eat," she says.

I still just look at. Cold food, plastic utensils, chain motel.

She's on the bed. I sit with her. I take her hand. She leans her head on my chest.

"We don't love each other," I finally say.

She lifts her head. Looks at me. We'd talked about it before, several times. Talked about breaking up.

"You can't have the baby," I say. "It doesn't make sense to have it."

She rises. Moves to sit at the little table. Pokes at the food. Doesn't eat.

"This is America, Laura. Women have abortions here all the time. They have sex before they get married, they accidentally get pregnant, and they get an abortion. There's no shame in it."

She keeps poking at the food.

"If we were going to get married," I continue, "it would be different. But we're not. I'm twenty-five, you're twenty-three. It makes no sense to have a kid now. We don't love each other."

"You don't need to keep saying that. I know you don't love me."

"No — we don't love *each other*."

"Don't tell me how I feel."

I sit silently. I know she doesn't love me. Lately she hasn't even liked me that much. She hates my van. She hates my lack of a normal career. She hates it that I haven't gone to college. I know it, and don't much care. Because just as much do I not like her obsession with "things." With who's got what and how good they look.

61

You go see a movie, or read a romance novel, and everybody who needs to love each other, does. But not in life, I don't think. Not in real life.

"You just like my ass," I say, to use her own words, to remind her of the truth, to lighten the mood.

She smiles.

"And you just like mine," she says.

I know my cue.

I move to her, take her arm, pull her over to the bed. I lay her down, and lie on top of her. We kiss, and look at each other.

"I care about you," I say. "You are the most beautiful woman I've ever known."

"You say that. But you look at other girls."

"You see my nose growing?" I say. "I mean it." I do. "You are so . . . succulent."

I kiss her on the neck, lick her there, and then down to her breasts. Her skin kills me.

"Turn the lights off," she says.

This delicious-looking girl always wants the lights off when we have sex. But she also knows the compromise. I get up, turn off the lights, but turn on the television, with the volume all the way down. We see by the set's flicker.

"You know what I was dreaming when you called?"

"What?"

I begin undressing her.

"I was dreaming about you, with your clothes off, on your stomach."

She stands, steps out of her heels, wiggles out of her jeans, and lies back on the bed. I take off her bra, her stockings, her panties.

I kiss her feet. Massage them.

"I was dreaming about licking your toes," I say, and do so, massaging her delicate feet.

I stand. Look at her. Undress. Go back to her.

"I was dreaming about very, very slowly kissing my way up your legs," I say, and do that, for ten, fifteen, twenty minutes. For a long time. No hurry.

And then I love her. When I make love to her, I feel love for her. And it shows. And she loves me back. And our weaknesses become vulnerabilities, and our vulnerabilities become endearing.

But then we finish. Lie together. But finish. And the love is gone again. I feel bad about that. I don't know why I love her when I make love to her, but don't later. Maybe it's just the intimacy, and then it's loss. Maybe it's just me and Laura. Maybe it's just me.

Afterward, I eat. She lies in bed, under the covers. I light a cigarette and eat.

I turn up the TV's volume to hear the evening news. Because I slept all day, I'm wide awake.

"Baby," I say, turning to face Laura, lying there with her head on her elbow, her beautiful dark hair spilling around.

She looks at me. She's all happy and warm.

"Baby, I kind of want to go," I say.

She looks at me like I should die, then turns away.

I'm in the wrong here, and know it.

"I'm just not tired," I say. "I know I'm not going to fall asleep, but I don't want to stay here all night watching cable."

"What do you want to do?" she asks, face down in the pillow.

"What do you think?"

She turns, looks at me. "You want to put me in?" she asks.

I'm pretty flush from the hit at Lotto's game, and pretty guilty for wanting to leave her after sex, and so smile, and nod yes. I'll put up her two-hundred-dollar buy-in to whoever's game we go to.

"Okay," she says. She loves to gamble. And just like that I'm off the hook. She probably wasn't all that sleepy herself.

SEVEN

After we quit the poker game, Laura drops me off at my van, which I had left at Nipa Hut. I drive home, and see Nug's car in the driveway. It's six-thirty in the morning.

Inside, I find Essay and Nug at the dining room table.

"Coffee and cigarettes, coffee and cigarettes," I say, joining them.

Nug is slender, narrow-shouldered, and about Essay's height, which is to say, five-eight. He grew up in Vietnam. Came here with his family when he was sixteen. Real boat people. Came here, went to school, and nearly flunked out because he couldn't speak the language. His father, who'd been a general in South Vietnam, drove a cab. His mother worked in a cousin's 7-11. Nug studied and eventually went to college for a year. But he never could learn to speak English well, and so didn't think he'd make it as any kind of professional, and dropped out.

We met four years ago and instantly liked each other. He might have an accent, but he talks straight. I can trust him with my life. I don't rank my friends, but if I had to, even he might be surprised to hear I'd put him number one. Like K.C., he's smart, and shares my code of honesty. Unlike K.C., he's not shy, and is actually pretty good-looking. Great with women. His real name is Dung Nguyen. I wasn't in on how we started calling him Nug, but it must have happened as soon as we didn't want to call him Dung.

"Where you been, man?" Essay asks me.

"No-Show's."

"Any good?"

"The game was good. I didn't do nothing in it."

"I see that by your face," Nug says.

"You move back in already?" I ask Essay.

"Last night."

"Cool."

"Coffee's fresh," he says.

"Nah. I'm going to sleep."

"No, sucker," Nug says. "Atlantic City."

"I ain't going up there. I'm going to sleep."

"You win last trip," he says.

"You ever hear of quitting when you're ahead?"

"So, just take cheese from last trip. Play with their money." Atlantic City had just recently permitted poker in the casinos, and that provided me with an opportunity to play higher stakes games. On our first few trips I had done real well. I was even thinking of moving there. The only problem is that to get to the poker tables there, you have to walk by the dice pit. No dice in Maryland. Safer for me.

"It ain't their money no more, sucker," I say.

"I call girls. We meet them." We'd met a couple of girls on our last visit.

"Meet them where?" I ask.

"Their house in Delaware. Then go A.C."

"No!"

"Come on," he says.

"I don't want to go to A.C. I've been a chip-dusting motherfucker up there this whole last six months. Everything I've made playing poker there I've lost in the pit."

"Then no A.C. Just see girls."

I shake my head. I'm going to surrender, I know. But I'm not happy about it.

"If we just go up to see the girls, are you still coming?" I ask Essay.

"I'm not going anyway. I'm broke."

"How'd you get broke already?" He'd mentioned at Larry Red's game that he had a couple of thousand bucks.

"Sucker play blackjack," Nug says for him. Essay shrugs. I laugh. Essay and Nug laugh. It is funny, kind of. After awhile.

"You pay your rent here yet?" I ask. Another dumb question.

Another cup of coffee.

Another cigarette. Another tug on my sleeve from Nug.

"Come on, man," he says.

"Why we got to drive two hours to see girls? We ain't got enough around here?"

"Nice girls," he says.

"Nice tits," Essay says. "He's been telling me."

"So you go with him," I say to Essay.

"Girlfriend like you," Nug says.

I pick up the sports section.

"Anyone seen Fat Boy?" I ask. "Sucker owes me cheese on the Eagles game."

Nug reaches in his pocket, pulls out a couple of hundred-dollar bills, hands them over.

"He give me for you."

I take the money, pocket it.

He tugs my sleeve again. I slap his hand away.

"Goddamn, man. Quit bugging me. You know I'm going to give in."

He smiles and says, "I say we leave this afternoon."

"So let me take a nap."

I shower, and lie down.

My mind is racing. I'm too wired to sleep.

Three and a half months pregnant! I've got nothing against kids, but I don't even know what a father is. Laura's got to see that.

I stay in bed, nod off, and wake up thinking someone's in my room.

I yell out, "Hey, she's stealing my money! Sam's stealing my money."

Only I'm not awake. I'm having a nightmare.

I sleepwalk into the living room, and as I go down the hall I start to come to. By the time I reach the kitchen, I'm pretty much fully awake.

Now it's Essay and Old Charlie there at the dining table. Drinking coffee, smoking cigarettes. Nug's on the living room couch, napping.

I shake my head, try to clear it. In my underwear, I sit with them at the dining table.

"You awake?" Old C. asks.

I nod. "Man," I say.

This isn't the first time I've sleepwalked around here. It isn't the first time I've dreamed someone was in my room.

"You got to quit this life," Old C. says.

"I got to quit keeping no schedule."

"That's what I mean," he says.

"Did you say Sam was trying to steal your money?" Essay asks.

"I think so."

"Why her?"

Her name was first on the list of people to hire that Freddy had given me.

"I don't know," I say.

"Too much caffeine and nicotine," Old Charlie says.

"Yeah. All of us."

I go back to my room.

Lie down.

Get up, piss, drink a glass of water.

Lie down again.

I light a cigarette. Think about Laura. Barely put the cigarette out before dozing off.

Wake up a few hours later when Nug knocks on my door.

One P.M.

We're in my van heading north in time to beat our own rush hour, and Baltimore's, too.

Nug drives. I try to sleep in the back, but can't. I join him up front.

"When you go L.A.?" Nug asks.

I'd picked up the *Card Player* — a poker magazine — and he'd seen me reading the ads for California card rooms. The past two years I'd spent January and February out there. Driving out, going to Las Vegas and Los Angeles and San Francisco and San Jose. The first year I'd gone by myself. Last year K.C. came with me. That was before he'd met Sam. Now he couldn't go.

"I don't know, man," I say. "I might not go this year."

"Why?"

"There's going to be a new casino. Up in Churchville. I've got the poker room."

"What nights?" he asks quickly.

It's important, because when a new casino opens, it can hurt another casino's business.

"Thursday and Friday."

"Good nights," he says, meaning they don't conflict with his. "Churchville? They open before."

"Yeah, couple years ago. Cowboy's place. Got taken down by the I.R.S."

"I remember. They busy, though. They do good."

"Yeah, it might work out all right. Good location."

"Who own it?"

"I don't know, but Larry and Kevin are running it."

"How you get poker?"

"They all know me. I been playing in their games a long time."

"Freddy help, too?"

"He says he did. I don't know what all is going on with that end of things."

"You talk to Freddy?"

"Yeah."

"He want you to hire some people?"

"A bunch. Including Sam."

"She thief, man. Everybody know she steal when she deal."

Poker players rarely cheat. Poker dealers, on the other hand, have been known to. Not in professional card rooms, which usually have video monitoring equipment. But in private games, in charity casinos around the country, yes. They're not card mechanics, though. They just steal.

The house makes money off poker by cutting each pot, usually one dollar per twenty in the pot, up to a maximum of three to five bucks. In Maryland, the dealers put the house's money in their tray. A tray is a rack of chips the dealers use to make change and sell chips for cash. The move by which they do this can be very quick, and except by tracking how much should be in the pot, and then counting the pot down, it's impossible to see if the dealer cut too much money.

Nug, to his credit, had been the first poker boss to really make an effort to weed out thieving dealers. Because he had hired only better people to begin with, he'd only had to fire one. I wanted my card room to be just as clean. Which meant I sure didn't want to hire Sam.

Because she was the dealer Nug had fired.

"Did Freddy ask you to hire her? When you first opened?" I ask.

"Yes," Nug says. "She owe him money."

"Why didn't I think of that? All the people on his list — they probably all owe him money."

"They pay two hundred a week. Ten dealers, pay him two hundred a week — two thousand a week."

"That's a good setup."

"Freddy, he slick. He like a credit card company. Get paid minimum forever."

"Maybe we should go into that business."

"No. We not tough."

"That's true."

"Freddy, he intimidate people."

"He what?" Nug has a very complete vocabulary, but his accent is tough sometimes, even for me.

"He intimidate people."

"Oh, yeah. Intimidate. Yeah, he does."

"He and Boulder press them. Never let up. No hit, but scare."

"Nah, they don't want to hit no one. You hit someone, and they panic and go to the cops, and the next thing you know you're in trouble for bullshit. For two hundred a week you want to go to jail? I remember Freddy telling us that wasn't worth it. My brother, too. Same thing."

"When he get out?"

My brother is in prison, in Virginia. My half-brother, younger brother, Jack. My mom's son by one of my stepfathers. Jack had been a major distributor of marijuana in Fairfax County before getting busted. He was now sixteen months into what would probably be a thirty-two month serve.

"I don't know exactly."

"He never turn?"

"Nah. Scared to. Dealt with Mexicans. He made his money, though. Had his fun."

"Sound okay."

"He told me once, he looked at it as a job. He goes to prison for a few years and gets paid a million dollars."

"Good hourly."

"Not bad. Except he got paid in advance and sloughed it all off shooting dice and nosing blow."

"He safe there?"

"Yeah. He's big. Big, strong, ugly motherfucker."

"How many white guys there?"

"Not many. But he's okay. Our high school was mostly black. He gets along with them."

"Bobby Lotto his lawyer, right?"

70

"Yeah, that motherfucker. You know, the more I think about it, the more that deal pisses me off."

Nug nods. "Lotto, he slick, too."

I laugh. "Yeah, Bobby Lotto — he slick, too."

Miles pass. Exit signs. Songs on the radio. Time.

I look out the window as we drive through industrial South Baltimore. The sky is still overcast.

The scene from the highway is always the same, somehow, to me. Driving to L.A. or driving to Delaware, it's still all the same. And I love it. Coffee and cigarettes and radio and driving — something's wrong with me maybe, but I'm always happy there.

My first road trip was at twenty-one, when I went to Las Vegas alone with a thousand dollars, which had seemed a lot of money at the time. I took a weekly rental near the downtown casinos and played low-stakes poker every day, and began for the first time to think of myself as a professional. Before, I had been a kid who played in private games and won more than I lost, and avoided having to get a job because I lived at home and only spent money on groceries and grass. But in Las Vegas I met people, lowlifes often, but sometimes very proud, free men who taught me that there is such a thing as playing the game for a living. My instincts had always been good; in Las Vegas's legendarily tight games, I learned patience. I struggled at first, but I won. I moved up, and played in mid-stakes games against well-known players and held my own with them. I also saw my first tournament action. I don't like tournaments. I think they are artificial, gimmicky additions to the game. But I loved seeing the high-stakes side action. And I had put in some play against some of the world's most famous players. And done well.

By the time I returned to Maryland six months later, I was no longer a thousand-dollar bankroll playing for spending money, I was a twenty-thousand-dollar bankroll earning a living. Then, old enough finally to play in the firehouses and Elks lodges and Knights of Columbus halls, I began sitting in the county's biggest games, the ten-twenties and fifteen-thirties. I had been winning forty to sixty un-taxed thousand a year since, working/playing twenty-five to seventy-five hours a week for the past four years. Not saving anything, because I had picked up the habit of shooting dice and betting horses and laying points on football games, and had also, in keeping with my day-sleeper lifestyle, become a regular at downtown dance clubs for a while. And even, about the same time, gone through a rather affected cocaine stage.

But if I wasn't working toward anything, I was at least free and happy — free from the notion that there was anything to be working toward other than freedom and happiness, and happy because I didn't meet many people who didn't envy me for something, and there wasn't anyone whose respect I wanted who didn't respect me.

But the prospect of a great-paying, easy-as-can-be, two-day-a-week job makes me think there maybe is a better, freer, happier life than even that of a card player. And the thought of becoming poker boss brings a smile to my face as we drive.

We cross a toll bridge — the woman in the booth makes me wonder how normal people work through their lives — and enter Delaware. I look at the directions Nug has, and the map. It's pretty clear how to get to the girls' apartment.

We turn off at the right place, and into a garden apartment complex of the sort found everywhere.

We cruise around the parking lot looking for their building number, find it, and go up.

We dressed nice. Me because Essay once made me buy a whole wardrobe after I came home one dawn complaining about being outdressed by the black guys at some hopping joint; Nug because his last girlfriend, a Korean blackjack dealer, a very nice, sweet girl I always thought he was lucky to have, used to buy him clothes. She spent all her money on him, I don't know why. He left her anyway.

Seeing him in good clothes makes me think of her. As we walk into the building, I tell him he was crazy to leave her. He tells me to shut up. In the four years I've known him he's left three women, each of whom I thought was too good for him. Too good for me, too. Don't get me wrong. I just mean they were all nice.

So why did we drive all the way to Delaware to meet girls he thought were nice?

As I said, we'd met these girls, Allison and Mary, in Atlantic City. Nug and I were walking by a craps game when he'd seen them, two fairly attractive, too-made-up, big-haired working-class types. Found out later that Allison worked in a dentist's office and Mary was a waitress in a diner.

Nug and I played alongside them a while, and explained the game to them, just for an icebreaker. They weren't gamblers. Just a couple of girls out for some fun. Civilians, shocked and maybe impressed by the recklessness with which we threw hundred-dollar bills around.

We'd gotten the casino to comp us, and had taken the girls to probably the best dinner in their lives. Fat Boy and K.C. had joined us for dessert and champagne. We were all so quick and funny, with our stories and jokes, that the girls never seemed to stop laughing. I guess we're not like the salesmen or clerks or managers these girls usually meet. I especially don't think they — small-town white girls that they are — had much experience with Asians. Allison, I could tell, had a lot of trouble understanding Nug's accent. But Nug's cute. And persistent. She liked him.

After dessert and champagne, Nug and I, without the other guys — but with the girls, of course — had gone up to our suite and had drinks, and then coffee. Flirted. Necked some; Nug with Allison, me with Mary.

And then we'd walked them to their car, an old Honda Civic, and seen them off. Mary was a pretty enough girl, except for that overteased, bleached-blond hair. She did have especially beautiful eyes, though. Real big, brown, know-what-you're-thinking eyes. But I didn't get her phone number, because I wasn't going to call her. I wasn't looking for anyone. I'd long ago had impressed upon me, by my mother, the idea that I should never be irresponsible with a girl's liking of me. That was about the only morality my mother ever tried to instill in me. To whatever effect.

EIGHT

"It's three-thirty, man," I say to Nug as we walk up the steps. "What are we going to do with these girls at three-thirty in the afternoon?"

"Shut up," he says, and knocks on the door.

Allison answers, greets us, and lets us in.

"Mary, the guys are here," she calls down the hall.

Their place is typical. Typical would-be cheerful single working girl's place. TV, stereo, nice couch; cheap nonmatching everything else. Baby toys and a high chair. They probably don't earn much money, and spend what they do earn on rent, food, and clothes. Which is no crime. It's not like I'm going to be the one to care.

Did I say baby toys?

Mary comes out. She has a little girl in her arms.

"Hey," she says.

I like the way she looks at me. She's more confident now than in Atlantic City. More assured. Maybe it's the home court. Maybe it's the baby.

Her teased-out hair is combed into a ponytail, so it isn't so big. Light brown at the roots.

Mary says to the baby, "Can you say 'hi'?"

The little girl makes that sound, very sweetly.

"Who's this?" I ask.

"This is Melissa. My daughter."

I come closer. The little girl stares at me. I smile.

"How old?" Nug asks, coming close, too.

"One year."

"She's cute," I say. Just to say it, really. I'm not a baby-type person.

Mary looks me in the eye. "I should have told you before. I'm sorry."

"It's not important." That's not true, but what am I going to say? Half the women I know are in the same situation as her. And I've been staying away from them.

Both girls are wearing jeans and sweatshirts and sneakers, and look good, natural, in them.

"You guys want to go hiking? Down by the river? It's nice," Allison says. She's not as pretty as Mary, and I don't think as bright. Very well built, though, which would be all that Nug would notice, if I'm not selling him short about this trip. She is very pleasant, too. Mary and Allison both, are not loud, but not shy, either. Even-tempered.

"They're not really dressed for hiking," Mary says.

"No problem," Nug says. "We buy clothes."

"You're sure?" Allison asks.

"No problem, no problem," Nug says, speaking quickly, excitedly.

I laugh.

"I don't know," Mary says. "You guys want to buy all new clothes just to go hiking once?"

"No problem," Nug says again.

"You don't mind?" Mary asks me.

"I've got some jeans and stuff in my van."

"He always got clothes," Nug says. "I forget. He stay out playing cards overnight all time."

"And you don't? Let's go," I say. "We don't have all that much time if we have to stop off at a store."

75

Am I a bit peeved, maybe? Had I been, maybe, a little more interested in seeing Mary than I had let on, and now been disappointed to learn she has a baby? That's not fair of me, I guess. But it does change things, that baby. Complicates them. And makes me think here, now, like I said, that I really must have been more interested in seeing Mary again than I had thought.

Mary picks up on my irritation. But what can she do? What can I do?

"We have to drop Melissa off at my mom's," she says.

"It's close, though," Allison adds enthusiastically. "Just take a second."

We go to some mall and drop off Allison and Nug so they can get jeans and sneakers. He figures he can wear his shirt and jacket.

Mary and I, with Melissa in a babyseat — which she had insisted we take the time to strap in — go to her mom's. We don't talk on the way over. Mary plays with the baby. I drive in silence.

At her mom's house, we unstrap the babyseat. While Mary brings Melissa and the seat inside, I go in the back of the van and change.

I'm not really liking all this. Hiking's not my thing, especially in October. But I feel now like I'm just along for the ride. Filling Nug's double date.

Mary comes back. We drive to the mall in silence.

Allison and Nug are waiting out front. Nug is wearing designer jeans, and black hightops, with his black and tan–checked dress shirt and leather jacket. He looks a little funny, because he's got short legs for his height.

They climb in the back of the van, and Mary gets out of the front seat and joins them. I guess I'm being a dick about the baby surprise.

I notice again, though, how natural the girls look. Comfortable. Their sweatshirts hang nice on their butts; they look cute in their little white sneakers and ponytails. All-American.

"You sit up front," Nug tells Mary, perpetually blunt.

"With Grumpy?" she says.

"You have to give him directions," Allison says.

So Mary returns to the front seat.

As she did when she saw me in the apartment, she eyes me deeply when she moves up. She has that habit.

I look away. I'm not in a poker frame of mind, competitive eyeballing and all that. Not that she's trying to read me; or rather, not that she's seeking ammo against me. Probably.

I look back at her, and she's still looking at me. She smiles a little. It's not an "Oh, I hope he likes me" look she gives me. More like a look that says she knows what my cards are. Which makes me smile.

I'm thinking, consciously, that I don't need this. I don't need to start liking this girl. In poker, if you want to win, you have to learn to ignore, or better yet, conquer your conscious thoughts. So if I'm thinking this girl likes me too much too fast? I like her too much too fast? This isn't practical? This doesn't fit?

We drive to a state park, and go walking through the nearly leafless trees. Nug and Allison are nonstop talk. They're hilarious; her with her chatter, him with his accent. But they get along. Anyone can see that.

Mary and I are quiet.

Fifteen minutes or so of downhill walking and we come to a river. Nug and Allison take off down the side. Mary and I sit on some big rocks. I light a cigarette.

I ask about her job. She tells me it's boring. Waitress in a diner. Evening shifts.

I ask how much she makes. Just curious, I say.

Fifty or sixty a night in tips; fifty on her paycheck. Three hundred a week on average.

She asks how much I make. I tell her I don't earn money like that. On a weekly basis, I mean. I win, lose, lose, win. Spend what I have, don't worry about what I spend.

When she and Allison, at that dinner in Atlantic City — after it, actually, when our buddies had joined us for drinks — had asked what we all did, the other guys had said poker dealer or home game operator or charity casino poker boss.

And me?

When asked, the guys laughed.

He just plays cards, one said.

No job? Allison asked.

The guys had laughed louder.

Now, I'm sitting on the big, overhanging ledge. Mary's a few feet away, on a lower part of the ledge.

"It's getting cold," I say. "Now that we've stopped moving."

"You want to walk down the riverbank?"

"Nah. We've got a nice view here." We do. "Besides, I'm too out of shape to be hiking around like this."

"You smoke too much," she says.

"Probably." I rub out my cigarette on a stone. "Smoke too much, drink too much, gamble too much, sleep too much. Stay up all night too much."

I use the same tone of voice I'd used in Atlantic City when she'd asked me if I gambled a lot. A defensive tone of voice. And again, as in A.C., she picks up on it quickly, and calmly diffuses it.

"I'm not judging you," she says. "Just trying to understand. You live different from anybody I know. You and Nug both."

"Not better, not worse. Just different. But I couldn't live any other way."

"You ever try?"

"A job?" I light another cigarette. "Everyone I know with a job is broke."

"You don't have bills?"

"Three hundred a month rent for my room. And I haven't had to pay that in nine months because the guy I rent from always loses it to me. My van's paid for. What else is there?"

"I've got rent, electricity, phone, and two maxed-out credit cards. Car payment. Car insurance. Health insurance. Groceries."

"See what I mean?"

"I know. You wouldn't believe what I pay every week for diapers and juice alone."

"And it gets worse the more you make. I know guys who own businesses and make good money. But they've got mortgages and taxes, bills of all kinds. Only if they skim cash off their company do they have anything to play with. Guys who make more money than me, have more money than me, are always worried about money. And I don't want to live like that."

"But do you have anything? I mean, your van's okay and all, but don't you want anything else?"

"I have the only thing that counts — my freedom."

"I guess you do have that. If you're happy, then great."

"I am happy. And I don't know many people with jobs who can say that."

She shrugs. Says, "I guess. God knows, I feel that way sometimes. But — don't you worry? I mean, you have no security."

"I know a guy who worked twelve years for a bank. Bank closed. Another guy, worked for I.B.M. *I.B.M.,* for Christ's sake. Got laid off. I'm the only one I know *with* job security. Because no one can fire me."

She's looking down at the ground.

"I get a little mad at the world sometimes," I say.

"I don't care. I kind of agree with you."

"It just bugs me to see so many people getting played for such suckers. What a bunch of losers people are. Working like dogs so they can have *things.*"

"You sound like a Communist."

I smile.

She stands, walks over to the water's edge, picks up a stick, kneels down, and pokes some stones around. Brushes her hair off her face.

I join her, kneeling by the water. I read her. Easy. She doesn't want to get involved with some guy who only wants his freedom. She wants a guy who'll make mortgage payments for her. That's cold of

79

me, I suppose. To sum her up like that. Defensive of me. But I'm not all that wrong.

I like her. I wish she could see that in my own way I am responsible. I don't say I'll be somewhere and then not show up. I don't lie to one woman about another. I don't fake friendship.

She's still playing with that stick. I'm kneeling very close to her. I look at her.

"You're not mad at the world," she says. "You're mad at me. For not telling you in Atlantic City that I had a daughter."

I'm impressed that she'd intuited that.

"You think if I cared, I'd be worth seeing again anyway?" I say. The obvious truth of that statement startles me as I say it.

"You're right. I was just having so much fun that night. And I'd decided beforehand not to bore any guy I met by showing baby pictures and gushing about her. That was my first time out since Melissa's birth, and all I wanted to do was have fun. Which we could have had, if you hadn't chickened out."

That's a joke.

"I don't sleep with strangers," I say.

"You're such a good boy."

I throw some stones in the water.

"Melissa keep you busy?" I ask.

"If you've never taken care of an infant, you have no idea how exhausting it is. I'm lucky my mom and Allison help as much as they do."

"Where's her father?"

"Canada."

"Why Canada?"

"Because he's Canadian."

"He doesn't care about the baby?"

"He didn't want it. I had it anyway. I don't hold him responsible for anything. It was my idea."

"Well, then . . . how many boyfriends do you have?" I ask.

She laughs.

"Just one," she says.

80

"Nice guy?"

She shakes her head no.

"Nice *looking*," she says. "Nice car, nice apartment, nice job. Nice family."

She faces me.

"But if he were all that nice, would I be here today with you?"

Wow. There is nothing sexier to me than an honest woman.

I say, "Maybe you're just helping out your roommate."

"Sure."

She stands, walks back to the ledge we'd been sitting on before.

"Why do you keep walking away from me?" I ask, still kneeling by the water.

"Maybe I don't like you."

I can't help but grin real big when she says that. *Smirk,* I guess, might be a better word. It's my main poker tell, that smirk. Unless I concentrate, I smirk when I bet with either the best possible hand or nothing.

I sit there now, smirking at her.

She eyes me warily.

"You think maybe you don't like me?" I say, mocking her.

"How come you got such a shit-eating grin when I said that?"

"Shit-eating grin, is it?"

I get up. Move over to her. Very close. But I don't touch her.

"You going to walk away again?" I ask.

"Maybe."

"Your stick's still there, if you want to play with the stones some more."

"That's okay."

"Sure?"

"I'm fine right here. Thank you."

I come very close. I'm a lot taller than her. I think she's about five-four. I lean down. "You think maybe you don't like me, huh?" I say softly.

She's quiet.

I kiss her, very lightly, behind her ear.

81

"Hey," she says, pushing me away.

I smirk more than ever. I know exactly where she's at. She's got an insensitive boyfriend who bores her. She's got a job that bores her. Lives in an apartment in a town that bores her. And, much as she loves her little girl, is bored with taking care of her every day.

And now she's here with me. A guy who is sensitive, in that he senses a great deal. A guy who lives differently from anyone she knows. A guy who carries more cash in his pocket than any of her friends have in the bank. But also a guy who'll never share a mortgage payment with her.

I reach out and pull her to me.

"It's cold," I say as I hug her. "And you really are nice," I add, not teasing her now.

"You think you know?" she asks.

I kiss her.

"It's really too bad you don't like me," I say softly. "We could have so much fun."

"Oh, yeah?"

"Going out drinking and dancing and eating at the best restaurants. Traveling all over. I have a lot of fun. You'd enjoy me."

"Uh-huh."

"But then again, compared with all the excitement you must have around here — why would you want to leave?"

She eyes me warily as ever. But smiles a little.

I brush her hair back. I put my face very close to hers and breathe in, along her neck and cheek.

"You know how they kiss in Thailand?" I ask. I do it a few more times. It's a very sweet move, really.

"No, but I'm not surprised you do."

"You know how they kiss in Alaska?" I ask, and rub her nose with mine.

"And I guess next you're going to ask if I know how they kiss in France?"

I don't answer. I just kiss her. I love kissing.

She gets all mushy. And folds. The hand is over, give me the pot.

And I'm disappointed.

How could she play so badly? I gave her a big tell — as soon as she said, even as a joke, that maybe she didn't like me, I got all interested. How could she not read me for the type who likes a challenge?

We stop kissing, and she looks at me all big-eyed. She's a pretty girl. Smarter than she knows. God dealt her a good hand. How come she doesn't know how to play it? I know how to play my handsome mug. Know how to move my body, my hands and mouth, in just the right way. Why doesn't she?

I'm not cruel. This girl likes me a lot — there is no way I'd ever give her what I can already tell she wants, marriage and all — so why fuck her? I didn't want the sex that bad (although, at the moment, she did feel pretty nice). And she would get hurt. She'd never play her cards well enough to get me to stand still. No one ever has. So what's the point in leading her on?

All this I decide in the space of a few seconds. Sense, feel, judge, act. In seconds. What do you need more time for? The cards don't change.

But I don't let on. I'm here for the evening. As long as I don't make any promises, spoken or implied, that I don't intend to keep, I cannot be accused of poor behavior. If something else starts growing I can't be blamed, but at least I'll keep my nose its current size.

Nug and Allison come back. They're holding hands, but let go when they see us.

"Come on, man," I say. "Let's go. It's cold."

"I know," Allison says. "It's going to be dark soon, too."

We go back to their apartment, change clothes again, and take the girls out to dinner at the nicest place in town. We go dancing at a Holiday Inn off the freeway, and stay pretty late. We go to breakfast at the diner where Mary works. By the time we get back to the girls' apartment, Nug and I are too tired to drive back to Maryland, so we sleep in Allison's room and she sleeps with Mary. In the morning they cook us a good breakfast, and we all say good-bye. Nug is telling Allison he'll call her tonight and try to get back up here next week. I'm not saying anything, which is conspicuous. Last night Mary and I had been kissing pretty heavily in the bar, and again at the apartment when we said goodnight.

NINE

Nug and I stop off at the track on the way back from Delaware, and I end up getting to sleep at about five-thirty in the afternoon. Wake up at three in the morning, feeling disoriented. Even for me it's a little strange to go to sleep when it's light and wake up when it's dark.

I walk down the hall and into the kitchen. We're out of coffee beans, but there's some old coffee in the pot. Cold, old, and strong, but I nuke it a minute.

The light in the kitchen is on, but the living room is dark. I decide to watch some TV there for a while, so I flip the switch. On come the lights; up sits a woman I don't know.

She looks at me, scared.

"Who are you?" she asks.

I've never seen her before, and she's in my living room asking me who I am. This isn't the first time I've found someone sleeping on the couch. Not even the first woman. But I've always known the person.

"I'm Joey. I live here."

"Is Essay back yet?" she asks.

"I don't know. Are you a friend of his?"

She lies back down, pulling a blanket over her as she does. It is a little cold.

"I'm his ex-wife," she says.

"No shit," I say. She sits up again.

"Charlie said I could wait for him here."

"Okay by me. I'll turn the light off for you."

"I'm up now."

"You want some coffee?"

"Do you have tea?"

"Sure. I'll make it." I go back in the kitchen and put some water on to boil. She, with the blanket wrapped around her, takes a seat at the dining table. The table is covered as usual with newspapers and junk mail and magazines and bills and ashtrays and cigarettes and dirty coffee cups and candy wrappers.

"What's your name?" I ask.

"Maria," she answers. She's about forty. Wearing a dark blue polyester dress. She's Italian-looking, but has a Baltimore accent, so American-born probably. Dark hair, dark eyes, olive skin. Five-foot-five, maybe. Might have been well built once, but definitely in a full-figured way. She was never skinny. And her face has looked worried before tonight.

Some of her story I know. Two little boys from ten years of marriage to Essay. Separated three years ago. Divorced two years ago.

The water boils, and I decide to have tea, too. The stuff I reheated in the microwave might be toxic.

I put two plain tea bags in two big cups.

"You want milk?" I ask.

"No. Sugar, though."

I bring the cups over, hand her one, sit across from her, and lift up a couple of newspaper sections until I find the sugar bowl.

"There are definitely no women living here," she says.

"Three gambling bachelors. Charlie cleans a little. I take out the garbage. Essay cooks sometimes."

"His cooking keeps him from being a good-for-nothing."

86

Something about this scene amuses me. Wrongly, I know. There's nothing in it an adult would find funny.

"I hope you don't mind me waiting here for him," she asks. She doesn't care if I do mind, though.

"Did he say he'd meet you here tonight?"

"No"— she looks at me —"he doesn't know I've found him."

He's been hiding from her. That was part of why he'd spent the last six months in L.A.

"You know, there's a warrant out for his arrest," she says. "Failure to pay child support. I can put him in jail."

"It's not my business," I say.

"You think I'm a bitch?"

Actually, I think, from her body language and tone of voice, that she probably is. But that's got nothing to do with Essay's obligations. And I've always thought that that ex-wife's-a-bitch thing was a chicken-or-egg kind of question. Kind of like gambling losses and suicidal tendencies.

"It's not my business," I say again.

"You're a gambler, huh? A sicko like Essay?"

"Sicko?"

"You know he had a good job at the bottling company? Made decent money? But I *never* saw it. He'd be gone for days. Gambling! Take his paycheck, cash it, lose it. Never see his boys. Never get the bills paid. Nothing! He was worse than worthless."

I shrug. What can I say? Essay has told me all this.

"If he could just send me some money every month. If he would just see his boys sometimes. You know how long it's been since he sent me any money?"

"A while."

"Twenty-two months!"

I can't defend Essay here.

"Do you think that's right?" she asks.

I stand up. "He's got a problem," I say. "He gambles down to his socks."

"You think that's okay?"

87

"Lady, it's none of my business. You wait, all right? He'll be home eventually. But you might as well go back to sleep, because it could be days. He's out dealing at some home game. He'll deal, he'll play with what he makes dealing. He'll lose. Then he'll deal some more."

"So you do know where he is?"

"No."

I don't. I could find out with a couple of phone calls, though.

She's got both hands on her cup of tea, the way people do when they're feeling weak. Who else needs, psychologically, two hands to hold one cup?

I feel sorry for her, but I know Essay's no monster. He talks about his boys all the time, but is afraid to call, because she runs him down to them. I can tell even from this brief meeting that she does that.

"Do you have any idea how hard it is to raise children by yourself? Do you?" she asks.

"Lady, look — I don't want to get involved, all right?"

I don't think it's funny anymore. I think it's ugly.

"Charlie understands," she says.

The old man must have spent some time talking to her tonight. Commiserating. And then agreeing to let her wait.

"I'm sure he does understand," I say.

The phone rings. I answer. She's studying my face.

"Don't say my name," says the voice on the other end of the line. It's Essay.

"Hey, what's up?" I ask.

"My ex there?"

"Yeah."

"Damn, man. How did she find me?"

"I don't know. Somehow."

"Shit. Have you talked to her?"

"A little. Where are you?"

"The 7-11. I was coming in, but I saw her car parked outside."

"Is that him?" she asks.

88

I'm in a spot. "Give it up, brother," I say.

He's silent a moment.

"Put her on," he says finally.

I hand her the phone. First thing she says is, "You motherfucking bastard!"

She's silent.

He's saying something.

She starts crying.

I go back to my room.

Fifteen minutes later she's tapping on my door.

"He wants to talk to you," she says.

I go out, pick up the phone.

"Yeah."

"Joey, give her five hundred for me."

"Come on, man! You owe me four bucks now. I'm going to make you nine?"

"She's going to call the cops!"

"Goddamn, man."

"I'll pay you back soon. I'll make six or seven a week once the new place opens."

She's standing next to me. I give her the phone.

I go back in my room and get the five hundred. I also get dressed. I'd been wearing a bathrobe and was cold.

I bring her the money. She doesn't thank me. Just wipes some tears away, puts on her coat, and leaves.

Five minutes later Essay comes in. He's bought coffee, so I put on a fresh pot. We sit down, smoke, in silence.

The old man comes out of his room.

"Look at the deadbeats," he says.

"Fuck you," I say. "How am I a deadbeat?"

"You don't pay no rent around here," he says.

"Three hundred a month's not rent?"

"Not if you don't pay it."

"I owe you money?"

"I never get no cash from you."

"When I owe you, I'll pay you."

"Pay me now, or get out."

"Charlie, *you* owe *me*. Don't blame me because you can't play worth a lick."

"Fuck you," he says, and sits next to me.

This kind of talk between us is standard. Means nothing.

Essay is staring out the window. He's got the look about him of a man who long ago gave up on the idea of coming out a winner on anything.

I get both of them, and myself, coffee when it's ready. We talk about Maria and the kids and the child support. Essay says the five hundred tonight bought him a Thanksgiving visit with his boys and two months of her not telling the cops where he is.

He gets up to cook. Osso buco. Charlie had bought some veal shanks.

I go into the living room and turn on the TV.

"There he goes, assuming the position," Charlie says.

"Fuck you," is all I say back.

I find an old movie. I like it, because it's from that time. That era. Forties, fifties. Black and white. Men in suits and hats, women in skirts. People living in cities and towns, not areas and sprawls. Traveling by train. A fictional time, almost, to me. One for which I was meant.

Essay joins me in front of the tube while the food cooks.

At some point we make eye contact. Then he shrugs. What can he say?

I think about his sons, and how they don't see him.

I think about my own father. He was a gambler. And I mean a gambler in the narrow sense. He shot dice, bet horses, and played cards. Especially the latter.

I never met him. Or at least, not when I was old enough to remember. He met me, though. When I was a baby. Met me, and took off. Not necessarily because of me. Not only. Not definitely. But, probably, mostly.

I don't know where he is. Neither does my mother. But I heard about where he might be. Last year, when K.C. and I were in Las Vegas, I was sitting in a pot-limit Hold 'em game at Binion's — side action at the Hall of Fame — when some old guy across the table, giving me funny looks, finally broke down and asked if I knew Biloxi Bill. Said I looked dead like him.

I said no. I didn't know him.

Someone else in the game asked if the old guy meant Billy Long Hair.

Yeah, that's right, the old guy said. Billy Long Hair.

Wild Billy Long Hair.

This other guy said he'd seen him about two years previous. In Lafayette. Played four-eight with him at the Ice House there. Said he'd heard since that Billy was back in Mississippi now that the river-boats had opened poker parlors. Said he'd heard from some bourre-playing old Cajun that Billy set up daily at a place in Bay St. Louis.

Bay St. Louis? the old guy asked. Maybe I'll swing through there some time. Ain't all that far from Tyler. And I don't mind driving a few hours for five hundred dollars.

Oh, yeah? the other guy asked. He owe you, too?

TEN

Essay and Charlie and I eat. The three of us, sitting around the table in jeans or sweatpants, T-shirts or bathrobes, at six-thirty in the morning, eat dinner. When we finish, Charlie brings the plates into the kitchen.

"What am I, your fucking maid?" he says to me. "How come you never do the dishes?"

"Quit nagging, you old bitch."

"I ain't your maid, is all."

"I never said you were."

"I ain't your secretary, either." That's his way of telling me I got a phone call. Must have come yesterday evening while I was sleeping.

"Just give me the message, man."

Essay laughs.

"He's always got to jerk us off."

"It makes him feel alive," I say.

"You want your messages or not?" Charlie asks.

"There's more than one?"

"You must be getting popular. You got three. Your mom called. Laura called."

"When did Laura call?"

"You want I should get one of those little pads for taking messages? Essay, look at this motherfucker — thinks I've got nothing better to do."

"Charlie, just give me the messages. Who else called?"

"Some girl I don't know."

"What's her name?" I say slowly, trying not to lose patience.

"Katrina."

"Oooh," I say, and smile.

"Oooh," Essay says. "Fresh?"

"Met her downtown."

I don't mention that she's Lotto's daughter.

"You write down her number?" I ask Charlie.

He's gone back in the kitchen. He bangs something. "I am not your fucking maid, boy," he yells.

"Ah, shut up," Essay says for me. "Did you get the girl's number?"

Charlie comes back in and throws a piece of paper at me. He walks to the drapes and pulls them open. Sun's rising.

"What you going to do today?" Essay asks me.

"I don't know. Wait until a casino opens, I guess. What is it? Saturday?"

"Yeah. I'll go with you. Wake me when it's time."

I nod. He goes to his room. What can I do at this time of day? I don't have my mind set to play cards, so I don't want to go to a home game. I read the paper, watch TV, drink coffee, and smoke.

At ten, I call my mom. She's sleeping, but asks me to come over tonight. I tell her I'll be playing late. She says drive by her house. If the front porch light is on, she's up. If it's off, come tomorrow. She lives nearby, so it's no hassle. Next call, Laura. Her mother answers. Doesn't chitchat because she doesn't like me. Just gets Laura.

"Yes?"

"Hey, baby," I say.

"What do you want?" she asks coldly.

93

"I'm just returning your call."

"That's all? That's the only reason you called? To return my call? If I didn't call you, you wouldn't call me?"

I laugh. "Don't be silly."

"You have a good time in Atlantic City?"

"When?"

"Oh, please. Do you think I'm an idiot? I know you and Nug went to Atlantic City yesterday. And you guys didn't go alone."

"We did not go to Atlantic City."

"You do think I'm an idiot."

"Of course not. But we didn't go to Atlantic City. We went to Delaware."

Click.

Gone.

I'll call her back later.

I don't want to call Katrina right after calling Laura — feels like a jinx move — so I call a bookie instead. Two of them, shopping the numbers. I put a couple of hundred bucks on Maryland. A fuck-of-it bet on a TV game. Then I shower, dress again, and wake up Essay. The man's not had five hours of sleep in forty-eight, but he'll play all day again.

Casinos are allowed to open at noon, and at eleven-fifty we walk in. By law, casinos must be located in public, noncommercial buildings. That basically means Elks lodges, Knights of Columbus halls, and fire departments, most of which have large meeting spaces. This law is designed to feed money to these organizations, which are, not coincidentally, politically powerful.

I'm saying hello to twenty people in five minutes, and there's another twenty I can only wave or nod to.

"Take your seat, man, they're going to start," Fat Boy tells me. He's a dealer here. Nug and K.C. might be my better friends, but Fat's my oldest. I've known him since junior high. He's a red-haired, red-eyed, red-faced kid. He and I were the only two white guys to start for the football team our senior year. He played center because he's big, and because the black guys all thought that position wasn't cool to play anyway.

"You get my two hundred?" he asks me.

"Yeah, thanks."

"I lost my ass, man. Lost two dimes. Fucking Eagles. Did you watch that game? They had no business losing the cover."

I shake my head. Nothing to say. Fat's worrying me some with his sports betting, but there's nothing I can say.

People gamble to put life in their life. Citizens sometimes ask me why I gamble. Why anyone gambles. I tell them, people gamble to put life in their life. To condense it, to magnify it. To juice it up. To electrify it. Gambling is anxiety. It's pressure. It's risk. It's action. It's fun.

And that makes playing poker for a living the hardest job in the world. I know plenty of lawyers, doctors, and businessmen who play cards. None of them are good enough to do it for a living.

Lots of people, going on three- or four-month-long winning streaks, think they can keep doing it. Here's the truth:

There's a young, working-class background white guy sitting next to me this day. I haven't played with him before, which is a rare occurrence around here. He's wearing a Regency hat. The Regency was a card club in L.A., now closed. It's an indicator that he's no card room virgin. Most Americans are kitchen-table players. No one gets good in kitchen-table games. You get good, if you're going to, in the card rooms.

He's got a California card room hat, and he's talking a lot. He's saying he's a pro. He's new around here, and he's the main noise. Some players like being the main noise at a game. This kid does. He's talking about the Bike and the Commerce and the action there. Telling stories that begin with "I was in this 40-80 Hold 'em game," or "I was in this 75-150 stud game."

This guy's sitting to my left. I'm there an hour and we never tangle. He gets off to a fast start, but he's not showing me much. Laying claim to being a pro, but not showing anything to make me think so. Playing fast and loose and lucky. Impressing everyone else though, except K.C., who, when he sees me step away from the table for a minute, joins me to compare notes. Independently we've come to the same conclusion — the boy ain't no pro. We aren't making that judgment on his winning or losing. We're making it on the cards he's turning over. He's giving way too much action, and not in a tricky way. And he's too eager to encourage others to think he's good, instead of taking advantage of any grace period before they'd learn it anyway, if it were the case.

We go back to the game. I'm not catching cards, so I do the boring, hard, mature thing — I fold.

The kid's giving more and more action. His luck turns, and instead of playing tighter like a pro would, he plays looser. Has some bad luck, sure. But poker's an emotional challenge, because unless you're playing for stakes you don't care about (in which case it isn't poker anymore, it's just cards), losing hurts, especially when it's to raw bad luck. The game can be brutally unfair, in the short run. All you can do is play each card of each hand the right way, hour after hour, and let your chips take care of themselves. But if you can't deal with it as you lose more and more, and it all becomes "impossible to believe," then you can't play the game for a living.

Here's a truth: You have to play good to run bad (because a bad player will lose his money eventually anyway, so bad luck just costs him time at the table, not actual money in his pocket) and you have to run bad to get good (because as long as you're having good luck, you won't bother developing the skill to win with average luck). I've learned most of what I know of the game during extended bad runs. And I never had really good luck when I was learning, so I didn't get seduced into bad habits.

This new guy's stuck four hundred, then six . He's embarrassed. He'd sat down thinking to impress us with his play, and he's getting chewed up. He thought his California poker experience would give him an edge here. He didn't know Prince George's County was spreading Hold 'em long before they legalized it in L.A.

This kid's on full tilt. He's in deeper and deeper. About seven in the evening, he quits. Dime-two loser. Because we had started talking a bit (turns out he knows some of the Maryland people now in L.A.) he asks to speak to me away from the table. I know what's coming. He asks me if I can loan him five hundred. A guy I've just met. I say no. He uses the name of one of the Marylanders in L.A. as a reference. I apologize, but say no. I've fallen for this stuff too many times. He says, how about two hundred? I say no, man, and retake my seat. I feel sorry for him. I think he lost a lot more than he'd planned to. I hate to lose, but I never lose more than I plan. This new kid? He was hurt by what he lost. I read him for that much, and feel sorry for him.

And I'll never see him again. Just another of a thousand faces I'll play against. Just another of a thousand stories.

The other big loser is a young Korean girl. Her father is rich. Wholesales to the Korean corner stores in the inner city. She's the quintessential spoiled, lost, second-generation American.

I hear from K.C. that she's been playing for three days straight now. Was at a casino Thursday day, at a home game Thursday night to Friday morning, at another casino all Friday day, another home game Friday night, and is now here, all day. Has written thousands of dollars in checks. Has called her family, and gotten into screaming matches with them over the phone.

She looks near death. I've known her a year or so, and ask her to step outside with me. The sun has come out and the air is fresh. Cold, but fresh. The card room is so smoky.

She stinks. She's got the smell real bad. The stinking ashtray smell.

"You got to go home, girl," I say in a sympathetic but no-bull voice.

"I will, I will." She has no accent. She's American raised.

"When?"

"Soon, Joey. Joey, can you take my check?"

"No, baby. Go home. How much have you lost?"

She starts crying. She breaks down. She's wearing some skimpy evening dress. I take my jacket off and put it around her.

"I lost four thousand, Joey."

I want to hit her.

"And I owe, too," she says. "I owe Sam two thousand."

I shake my head. She'd gone to Cambo Sam's home game last night. With no cash. But that's no problem. It's called playing on the book. The home games get beat for some money doing this. They have no way of collecting from people who really don't want to pay. But Sam's pretty good at getting what's owed her. A great nag. And in this case, she knows the girl's afraid of her parents. She'll tell the girl to pay, or she'll go to her father. The girl, fearing the humiliation, will get the money. Sam will get the money. The hawks who preyed on the girl in the game last night — I'd have been one if I'd been there — will get their money.

Then she'll be gone for a few weeks. Telling herself she'll never gamble again. Meaning it.

And then she'll come back when she's got cash again. When she's bored. When she needs to live a little.

"I need a ride home," she says.

We go back in. Sam, who's also been up all night of course, comes up to us.

"Hey, hon," she says to the girl. Full of concern. "You feeling all right?"

"She's ready to go home," I say for her.

"Good. I hate to see you play too long. I'll get you a ride, okay?"

Sam would drive her home herself, but she doesn't have a car. Uses K.C.'s. His car, his apartment, his money. What she makes off her home games, she loses playing. She's as addicted as anyone. I try to remember that about her.

I play some more, take another break. Cigarette break. I don't smoke when I play cards. Can't. Quit when Nug told me I had a tell. The way I held my cigarette was giving me away. Nug, who's played with me more than anyone, had known about it for months. He pulled my coat when he saw others picking up on it. That was smooth enough. Even the best of friends play each other for money. I don't mind that he used the info against me. I'm grateful he told me when he did. And if other people ever figure out that he makes a certain downward glance with his eyes when he's betting with a really good hand, I'll be the first to let *him* know.

When I take this break, Nug comes outside with me.

"Hey, man, who'd you tell about Delaware?" I ask.

"Essay knew."

"Oh, yeah. Well that explains how Laura heard about it."

Nug laughs. "She mad?"

"Hung up on me this morning."

"Why you stay with her? She crazy."

I drag on my cigarette, shiver in the cold evening air. We'd gone out the back door, and we're standing in the parking lot. I sit on the hood of a Mercedes. Belongs to Laura's father. Nug's boss. The civil servant with the charity skim. I sit on the hood, drag on my stick, and say, "She's pregnant, man."

"Laura?"

"Yeah."

"How long?"

"Three and a half months."

"Hard to lose baby now."

"She won't do that anyway."

"Why? She want you for husband?"

We laugh.

"Nah. Just doesn't believe in abortion."

"In this country, women choose belief after they choose answer."

"Well, then I don't know why she wants to have it. But she says she does."

"Bluff. Tell her you want baby. Maybe then she lose it. Reverse psychology."

"She'll talk herself into believing that we can be married and have a family and all that. She'll convince herself she can change me. I've seen women believe that shit. Never seen a man change, but seen plenty of marriages end that only got started because some woman thought he would."

Nug nods.

Everything I say about poker applies to life. How many of those women, marrying the wrong guy, failed to play with courage? Courage isn't just calling someone's bluff. It's also folding when you're beat. Because it can be scary letting go of an investment for which you still hold hope.

K.C. comes out. He's as tall as me. Lights a cigarette off mine.

"K.C., I was just telling Nug — Laura's pregnant and won't have an abortion."

He shakes his head.

Back inside I see Kevin.

He reaches into his coat and pulls out some papers. "These are the membership applications," he says. "Anyone you want to hire has to fill one out. Make sure the dates on the application match the ones on the affidavit."

"Sure. I can start hiring?"

"And spreading the word to the players, too."

"Cool. When do we open?"

"Hopefully, first Thursday in November."

I see Laura, and go up to her.

"You hungry? Want to go eat?" I ask.

She looks at me with cold hate.

"Why are you being like this?" I ask.

She's seated at a crowded blackjack table, and everyone is hearing us.

She ignores me, plays a hand. I'm standing there looking lost. I lean over to whisper in her ear.

"Come on, baby. This is stupid. I didn't do anything. I just went along because Nug needed me to double date with him."

She ignores me. Plays another hand.

I'm still leaning over her shoulder. A guy, a serviceman, sitting next to her, says, "Is he bothering you? Hey, man, why don't you leave the girl alone?"

I look at him. I know the type, and the situation. Laura draws lots of men like him.

He's been flirting with her a little, but not too well, I'll bet.

I look at him like he's a nobody. Laura doesn't say anything to him, but maybe she's enjoying this a little. I know her. I know she'll blow him off right after I leave. But I'm pissed at her for using him against me.

I stand up.

"I'm leaving, Laura. Come or don't."

It's a risky play. Could backfire. But I know her. And I so rarely show anger that it's effective when I do.

She hesitates a moment, finishes the hand she's on, picks up her chips and gets up.

"I just wanted to play out the shoe," she says.

I'm in no mood. I say nothing. I give the guy a look, though. A look that says, who's she leaving with? A look that says he was an idiot for ever thinking he could land a girl like her. It's a petty thing to do. But he pissed me off.

I've got to cash out. Laura walks with me to the poker section.

I say good-bye to everyone real fast. Nug, Fat Boy, Essay, Kevin, K.C., others. Laura says good-bye. Takes her a while.

"Where you going?" K.C. asks.

"Eat. Movie maybe."

"You coming to the game tonight?"

His home game comes off this casino. Like a lot of professional players, he likes to have a little piece of something, to get back in his own game what he puts into others in cut and tips.

"I don't know," I say. "I'll call if I want a seat saved, but I was up early this morning, so I think I'll probably pass."

Laura's over talking with the older Filipina women at the cashier's cage. Relatives, or her mother's friends. I say hello to them. They give me that suspicious white-guy-with-one-of-our-girls look. I don't tell them to fuck themselves. I just take Laura's arm and lead her away. Quickly, because I see her parents nearby, and I don't feel polite.

ELEVEN

Laura and I drive in her car to a shopping center Chinese restaurant where we know the waitresses. From poker, we know them. Seriously bad players, but always very nice.

The place is busy. It's a Saturday night. Mostly blacks. Some Asians. Me.

Laura small-talks on the drive over, and she's small-talking now. I'm quiet until I say, "We've got to think about this pregnancy thing."

"No, we don't," she says. "*We* don't. I do."

"I've got no say in it?"

"It's my body."

"This thing doesn't affect my life?"

"It doesn't have to. Just go your own way. I'll raise it."

"I don't want a child of mine in this world not to know me. If you have the baby, then I want to be a part of its life."

"Good. Because I'm having it."

"Laura — are you ready to be a mother? What about singing?"

She sings nice, but not great, and has no chance of ever being a star. But I'm desperate.

"There's nothing more important than being a mother," she

says. I guess pregnant women keep that statement ready like a robber does a gun.

I sip some hot tea, and pour her some. The food comes. We pretty much eat in silence.

"Anyway," she says softly, "it might not be yours."

Well, I'm just getting quieter and quieter.

She goes on. "We were broken up back then, remember?"

I remember.

"In fact, that night, at the Red Roof, was when we made up."

Yeah, yeah, go on, I'm thinking.

"So," she says, still real softly, "for the couple of months before we made up, we were both seeing other people. Right?"

"Who's the guy?"

"I think you are. I mean, I'm ninety percent certain."

"Who's the other guy?"

"I don't want to say if I don't have to."

"What do you mean, if you don't have to? You have to. Who's the other guy?"

"Bobby," she whispers.

"Get the fuck out of here!" I say, incredulous. "Bobby Lotto? You slept with Bobby Lotto? He must be fifty years old!"

"He's not. He's forty-eight."

"He's not twenty-three."

She starts to cry.

"What the hell were you thinking, Laura?" I'm dumbfounded. I could not be more shocked.

She's bawling now, and I know I've got to let her calm down before she can talk again.

If she says he's forty-eight, then fine, he's forty-eight. But he looks older. He's in no kind of shape.

"Laura, how could you sleep with him?"

"He's a nice guy, Joey."

"He's got kids your age!"

That gets her crying again, so we have to pause. When she settles down, she says, "He's divorced."

"I know. So what?"

"He treated me well." Then she adds with a glare, "He didn't try to get me into bed the first time we met."

She's referring to the enthusiasm I'd shown on our first date.

"Because he knew you were with me! He's had a crush on you for a long time."

"You were gone, Joey! I didn't know if we were ever getting back together."

K.C. and I had gone to Colorado for a month. They've got little casinos there, with poker rooms. Real small stakes, so we didn't play much. But we hadn't really gone for the play. We mostly just had a road itch.

"And my dad likes Bobby," she says. "You know they're friends. My mom, too."

"So you fucked him? Because your parents like his house?"

More crying.

Now I feel sorry for her. I take her hand, shake my head.

I could just imagine how much a pudgy bad-skinned rich old white-bread geek like him would want Laura. Slender, long-legged Laura. *Young* Laura.

I stroke her hand. I move to sit next to her, and hug her. She looks up at me. I can tell she really does regret what she's done.

I kiss her.

"Okay. It's history," I say. "I've made mistakes, too, so . . . We'll just go on, all right?"

She hugs me back.

"What if it's his?" she asks.

"Well, I'm going to have to ask you some questions. Practical questions."

She nods.

"How many times did you sleep with him?"

"Three."

"Did he wear a condom?"

She shakes her head no. "He said he couldn't have children."

I wasn't going to give her a lecture right now, so I let it pass that there are other reasons to wear one.

"But after," she says, "he told me he could."

She sits up, looks at me. "He lied, Joey. He told me he'd only said that because he wanted me to get pregnant so I would marry him."

I shake my head. The magnitude. "What a scumbag," I say.

She can't argue.

"How long before we got back together did you sleep with him?" I ask.

She thinks a moment. "About two weeks."

I think. Figure the dates. "That should be me, then."

"I know. That's why I said you."

She looks down.

We don't need to say again, though, that it might not be me.

We finish eating somehow, pay, and leave. A wind has come up, and the cold hits us hard.

"You want to come home?" Laura asks. "Watch some TV? My parents are at the casino until almost three."

"Nah." Her grandmother and kid brother will be there.

She reads my mind.

"Everybody goes to sleep by ten."

"Nah. Thanks, though."

There's a ten-screen movie theater almost next door to the restaurant.

"Let's see what's playing," I say.

We walk over. Pick out a movie. It doesn't start for forty minutes, so we walk to an ice-cream parlor and have some hot chocolate. Then we see the movie. Then she drops me off at the casino, where my van is still parked.

We say good-bye in her car. She tells me again how she feels she has to have the baby. She's scared to, but she has to. And she tells me her parents know, and approve.

105

And I can't argue with her. I can't stop her from fucking up my life. She's got all the power.

She tells me she loves me and hopes I meant what I said about being part of the baby's life. She says she knows we aren't going to get married, but the way she says it makes me think she's hoping otherwise.

I don't argue with her. I'm not going to marry someone I don't love. Someone who, even if she's trying to convince herself otherwise, doesn't love me, either.

I give her a kiss, tell her to drive carefully, get out of her car, and go into the casino. First person I see — swear to God — Bobby Lotto. I walk by him without saying hello, but without hitting him, either.

He calls after me, though, and I stop.

"What?" I ask.

"What are you pissed off about?"

"What do you want?"

"Just wanted to know if the police had talked to you about Mikey the Cop."

"No."

"What are you pissed about?"

I step closer. Look down at him.

"I just had dinner with Laura. She told me about the two of you."

His eyes widen. "Hey, Joey — you were done with her. You went away."

I walk off. I really don't want to hit him.

TWELVE

The casino is busier than before. Prime time. Packed solid. Saturday night fever.

I meander through the blackjack tables and roulette tables, saying hi to players I know, dealers I know.

I nod to Laura's father in the blackjack pit. He smiles back. Chito likes me well enough. Not especially happy I got his daughter pregnant, I'm sure. But we've known each other a few years now, from poker, and I've earned his respect as a man across the table. All the Filipinos know me. And gambling is a big part of their culture, so they can't get too high and mighty. Chito especially. We've spent too many all-night card games together, playing Filipino poker. (High-Low Omaha Criss Cross eight-or-better with wild cards. Pot-limit. I'm not making this up.)

Laura had said her father wanted her to marry me. Her mother wanted her to marry Bobby Lotto. Wanted her to tell Bobby the baby was his, and to marry him like he wanted.

There's no seat open in the 10-20, and I won't play smaller, so I sit with the off-shift dealers and play Pai Gow. We talk about the usual shit. Bad beats. Who's losing these days, who's winning. Who's how good. How the different home games are doing. How the different casinos are doing. I tell them we're opening up Churchville and they're all interested.

I dust off an hour that way, and get bored. Nobody's moving out of the main game.

I feel a heavy hand on my shoulder. I look up. It's the Greyman, Kenny Jones. I haven't seen him since that night I punished him at Lotto's poker game.

He motions for me to move away from everyone. We step off into a corner. He speaks in a low, steady voice. Same school of speech as Freddy Sorenson.

"You're in with the blacks up at Churchville," he says.

I nod. He's got to look up at me because he isn't real tall. I don't think he likes it.

"You got that list from Freddy?"

"What list?"

"People to hire."

"I got it."

"Any problems?"

"I ain't hiring no thieves."

"Nobody's asking you to."

"Some of those people are thieves, Kenny."

"They've all been talked to. They'll stay in line or they won't just be in trouble from you."

"What's your interest in it?" I ask.

"That doesn't really concern you."

I look at him.

He fish-eyes me.

A moment passes.

"What kind of promotions are you going to have?" he asks.

"I haven't decided yet."

"Have a tournament. Just like here. Early. Then high hand bonuses every two hours."

"I'll probably be doing something like that."

More fish-eye. He tries a different angle.

"Joey," he says, with as much warmth as he can muster, "I've known you all your life. And you know I've been in this business a long time. I want to see you be successful. It's something I owe your mother. You've never had a father around, and your mother's always worried about you. So I want to give you some guidance on this. Me and Freddy both do."

He puts his arm on my shoulder.

"I've known you since you were a pup. I even changed your diapers."

My mom must have passed me around the neighborhood when I was a baby.

"You'll be all right, son," he says. "Just listen and learn, okay?"

"Yeah, sure."

"Good boy. And trust me about the people on that list. They're all fine dealers. They're all well known in this county, and can help you talk the place up. And they will all stay in line. Okay?"

"Yeah, sure."

"All right. Hey, I see someone getting off the ten-twenty game. That's your seat, right?"

"Yeah, I'm next up."

He pats me on the butt. "Knock 'em dead, tiger," he says, and points me over.

I play, but not well. Play foggy. Inattentively. Without confidence. I don't know why at the time, but figure out later that Kenny had made me feel bad, somehow. Tried to be fatherly to me, and then gives me that slap on the ass? There's something sick about him.

The casino closes at two A.M. I go home. As I pull in the driveway, I remember I was supposed to see my mom. She only lives a mile away, on down Marlboro Pike some, so I pull back out and drive over.

♣   ♣   ♣

She lives in a little white brick rambler. The small side of a duplex. A block off the main drag. Not the same place I grew up, but near.

Her porch light is on, and I can see a television's flicker through the front window.

I knock lightly. A moment passes, and the door opens. She smiles. I come in. We hug.

"How you doing, boy?" she says in her raspy, smoky voice.

"I'm all right. How about you? How you doing, Mom?"

"Just fine, just fine."

She leads me in, and we sit in the living room. Her house is not well furnished. She's never been much of one for holding on to money. Or things. Used to judge people all the time by what things they had. By who had how much. But she's stopped that somewhat. Made her peace, maybe, with the fact that she's going to be the one without things.

There's no booze out. That's a good sign.

"You drinking less, Mom? Seems like it."

"Mind your business, little nose," she says.

"Just glad to see you doing better." Only when real depressed had she ever been one to drink alone.

"Well, let's not jinx it with talk."

"Okay. How's the job?"

She works, of all places, at a liquor store. Mostly selling lottery tickets. She buys them, too. Like a hundred other people I know. Talks about them like they have meaning. Plays my birthday. Plays my half-brother Jack's birthday. The poor, they love the numbers. I've been in the store with my mom as she works. She talks the numbers with the customers, and they talk it back:

"I just knew a four was up. Had to be. No fours all week!"

"You know, I been playing that 3-8-3 for two months, and I get off it last night, and you see what it come? 3-3-8!"

"Oh, I know it. *Don't* I know it."

"My little grandniece? She had a dream all twos and fives last week, and I swear it ain't been nothing but twos and fives since. But in Virginia! Why she going to dream the Virginia number?"

They go on and on. I've tried to explain how bad a bet the lottery is, but my mom won't listen. I mean, she'll listen, but she won't stop playing.

"What are you doing up so late?" I ask her.

"Just watching old movies. You seen this one? *Dark City*. It's a good one, hon."

I sit with her.

The movie ends, and we go to the kitchen to cook some pancakes. The sun's coming up, and the room fills with soft light.

"Mom," I say.

"Uh-huh?" She's mixing the batter.

"You look good, Mom. You know that? You look good."

She does. She has good skin for her age. Especially considering she's always been a smoker. Her dark hair looks older than it needs to because she's always permed it. But she has a great body.

"Thank you, son," she says matter-of-factly. I guess I'm always telling her she looks good.

"Mom," I say again.

"Uh-huh," she answers again.

"Laura's pregnant."

That gets her attention.

She takes my measure.

"She going to have it?" she asks.

"Says so."

She looks at me and says, "Wait and see if she does before you start worrying too much. You're not going to know how you're really going to feel about it till it happens."

She looks down then. At the batter. A bit of harshness comes over her face. Maybe she's thinking about my father and her when she had me.

The pancakes are ready, and we eat in the kitchen.

"I heard you got some piece of the new casino," she says.

"Not a piece. The poker boss job. But I get paid a percentage of the cut, so it's like a piece. Who told you?"

"Kenny Jones came by yesterday."

I nod.

"I know you don't have a *piece* piece. The Jones boys and Freddy Sorenson got all the real juice there. But it's nice they gave you what they did."

I sit back in my chair, spooked.

"What do you mean they got the juice? Freddy's just renting them the equipment."

"No, hon. Freddy and the Jones boys got the whole thing."

I'm quiet a second.

"What I heard, from Boulder —" she starts to say.

"From Boulder? When were you talking with Boulder?"

"Oh, I don't know. Friday night, Thursday night. Went to some bar with him and Kenny. You know he's had a crush on me forever."

"Boulder?"

"Sure. Well, Kenny, too. Both of them. Since high school. You know Boulder is Kenny Jones's cousin?"

"Yeah, I know."

"Sure he is. Used to tag along with our gang when we ran around Georgetown. Oh, those were some wild damn years. That was back when Georgetown was biker heaven."

I light a cigarette. Light one for her, too.

"What he tell you?"

"Boulder? The blacks got the charity set up, and filed the paperwork and all, which costs ten thousand for the application to the county. Freddy put up the money. Now he's backing the place."

I nod. I'm following. If she says it's so, then it's probably true.

"What's your friends' names? The black ones?" she asks.

112

"Kevin and Larry?"

"Yeah. Larry Red? I know Larry. Know him from Silver Hill. I don't know Kevin. Is he all right? Freddy was asking me."

"They're both good people."

"Don't trust them *too* much. You always think no one cares about color any more than you, but you aren't black, you know. Don't trust too many people, okay?"

"Including Kenny Jones?"

She flicks an ash. "Don't trust anyone too much. I know you're a good judge. I never was myself. Jack neither. But you always were. You still got things to learn, though. So, yeah — don't trust Kenny Jones or Freddy too much, either."

"Mom, it ain't that big a deal, really, if you think about it. Ain't no one ever gone to jail for none of this. Look at how many Las Vegas Nights have been raided. Home games, too. No one ever goes to jail for this shit. And I'm just running the poker room."

"You know I'm going to be working there?" she says.

"Yeah? Dealing blackjack?"

"Pit boss."

"Good. Yeah, that's good, Mom. How much money?"

"Three hundred a day."

"You going to quit the liquor store?"

"Cut down to part-time. Hey, you want some coffee?"

"Coffee? Nah. I'm going to sleep."

"No, this is decaffeinated. It's good, though."

"Wow, Mom, decaf. Next you'll stop smoking."

She gets up and grinds some beans she had in the freezer. Puts the grounds in the coffee maker and adds the water.

"I didn't really know Freddy and Kenny and them were back together," I say. "I mean, I knew they knew each other and all. But I didn't know they were partners again."

She stands over the coffee maker, looking out the kitchen window to the little bit of yard, the small tree, the four-foot-high chain-link fence, and the neighbor's dog. She drags on her cigarette. She's wearing some ratty old bathrobe. Now, because of the morning light coming through the window, she does look old. But she isn't. Forty-five, I think. Had me when she was about twenty.

The coffee's ready, and she pours two cups. We both take it black. She taught me to appreciate good coffee. Raised me with it. Always fresh ground, never instant. I was the only nine-year-old I knew who started off his day with a cup of French roast.

She sits back down. Beside me. I read somewhere, and have found it to be generally true, that women prefer to sit across from someone, and men prefer to sit side-by-side. But my mom's a side-by-sider.

"When Freddy first came around here, he didn't know anyone," she says. "And he was so Jewish. New York Jew, too, so it showed. Back then this was all almost rural. Very white. And of course, down in Waldorf and Upper Marlboro, it was just plain redneck. Anyways, he meets Kenny and the other Joneses, and Boulder, at the old Bowie racetrack — that's closed now — and through them he got into the gambling around here. It was a good partnership, because Freddy knew everything about running any kind of gambling, and the Jones boys had all the energy in the world. And all the balls. Ignorant, wild-assed boys, but with Freddy teaching them, they all made money. You know they had Painter's Branch when it was open? And they had the Waldorf Elks, too."

"I played there."

"That was Kenny and Freddy's money."

"They clean up?"

"They made so much money, my God. Used to run the casino on the weekend — it was only allowed to be open two weekends a month in Charles County — and then charter a plane to Atlantic City. I went with them sometimes. We were treated like royalty."

I remember her going off to Atlantic City. I didn't know it was with Kenny and Freddy.

"You sleep with them, Mom?" I ask softly.

She rubs out her cigarette. Shakes her head. No.

"Lord knows they used to try. But I never did go for any of them. Which is why they all still have crushes on me."

My mom talks about crushes like I talk about poker hands.

"I thought you used to go out with Freddy," I say.

She shakes her head emphatically. "Go out with him, sure. But I never slept with him. I hung on his arm when he met the wiseguys up north."

"He was with the mob?"

"No. Knew some of them."

She lights another cigarette. Sips her coffee.

"Gangsters love to gamble," she says. "That's the main thing they do is gamble. Gambling isn't run by the mob because it's illegal. It's run by the mob because mobsters love gambling. They love the action. That's why they become criminals. The action. So sure, Freddy, from gambling, knew people. But it's hard to say what the 'mob' is, outside of the real Mafia. Which never was down here. I don't know why that is, but there never has been much mob action here. In Baltimore, but not down here. Not much, anyway."

I get up, pour us both some more coffee. Put the pot back and see, out the window, the neighbors going out, dressed for church. Picture-perfect middle-class black family.

"Grizzly gave me eight hundred," she says. "Says you won a bundle off Kenny."

"Yeah. Thought you'd want a slice."

"Why'd you ask about me and Kenny?"

"I don't know," I say. "It's no big deal."

"Didn't want to think your mother had sex with all these guys?"

"Who would?"

"Well, relax. I started hanging out with the Jones boys about the same time your father was around, and they have always paled by comparison with him."

"They all knew him, huh?"

"Sure they did. Knew him. Hated him. He breezed in here, up from New Orleans, and whipped all their butts in poker. And he got me. Got me easy."

She laughs. I do, too.

"Your father was slick. Smooth. Dressed so sharp. And no one else around here did. Best-dressed, best-looking, best-built, most arrogant man I ever met. Had that beautiful long hair. This was in the sixties, when only hippies had long hair. He had it, though. And he was no hippie. He was just himself. Had that way about him. Good-humored, smiling man."

"I wish I'd known him," I say.

In my whole life, I've never said that.

She looks at me. Tenderly.

I shake off the emotion.

I look at her. "Who knows what brings what on, huh?" I say, forcing a smile.

She smiles with me.

"Would you believe I was a virgin when I met him?" she says. "Eighteen. Not so unusual, then. Catholic upbringing. I did a lot of running around, but I never had sex with anyone before your father. Then I met him, and fell for him, and for two years we had the most fun in the world. He was a hell of a card player, and had brought a big old bankroll up from Houston with him, and we just owned the world. Drank and danced or gambled every night."

"And then you got pregnant."

"Yes, I did. And not on purpose, either. But he was happy. Said he'd stay with me. Try to settle down."

She looks away a moment. Then says, "But you know, he couldn't do that." Looks back at me. Says, "He left the day after I brought you home. He took a cab."

I shake my head in amazement.

I look at her carefully. She's not crying. Not close to it. Sad, but not close to crying.

"How come you wait till now to tell me all this?" I ask.

"Isn't that funny? We're just sitting here on a regular old day, and out it all comes."

"Ain't all that important anyway, though, I guess."

She shrugs.

"I just wanted to know the full scoop on Freddy and them," I say.

"It's good you do. It's good you do."

I get up, clear the table, do the dishes. Take out her garbage. Come back and kiss her good-bye. She hugs me tight, and walks me to the door.

"You know more about your father than you think you do. You got all the best of him, believe me. All the best."

"Thanks, Mom."

"That's why I love to see you with women. Same as him, you know what they're thinking. Know how to charm them."

"Yeah, yeah, yeah."

"You don't dress as sharp as him, though."

"Why would I want to spend my money looking good for women? Women are easy. It's money that's hard to come by."

"Okay, okay. You go on, now. Oh, one more thing — you got to go see your brother at the prison. You know I got that friend of his coming up here?"

"That guy?"

"Yeah. I put him up for parole. He's going to be staying with me for about six months. Grizzly's giving him a job as a carpenter's helper. That's all he needs for parole."

"Mom, you want to do that? He's a convicted murderer, right? You're going to invite him in here?"

"Jack made that deal with him. I don't know exactly what it all is. I just know my end. You met him that time you went to see Jack down there. You thought he was okay."

I had met him. He did strike me as okay. But still, he had murdered someone to get sent to prison, and later killed an inmate. Jack had some kind of obligation to him, though. A prison thing. My mom wasn't as good as other moms at a lot of stuff. But this she could cover.

"He gets out in two weeks," she says. "I want you to drive down there to pick him up, okay?"

"Yeah, okay."

"You take care, now, then."

"I guess I'll see you at Churchville for the first training sessions."

117

"Yes, you will. I'll be teaching blackjack. Thank God I won't be dealing it no more."

"Yeah, you're a boss now."

"Isn't that something? And you say hi to Laura for me."

THIRTEEN

I wake at six in the evening. Old Charlie's baking, and I pour some cold coffee into a cup, microwave it, and drink it while I wait for his muffins to finish. The coffee is double strong, but I sometimes like it that way. No cream, no sugar. Just double-strong, reheated coffee. (Did I just say something about appreciating fresh ground?)

I light a cigarette and notice how happy the old guy seems.

"What's up with you?" I ask.

He waves me off. He's wearing his usual around-the-house clothes — blue sweatpants, black dress socks, and a flannel shirt.

"No, really, man, what's up? Why are you so happy?"

"I'm not happy."

"You're walking around humming because you're hating life? Baking blueberry muffins because you're miserable?"

"You're going to be a daddy!"

"Why does that make you happy?"

"It'll make you be responsible."

"Aw, shut the fuck up. What do you know about responsibility? Haven't had a job in twenty years and you're talking to me about responsibility."

Charlie wasn't happy about my becoming a father because he liked kids or believed in family. He just liked the idea of me being in trouble. If I ever went broke he'd bust his diseased old liver laughing about it.

I look at him humming and baking. I laugh.

"You're not altogether here, are you Old C?"

"What do you care? Huh? Since when do you care about anyone but yourself?"

"Who drives you to the doctor every other week? Who visited you every day you were in the hospital last year?"

"You're such an angel. Such a fucking angel."

He takes the muffins out of the oven, and sets them aside to cool.

"Come on," he says, picking up a deck of cards and sitting across the dining room table from me.

"Ten-twenty Hold 'em?" I ask, reaching behind me to get the chips we keep there.

"What difference does it make? Huh? I'm playing with the greatest card player in the world. In the world!"

"You got cash?"

"Do you?"

"You owe me now, sucker."

"You got a fucking attitude."

"Shut up and deal, you Cheese-Whiz-eating, cheap-wine-drinking, porno-watching old bitch." We spend a few hours this way. Cussing each other, eating muffins, drinking coffee, smoking, playing. Someone comes in the door — Essay.

"Where'd you go?" I ask him.

Kevin comes in right behind him.

"Pick him up," Essay says.

"Hey, Joey. Hey, Charlie," Kevin says.

"Look at the Rainbow Coalition," the old fart says. "I got a black, a white, and a Latino here. What a country. What a fucking country."

"Shut up and deal, man," I say.

120

"It's your damn deal."

"Then give me the deck. What's up, Kevin? Where you been?"

"Knights of Columbus," Essay says.

"Eat some muffins," Charlie says.

"Where's your cigarettes?" Kevin says.

"Eat the damn muffins," Charlie says.

"Here, brother," I say, tossing my pack.

Essay pulls up a seat. "Deal me in," he says.

"Me, too," Kevin says.

Fat Boy comes by about midnight. He's dealt all the previous day for Nug, and then played and dealt all night at K.C.'s, and then gone to the Elks' today. He's been awake for thirty hours.

He pulls up a chair.

"Cash game," Charlie says to him.

"Fuck you, Dago-face," Fat Boy says. "You got cash?"

"I got a dick good as gold," he says.

"Just cause it's yellow don't mean it's gold," Fat Boy says.

"When's the last time you got it to work?" Essay asks.

"The last time you had money," Charlie answers.

"Let me see," Fat Boy says, throwing a chip at the old man.

I grab the chip and toss it back. "Don't, Fat. This is one of them 'be careful what you ask for you just might get it' things."

"No, shit," Kevin says, fearful. "Just keep that old dog wrapped up, Charlie. We believe it still barks."

"No, he wants to see it," Charlie says, standing up.

"Man, don't do this," I beg.

"Show me what you got," Fat Boy says, egging the old guy on. "I don't think he's got one."

Charlie stares at us.

"Fuck you," he says, and drops his sweats. He's not wearing underwear, so there it is — the sorriest looking penis in the world.

Charlie, with his pants down around his ankles, starts chasing us. We're scrambling, jumping over the couch and diving under the table, scared to death he might touch us with it.

We calm down and go back to playing cards. Essay puts some pasta on. I finally break down and make some fresh coffee.

"Hey, man," Fat Boy says. "I heard Laura's pregnant. Like five months, now, or something."

"Four months," I say.

"Damn, brother. Papa time?" Kevin says.

"Looking that way," I say.

"Why's she so crazy about you, anyway?" Fat Boy asks. "She's crazy about you. It don't make no sense."

"None," Kevin says. "Girl as fine as that."

"And look how he treats her," Essay says.

"Fuck all y'all," I say.

"We just don't see what she sees in you," Essay says.

"I notice women don't have to ask what she sees in me."

Fat makes a jerking-off motion with his hand.

When I get a chance I ask Kevin back to my room. I tell him what I heard about who's backing the casino.

He says, without being happy about it, that it's true. Freddy and Kenny Jones are the money. But he's still in charge. He and Larry. The charity's license is in their name.

We go back to the game.

The phone rings. Essay gets it. Listens. Motions to me.

"Girl," he says, as he hands me the receiver. I take it.

"Yeah," I say.

"Hi," a girl says.

"Who's this?" I have to ask.

"Katrina."

"Oh, shit — I forgot to call you back, didn't I? I'm sorry."

"That's okay. What are you doing?"

"Nothing. Got some friends over. Why are you calling at one in the morning?"

"It's not okay?"

"Probably the best time."

"Your roommate, Charlie, said it would be all right."

122

"I get on a day-sleeper schedule sometimes."

"Sounds like you're having a party."

"Kind of. What's up? What are you doing? It's not past your bedtime?"

"Me and a friend from school are at the Pig's Foot. It's our favorite place to pull an all-nighter."

"Where?"

"Au Pied du Cochon? It's a place in Georgetown. Just down the street from us. Open all night."

"I know it. Wisconsin Avenue. What are you pulling an all-nighter for?"

"That paper's due. The one about *The Hustler*, remember?"

"Yeah. How's it going?"

"Okay. Hey, you want to help me?"

"Now? No."

"Come on, Joey. It'll be fun."

"I'm already having fun."

"Okay. Just an idea."

I laugh. "Au Pied du Cochon, huh?"

"Yes. You're coming?"

"Sure."

"Why?"

I laugh again. "Because you're still up."

"You know how to get here?"

"If it's open all night in the D.C. area, I know how to get there."

I shower, shave, dress. Light-blue jeans, black leather shoes, white socks, dark-blue cotton sweater, brown leather jacket. Red silk scarf on, and then off. Too much.

Hair, getting longer and longer, combed back. Skin, vampire pale, clear. Dab of cologne. Spray of deodorant. Cut a nostril hair, trim my nails.

I check out of the game. The guys ask who I'm going to see. Who's the girl.

I can't think of an out. I know these people — word will get back to Laura. So I don't answer. Just say see you.

I'm in my van, and all I've got to do is go to Pennsylvania Avenue, turn right, and keep on it all the way through D.C. to Georgetown.

I'm going through the city. Late on a cold night. Nobody good or lucky is out. The streets aren't quite empty. But nobody good or lucky is out.

I see the winos shivering in an alley; young bloods tooling in their Blazers.

I'm smoking, so I roll down the window a crack and the air feels good. The radio's off, and the silence feels good. No gunshots, no sirens.

Over a little bridge and I'm in Georgetown. My mom was talking about it, but it's a different place now. Used to be biker bars and dive joints. Now it's yuppie central. Empty streets, though, this late. Parked cops. Couple of couples falling out of the last places open.

Turn on Wisconsin Avenue and go up a few blocks and park just a block away from the place, which is a lucky pull for this neighborhood.

It occurs to me as I walk over that I feel uncomfortable about this. I know what it is — I'm coming down here alone. Like I got nothing else to do, and nobody to do it with. She calls me and I hardly know her but I'm on my way.

I pause before turning the corner to the restaurant, trying to think of how to handle this. Nothing comes to mind. Fuck it. Deal.

I go in, and I see her sitting in a well-lit corner. Her head's down; her hair's a mess. Dark-brown, tangled, falling all over. I like it.

How many men, out of a hundred, would think she's attractive? More than a couple?

I think she's wearing the same clothes she had on when we met — blue jeans, black T-shirt, black windbreaker. Black sneaks.

There's only one coffee cup on the table.

I pull up a seat and sit down.

She looks up, smiles a little. Starts to say hello, but I interrupt.

124

"I give up," I say.

"What?"

"I give up. What kind of person are you?"

She laughs.

"I'm serious. Your mother's not white."

"She's half-Chinese and half-Italian. Is it important?"

"Are you sensitive about it?"

"If someone doesn't like it, I don't care."

"What if someone does like it?"

She smiles. I make her a little nervous. That makes me a little calmer.

The waiter comes up. I order a coffee.

I lean back in my chair. Light a cigarette. Look around at the few other people still there. New bohemians.

Look back at her and find her looking at me.

"Your father likes exotic types, huh?"

"You know him."

"Grows up in an old Virginia whitebread family, but marries a Eurasian. Born into money but becomes a criminal defense attorney and loves the gambling life. Why do you think that is?"

"Daddy's consistent, isn't he?"

"That doesn't answer my question."

"I don't have an answer."

"But you pose the same question."

She looks at me, not following.

"You like 'bad relationships.' Try drugs. Go to college, but study film, not business or law. Probably meet lots of nice boys, but call up a guy your father has warned you off."

A moment passes.

"What am I supposed to say?" she finally asks.

"Nothing."

"Are you mad about something?"

"I have a girlfriend. Kind of. We break up, get back together, break up again, get back again. We don't love each other, but we have fun."

"That's every relationship I've ever been in."

"Last time we broke up, your father started seeing her."

A shocked look comes to Katrina's face, followed quickly by a pained one.

"He slept with her," I say. "I only found this out a few days ago."

"Oh, God," she says. "How old is she?"

"Twenty-three."

"White, Asian, black, what?"

"Filipina."

"Pretty, I guess?"

"Of course."

Pause.

"It's sick," she says.

"I'm not happy about it."

"Because it's him? Or because it's anybody?"

"Him. I don't love her, but I do care about her. She's not a toy."

"My dad has some problems. He loves low society, not high."

I grab her elbow. "Who's low society?" I ask.

Her eyes widen. "I'm sorry," she says.

I let go of her. Take a deep breath. Sip my coffee. She didn't mean anything.

"What was going on at your apartment?" she asks, making conversation.

"It's a house. In Forestville. You know Forestville?"

She shakes her head.

"Nah, I guess you wouldn't make it out that way."

I smoke my cigarette and say, "Poker. A poker game. We don't usually play there, but this one just kind of happened. The old man I live with likes to play. We were playing tonight for the rent and some people came over and then some others, and it just happened."

"At this time of night? You all just do what you want, huh?"

I give her a look. She has a small, rosebud, full-lipped mouth. Very nice.

126

I smile. Let my anger go.

"Is that the paper you're writing?" I ask. She's got a notepad in front of her.

She nods. "It's coming along. I really should give you credit. I'm using a lot of stuff you told me."

I had talked a lot about the movie that day we'd met.

We're silent a moment. I look at her.

She's not tough. I meet more than my fair share of tough people, male and female. I know them when I see them. They're all weak, mind you. I got no problem playing with "tough" people. They try too hard.

But the sensitive? They play too soft, until backed up, when they usually overreact. This girl — definitely sensitive. Rich girl, college girl, no idea what to do with herself.

I look at her.

I laugh.

"What?" she says.

"Why are you here alone? Where's your friend?"

"My roommate? She went home. Got tired."

I read her for a lie there. But I don't care. So she didn't want to say she was alone when she called. So what.

"You're not tired?" I ask.

"No. I'm a night owl."

"A night owl who sits in cafes writing. Who goes to old movies with her dad. Who calls a guy she only met one time. Who calls him back when he doesn't return her first call."

She looks embarrassed.

I just look.

"You hungry?" I ask.

"Yes, a little. But let's not eat here. I like this place for the atmosphere, not the food."

She'd walked to the cafe, so we drive to a diner, the Howard Johnson's by the Watergate, in my van. I tell her about me and K.C. traveling out west in it. She thinks that's great. Tells me about traveling to Europe. Spending a summer in Paris.

While we eat, she talks about her family. Her stepfather is a clothing importer. Her mother's an interpreter, always in demand.

"And you want to make movies?" I ask.

"Yes. I think. Or write them. Or both. You know."

"Not really. I have no idea how movies get made. I know what I like, though."

"You talk well about them," she says, with a certain encouraging tone of voice.

I give her a carefully measured look of displeasure.

She absorbs it. "Sorry."

I like her. I'm thinking she's a loner. And she's not obviously good-looking and has no body. But she's smart, and sensitive, and that flippant rich-girl scene she'd put on when we'd met was an act, or a small side to her, or a reaction to being around her father.

After eating, I drive her home. Glover Park. She invites me in. She and her roommate have a ground-floor apartment in a three-story house, with a back garden. Costs some money, I'm pretty sure. It's nice. Poorly furnished, but different, somehow, from the poorly furnished places of the other people I know. Her place seems deliberately poorly furnished. Fearlessly, maybe I should say. Like there's no mistaking it's only for a while, and not a life.

"You want something to drink?" she asks.

"No. Can we open a window?"

We parked a ten-minute walk from her building, so I warmed against the outside cold, and feel hot now, indoors.

I take off my jacket and shoes, and reach up to open one of those little, set-in basement windows. The back of her place has sliding-glass doors, but the rest of it is underground.

I sit on the couch and look at her.

She has no idea what to do with herself. She's taken off her jacket and shoes and is sitting on a chair across from me. Her hair is a mess, her clothes baggy, and her body almost undetectable underneath them.

"How come you don't get hundred-dollar haircuts?" I ask.

"I do sometimes. I need one, I know. I just haven't felt like caring about it lately."

She looks around the room, not at me. Fiddles with her earrings.

I laugh. I'm surprised by her awkwardness. When we'd met she'd been practically bragging about her bad relationships, about her therapy and treatment. Now she's shy. Could be just an act. But I don't read her for that. I think that day with her father had a lot of show in it.

She looks at me and I smile.

"What?" she says.

"What time is your paper due?"

"It's a night class. Tomorrow night."

"You want to come here, then?" I say, a little nervously maybe. But in this spot it's okay to show a little nervousness. I've known it to help a woman relax.

She takes a deep breath. Like she's diving into something. Then she comes and sits next to me. Looks at me.

I laugh. Smirk a little. Laugh again.

"What is so funny?" she says, smiling herself.

I kiss her. And bad as it may sound, I say without thinking, "Umm, baby . . ."

I couldn't help it. She just had the sweetest, most pliable little mouth.

I take her T-shirt off. She has no bra on. Doesn't need one. Her breasts are small enough and young enough.

And as I lift off her shirt she again takes a deep, ready-get-set-go breath.

I kiss her neck, and her earlobes. I take a long time. She has a beautiful complexion. I love it.

She doesn't know where to put her hands.

I take my sweater off, and put her hands on my chest. Hold her. Kiss her.

In the softest voice, she says, "Let's go to my room."

129

I pick her up, which is easy because she doesn't weigh a hundred pounds, and carry her.

And love her head-to-toe for hours. She is so fragile. So delicious. This change in her personality from when we'd first met fascinates me. And her rich-kid background and being a college student fascinates me, too. When a woman arouses my curiosity, makes me want to learn about her, how better to do that than through sex? I don't mean that in a calculating way. I just mean that I don't understand her, and want to.

I'm supposed to have slept with a lot of women, but in truth I haven't slept with all that many. Don't like to, really. Sleep with them just to sleep with them, I mean. The few one-night-stand type things I've had were pretty bad. The sex as much as the morning after. It takes me a while to feel comfortable with a woman. To figure out how to touch her.

But tonight's different. And very nice. Very, very sweet. Right from the start. Better for her, though, maybe, than for me. It's easy to be wrong about such things, but I think she liked it or needed it more than me. Which is fine.

FOURTEEN

A few nights later we're at the bar One Step Down. A black quartet is playing: sax-playing singer, bassist, drummer, keyboardist.

Katrina and I and a couple of her film student friends are drinking — one round, two rounds, three. Sitting in a corner, in the dark, where, when her friends go to the bathroom, I can put my hands all over her and only someone nosy could tell.

"I'm drunk," she says, smiling.

"You're horny, too."

She laughs. "Look where you've got your fingers!"

Her friends return. I pull back. Drink. Beer.

The band breaks. Katrina drunkenly applauds.

The keyboardist comes up. I stand. We shake.

He reaches in his pocket. Pulls something out. Slips it to me. I can tell by feel that it's money.

"Thanks, man," he says.

"No problem. You running better?"

"This gig helps."

"Stay off the tables."

"Give me lessons."

"Stay off the tables."

"I'm hopeless."

We laugh. He goes on.

"What was that?" Katrina asks.

"He called me to meet him tonight. Owes me money. Four hundred, all here."

"What did he owe you for?" one of her friends asks. A blond girl, here with her blond boyfriend, the both of them dressed in black. Kids. My age, but kids. Could probably beat me at Jeopardy. Not at Monopoly.

I drag on a cigarette, let the smoke find its way out my nose.

"Rent," I say. "I chipped up his rent money last summer."

"You know what?" Katrina says, sloppily.

"What?"

"I know what to do for my senior project."

"What?" her girlfriend asks.

Katrina holds up her arms and dramatically spreads them apart. 'A documentary on gambling. On the real world of gamblers."

"I like that," the blond kid says. "Black-and-white."

"Yeah," the girl says. "With a *Cops*-type tone. That real-life tone."

"Only," Katrina says, "instead of taking a camera out with the cops, we take it out with Joey here."

"Get jobs," I say.

"Come on, Joey," Katrina says. She's dressed in black, too.

"You can't go wrong wearing black, can you?" I say to them all. "Safe as can be. But you want to do a movie about gambling."

"A documentary," Katrina says. She smokes. Drinks. "We'll call it 'The Picture of Gambling.' Chez Joey. My Pal Joey. The Man With the Golden Arm."

I guess three drinks for her is like five for me, small as she is.

"*The Cincinnati Kid. Dark City. The Set-Up*," says the blond kid. "*Generation X* meets *The Hustler*. The ultimate slacker hero."

"We'll get Kenny Rogers to do the soundtrack," his girlfriend says, giggling. "No, I'm kidding. Pearl Jam and Soundgarden."

132

"Have another drink," I say. "Might clear your head."

She laughs.

"What would you be doing if you weren't with me?" Katrina whispers into my ear, one hand on my shoulder, one in my hair.

"I'd be going to a home game."

"Let's do it," she says.

I look at her. Think about it. "Okay, baby," I say. "I am going to take you out. Show you, this one time, what I do. Show you how grey this little black-and-white film you want to make would end up."

We drop the blonds off at their apartment, then head out of the city. To Prince George's County. The first time she's ever been out this way. Grew up in the area, but has never gone out across the Anacostia River. Amazing.

I've got the window down hoping the cold air will sober me up. Katrina's in the back of the van, on the fold-out bed.

"Joey, put the window up," she calls out. I ignore her. "Joey, it's too cold. Come on."

"There's a blanket by your head."

She giggles. "What's that about head?" she asks.

I put on a Kenny G tape. White girls love it.

"I might be serious about that documentary," she says. "I've got to do something. It could be good."

"Yeah? You sleeping with the class project?"

"You fucking my father's daughter?"

Pause.

"Come back here," she says. "Pull over. I want to fuck you in the middle of the night, in the back of a van, on the side of a highway going over a ghetto, with jazz in my ears."

She says that like it's a triumph of imagination. I keep on driving, of course. Carefully. Afraid I'm drunker than I feel.

Out 295 we go. To Oxon Hill. Down a strip of shopping centers and motels and fast-food joints and gas stations and banks. The same stuff as everywhere.

Off the strip to the homes. Little homes. Working-class,

middle-class. The poor in their apartment complexes. Late night, and the cold's whipping through.

It's K.C.'s game we're going to. I find the house. Cars fill the driveway, spill out onto the street, crowding the neighbors. But the homeowner is Filipino and some of the neighbors are Filipino, so things have been worked out.

I park a block up, jam my bankroll into a slit in the carpet under the front seat, and get out.

"What's that for?" Katrina asks.

"I don't bring cash to this game," I say. I don't like bringing cash to private games because if they get raided or robbed, the police or the robbers will take your cheese, and you're not getting it back from either one.

She nods.

I tell her I park a block up because, also if the police raid the joint, they'll search all the cars parked out front.

As we walk, she asks me how often these places get raided.

I say it's been years, but that there are rumors out that the police are pissed off because a cop who played around here killed himself recently.

The house is dark except for a light over the side door. The game is in the rec room downstairs, and the windows are blacked out. But the noise escapes. The talking and the clicking of chips. Muffled, but present.

I knock. A curtain pulls back off the door window, and an old Filipina woman peers out. The curtain drops, the door opens, and she steps back. I say hello. She smiles.

We go downstairs, and the heat and smoke and noise hit us square on. From the cold, fresh, late-night air outside to the enveloping staleness of a basement with eighteen people in it, most of whom smoke.

K.C. runs a good game. Nice table. Professional dealers and waitress. None of the more vulgar, angry players invited. Women feel comfortable coming here.

The crowd tonight is typical. Young, old. Male, female. White, black, Asian, Middle Eastern. A lawyer, a banker, a doctor. A real estate broker, a restaurant owner, a gas station owner. A cab driver, a bartender, a waitress, a schoolteacher, a government accountant, a fireman. Couple of housewives. Couple of retirees. Poker dealers, home game operators, bookies. Professional players. Everybody.

"What's up, sucker?" I say to K.C. as I come in. We shake hands. Nug's here. Fat Boy. Essay.

I introduce Katrina. The guys are all nice to her, but otherwise she attracts no attention. She's not their type.

A player gets up, cashes out his chips with K.C., and leaves.

Nug's next up for the game. He goes into K.C.'s chip case and takes two hundred in red, forty five-dollar chips.

"Come on," he says to Katrina. "You watch over my shoulder."

"Okay," she says. Happy to.

She looks at me.

"Yeah, it's a good idea," I say. "It's the second best way to learn."

"What's the best way?"

"Losing your ass."

"I'll just watch."

"Good. Because you ain't got no ass to spare."

The guys laugh. She smiles along. Drunk.

I must have had something in the back of my mind, taking Katrina into the heart of the gossip-hungry poker world. About three days later, Laura and I have dinner together. Some Vietnamese restaurant.

She is silent during the drive there. The girl loves to talk. Hates to let a silence go unfilled. But this night, she's quiet.

So I'm quiet. Does she think I know what to say?

We order.

We eat.

The plates are cleared. The waiter brings a fresh pot of hot tea.

"You really made a show of it, didn't you?" she says.

"I did what?"

"Bringing that girl to K.C.'s game. So everyone could see her."

135

"I always go to his game. She was with me. What am I supposed to do — sneak around? You and I are not together."

"Do you like her better than me?" she asks.

I sigh. I say, honestly, "No. Not 'better.'"

"Where did you meet her?"

"Downtown."

"What does she do?"

"She's a film student."

"I heard she's not very cute."

I give up a line here. Say something like, "She's not as pretty as you."

"Oh, yeah. I must be beautiful. You must really think I'm beautiful."

"Laura, our problem has never been physical."

"Are you going to tell me how I feel again?"

"No."

"I don't want to marry you, Joey. You can relax about that. Why would anyone want to marry you? You don't even have a job. In fact, as far as I'm concerned, we don't have to see each other ever again. I don't need you."

"What about the baby?"

"It's not your concern."

"I want to help."

"You don't have to. My family will take care of me."

"You don't want money?"

That cools her. She won't even bluff that she doesn't want money.

"You can just send me a check."

She's saying this in one of those "what a pig you are if you *don't* argue with me" voices.

"Joey, I can marry someone else. You'll be off the hook. The baby never has to know you. I think that would be better. My mother definitely thinks it would be better."

I think about all that. I've thought about it before. She could be right. She's bluffing here, but she could be right. If she married

136

someone, and the child took that man's name, maybe we'd all be better off.

But I say — because I think I feel it —"Laura, I want to be a part of its life. If it's my baby, I want to be close to it."

Oooh. I said "if" it's my baby. That's about my only ammo in all this.

"It's your baby. Believe it."

"I do."

I really do. The timing is right. Bobby Lotto was gone for three weeks to California when she and I were getting back together. If the baby is born in early April, it just about has to be mine.

I take her hand. Look at her.

I don't know what to say, but feel, and so voice, "Laura, we have got to work out some kind of relationship."

"Why? I told you — you never have to see the baby."

"You know, you always say the opposite of what I say. If I say I don't want to be involved, you say I'm an irresponsible bum. If I say I do want to be involved, you tell me not to bother."

The truth of that gets her. She looks away. Tears well in her eyes.

What am I doing? I can't be tough with her. How could anyone? She is so lost. I'm lost, sure. Everyone is, maybe. But she can't even begin to see straight.

I move to sit by her. Bring her head to my shoulder. Feel a lot of emotion myself.

I suppose most people would say I'm being a pig. That I should marry her. But most people get divorced, or don't get divorced but cheat on each other and fight all the time. And I'm not most people.

She sits up.

"Bobby's been talking to my parents," she says.

"Why?"

She shrugs. "He wants to marry me."

I want to say, Laura, please don't ever marry that asshole. But I think, how is it my business? If he has money, and loves her? I shouldn't say anything. If she is going to marry him, it should be with the best possible attitude.

"Laura," I say, "I will never forgive you if you marry that asshole."

She laughs. Finally.

"Your father wants to marry my ex-girlfriend."

Katrina shakes her head. "He is such a mess."

"She's pregnant."

"Whose kid?"

"Probably mine. Maybe your dad's."

She shakes her head again. Puts her hands over her eyes. Says, "My therapist will love it."

FIFTEEN

I'm on my back, on the ratty living room couch, listening to Old Charlie's old jazz tapes. The phone rings. "Yeah?"

"Joey?"

"Yeah?"

"Jack."

"Yeah?"

"What's up?"

"Nothing."

"You got to do that Calvin thing today."

"I know."

"You going to do it?"

"Of course I'm going to do it. All I got to do is pick the sucker up, right? Mom's the one who's got to live with him."

"Calvin's all right. Just stupid. Can't read."

"He's a killer, and you got Mom putting him up."

"I got to! Look, man. I'm in a thing here. It's a white thing. Can't tell you the name. Not Aryan Brotherhood, but like that."

"A gang?"

"An organization. It's not really even racial, except that who else we going to be with? This place ain't got but so many white men, you know."

"So you got to do what you got to do. I'm not saying nothing about that. I'm just saying, why you bring Mom into it?"

"She don't mind. And Calvin's all right, I'm telling you. I can tell. Everyone here knows Calvin don't start nothing."

"You told me he killed an inmate, too."

"But he didn't start that. He just finished it. See?"

"No."

"Joey, why are you being so stupid? All I'm saying is that, yeah, if someone pushes the man, sure he's going to take them out. But the difference is, Calvin don't never look for trouble. In thirteen years here —"

"Thirteen years? How old is he?"

"Thirty-three. In thirteen years here, he's never started nothing with no one. You understand? He's not aggressive. You think I'd send some maniac home to Mom?"

"How do you know, though? How can you be sure?"

"Joey, listen to me. In here, we all know who's what. We know who'll do what. We know who'll start what. We know. The shrinks don't know. The counselors don't know. The preachers don't know. But *we* know. Okay? And Calvin don't do nothing."

"Why'd he kill the inmate?"

"It was a white guy ratting on someone. Long time ago, when the organization first started. Calvin got given the hit to test him."

A moment passes. What can I say? There's nothing I can say.

"So what do you need me to do?"

"Just pick him up. Take him to Mom's. Get him settled in."

"What do you get out of this? I mean, we'll help you. I'll help you. But how does helping him help you?"

"I don't want to kill no one, Joey. I don't want to get into the heavier shit around here. So my *in* is to help get this brother con *out*. He's got no family. No one to parole to. So we're putting him up. I got to get this done, Joey."

There's anxiety in his voice.

"Yeah, yeah, yeah," I say. "Okay. Today, right?"

"That's why I'm calling you. Make sure you're up in time."

It's a few hours drive down there. Powhatan Correctional is well outside Richmond, on the James River. Nice enough looking place, actually, for a prison.

I pull in, go in, check in. Wait. Two o'clock when I get there, three before a steel door opens and a man steps out.

"Calvin?" I say, checking. I only met him one time, a year ago. He nods.

I stand, put my hand out to shake. He nods again, shifts a box he's holding from one arm to the other, puts his right hand out, takes mine, pumps it.

"How you doing?" he says in some kind of thick country accent.

"Let's go," I say.

He nods. Follows me out.

Calvin's no taller than me, but he must be seventy pounds heavier, and it's all muscle. Lift weights every day for so many years, and it'll show. He's a tank.

He's otherwise tough-looking, too. Pock-marked skin. Long, greasy brown hair. Brown eyes, narrow-set. Wearing tight-fitting bluejeans, black work boots, a couple of white T-shirts, and a jeans jacket. A strong-jawed man, yet dull. Not scary, if you study him. Not sharp. Not "looking." Doesn't study the world to figure how to beat it. Just studies it to see how it's next going to try to hurt him. That was my instinct about him the first time we met, and is again.

We walk outside, and he smiles. I smile with him.

"Congratulations, man," I say.

He smiles again, sheepishly. Looks around, sheepishly. Says nothing.

We go to my van. His box has a radio in it, some clothes, and some toiletries. He climbs in the passenger side. Puts the box down between his legs.

"Can I smoke?" he asks.

I start the engine, and then reach down under the front seat and pull out a carton I'd had there.

"Welcome out, man," I say, handing it to him.

He nods, takes it.

We drive across the almost campuslike grounds. Past a ball field.

"Hey, pull over, man," he says.

I do.

He gets out. Waves to the inmates playing softball there. Lets out a wolf howl.

Several wave back. Howl back. He howls, they howl. Laugh.

I see Jack. He's got a beard now, and hair longer than ever. He's gained weight. I wave to him. He waves back.

Sad.

Calvin stands looking at them all. One finally yells, "Go on, motherfucker. Get the fuck on."

Calvin nods, climbs back in.

A few miles on down I stop at a gas station. Calvin comes in with me.

"You want some coffee?" I ask.

"You fix it yourself?" he asks back.

"Yeah. Then just take it to the counter and we'll pay for it with the gas. You want anything else?"

He gets a few candy bars.

"I got it, Cal," I say.

"I got money."

"Not much, you don't."

He smiles. Not too sensitive.

In the van, he gobbles down the candy bars, slurps up his coffee. Rips open the carton of cigarettes, yanks one, lights it.

"What kind of music you like?" I ask him.

"Whatever."

I put something on.

Miles pass. He doesn't speak, but we're both comfortable. He just looks out the window, periodically smiling, nodding to himself.

"Thirteen years?" I say.

"Yep."

More miles pass. On 95 north to D.C. we pass a sign and he asks me if the "E" stands for East.

I nod yes.

"How's your reading coming along?" I ask him.

"A lot better. Since I knew I'd be getting out, I worked harder."

"Can you drive?"

"Ain't done it so long, I don't know. Scares me to."

"Why?"

"I get lost easy."

"Keep a map."

"Can't figure them out."

"They're a bitch sometimes. But I'll teach you."

"Cool."

"You never met my mom, have you?"

"No."

"She's all right about things."

"Jack said she was."

"And this guy Grizzly you're going to work for — he's a good man."

Calvin nods.

"They'll be as square with you as you are with them."

He nods again.

What's my point?

PART TWO

SIXTEEN

The next few weeks, I'm working. I'm going to every card room and home game around, talking up the new casino. Telling everyone it's my card room, come by and give me some action. I get flyers printed up. Business cards. Pass them out.

Word spreads, and everywhere I go someone asks me for a job. I've got to say no to most of them. That's a new spot for me.

K.C. asks me point blank if I'm going to hire Sam to deal, and I say yes. Freddy Sorenson, Kenny Jones, K.C. — they all want me to hire her. K.C. tells me she's not going to steal this time. She's learned her lesson. He's one of my best friends. I can't tell him I don't think she'll ever change. He loves her.

Another dealer on the list of people I'm supposed to hire, another guy with a greed problem, I also give a job to.

Two more people from Freddy and Kenny's list I don't mind, because they are good dealers, and not known to be thieves.

Essay and his new girlfriend sign up. Fat Boy. That's seven. I can handle four or five tables with seven dealers. There's a couple of people hired to deal blackjack that can jump in a poker box if I need them. My mom can, even, in a pinch. And they'd love the chance. The blackjack dealers are getting twelve to fifteen dollars an hour. If we're at all busy, the poker dealers will make six hundred for the two days.

Opening day gets postponed one week because the pit crew is late getting together. Too many rookie dealers. They need more time.

But then we open, and at noon I'm a little nervous. My first ever job. Part job, part business.

Running the card room is the easy part. Greet the customers by name. Seat them if I've got something open. Shoot the breeze with them if I don't. Rotate the dealers and keep an eye on the ones I doubt. Make rules decisions when questions arise.

The hard part? I can't *make* people come in. All I can do is sweat the empty chairs.

At noon the first day I've got Nug and three dealers from his place; K.C., brother pro, shows up on time for me; Grizzly; a yuppie couple I've known a long while; and maybe two other players. In other words, besides personal friends, I've only got two people, out of hundreds, who said they'd be here.

But we play. A few more people straggle in. We get up to two full tables at one point. In the evening, back to one table.

It's the first week, people tell me. What do you expect? My mom's there, working in the blackjack pit. She tells me I did better than the rest of the place.

I thank my buddies. I really am grateful they came. Especially considering I had so little action to offer them. Nug and K.C. sat in a 2-5 game all day for me. I know they haven't played that small in years.

The next day, Friday, we get two tables early, and make it up to three at one point. That's a little better.

Kevin and Larry are satisfied. At least I brought some money in for them. They've got a twenty-thousand-dollar nut to meet every week, between food (customers eat well, and free), rent, and payroll.

That's before they themselves get anything. Before the charity gets anything. Before Freddy Sorenson and Kenny Jones get anything.

This first week, they only made five thousand off blackjack, and two thousand off roulette. They got close to four thousand off poker. I get eight hundred off the top, and the dealers work for tips, so the casino profits three thousand some.

I call Freddy. We talk. He tells me not to be discouraged about the slight poker turnout. That it will pick up.

I don't tell him, but I'm not discouraged. The eight hundred I made undiscouraged me pretty well.

The casino's second week is better all around. I've spent a lot of time going around the county telling everyone again about our place. This time I get to tell them that we are open and having tournaments and bonuses. So I get two games all day Thursday, three at the peak. Three games all day Friday, four at the peak. We cut about fifty-five hundred. I take home eleven hundred. Sure, I've been putting in a lot of hours traveling around brushing up the action, but eleven hundred! I'm a happy puppy.

The next week is busier still. Three or four tables Thursday, four or five on Friday. Seven thousand cut, fourteen hundred for me.

And by our second month we've leveled off at almost fifteen thousand dollars a week in cut, three thousand a week for me.

And *that* is the definition of loving life. I don't have to advertise anymore. I've got Essay rotating the dealers for me. I've hired a girl to work the seating board. All I do now is greet people and make an occasional rules decision. Sit on my ass and play Tonk, gin, or Pai Gow. Read the sports section or *Racing Form*. Talk on the phone. And count my money.

My bankroll, before the casino, was probably pretty typical of a mid-stakes professional poker player. Usually around twenty thousand dollars. If it got down to ten thousand, I'd start getting nervous and play a little lower, a little longer. When it got up past thirty thousand, I'd start shooting dice or playing the horses with it. Just spending it, maybe. I was never working toward anything with the money. Had to have enough to operate with. Didn't need much more than that. To some people, twenty thousand is nothing. To others, it's a ton. To me, it just was what it was. Enough. No worries either way. No too-much-money worries, no too-little-money worries. Everyone's got their comfort range. Mine was twenty dimes.

Then this casino opened. The money started jumping in my pockets faster than I knew what to do with it. I actually started worrying about the I.R.S. for the first time in my life.

Freddy gave me his advice on that. He said I should start putting five hundred a week in my checking account, and then withdrawing two hundred a week, and writing checks for my rent. He said, at the end of the year, report that five hundred a week as income, and pay taxes on it. Don't do anything that would indicate a bigger income. Because I was being paid illegally, and in cash, the I.R.S. could only judge the accuracy of my reported income by comparing it to the income they would estimate to be necessary to maintain my lifestyle. As long as I didn't have any visible signs of a greater income, they would have to accept the five-hundred-a-week story. This meant, don't put anything else in the bank. Don't buy a new car in my own name. Don't move into a more expensive place.

But also, don't worry. You're a small fry, he said. They'll only go after you if they stumble upon you somehow.

"Like if the casino gets raided?"

"Report that five hundred a week, and stick to your story. There won't be any written records to contradict you."

I do what he says. Five hundred a week in; two hundred a week out for "spending." That's three hundred a week saved officially. I already have a couple of thousand in a checking account. I'll just build on it and forget it.

The rest?

I have a reserve five thousand stashed at my mom's house. A month after the casino opens I add another five thousand. I decide to forget it's there. That's what a reserve is for.

Two months after the casino is open, I've got five thousand in the bank, that ten thousand at my mom's, ten thousand stashed in my van, five thousand in my bedroom dresser, and three thousand in my pocket. I've always kept at least a dime on me, because I hate walking around with less than that. But now I'm out with three thousand.

"Why do people love the feel of money?" I ask. "Why do they love physically playing with it?"

Katrina laughs. Drinks white wine from the bottle.

We're in my bedroom. She's in bed, naked. I'm at my desk, counting hundred dollar bills. When I finish, I sit there, looking at her, holding them.

"How much?" she asks.

"Three thousand."

I put the money in a drawer and climb into bed with her. She passes me the bottle. I drink. We've got Chinese food and wine and candlelight. Four in the morning. The casino closed at two. I needed a half-hour to finish off the paperwork and pay the dealers and see Kevin in the office. Then Katrina and I went to Chinatown, grabbed food to go, and came here.

"Poker grossed fifteen thousand for the two days," I say to her. "Three dimes for me."

"And then you come here and get your cock sucked and fucked while you lie on your back taking it easy. And then you eat, and drink expensive wine. And then you count your money. You really are the luckiest man alive."

"Why do you like talking dirty?"

She laughs, drunk. "*This*," she says, waving her hands around, "brings it out in me. *You* bring it out in me."

"I don't like it." I really don't.

"Why?"

"Forget it. Let's go to sleep."

"Let's go out to the living room and watch Old Charlie's porn movies."

"You get drunk too easy," I say. And her personality changes so much when she does.

She rises. "Come on," she says, starting out the door, still naked.

I grab her. Pull her back in. Shut the door.

"What if Charlie wakes up?" I ask.

"Then he'll finally see what he's been listening to."

I gather the food boxes and take them out to the kitchen. When I come back, she's in the bathroom, brushing her teeth. I do the same, blow out the candles, put her in bed, and join her. We cuddle in the dark.

"I can't believe how much money I'm making," I say.

Her head is on my chest. "More than playing?"

"Hell, yes. Easier, too."

"That's for sure. I never see you do anything except sit around talking to people."

She's been coming out sometimes, playing low-stakes poker. Learning pretty fast. Plays blackjack some, too. Never loses.

"Hey, I have to make rulings. Rotate the dealers."

"Count the money."

"Count the money."

"Read the *Racing Form*."

"It don't read itself."

We laugh.

"I just can't believe it," I say. "I mean, I worked hard, sure. But still — to have the busiest poker room in the county — wow. Three thousand for two days work."

She climbs up on top of me. Kisses me.

"Don't change," she says.

"What?"

"Don't start caring about money now. Now that it's coming easy. Wouldn't that be ironic? I go out with a guy who first is playing for money, but working hard for it, and doesn't care about it. But when he starts working for it, but having it come easy, *then* he starts counting it. That really is ironic."

I stroke her hair.

152

"Don't start caring about it, Joey," she says.

"It's just fun," I say. "Like I won a lottery. I've never had it easy before. I like it."

She rubs my chest.

I hold her. Think about things.

"You said all of 'this' makes you talk dirty?" I ask.

Katrina, kissing my chest, murmurs something.

"What did you mean?" I ask.

She sits up. My eyes have adjusted to the dark, and I can see her a bit, from the slight light coming through the window.

Christmas Eve, she brings me to her mother's home. I meet her mother, her stepfather, her sisters, their blow-dried boyfriends.

"Joey, Katrina says you work for a charity in Prince George's County?" her mother asks me.

"Yes, ma'am," I say.

"A charity that gets girls off welfare," Katrina says.

Later, in her old bedroom upstairs, Katrina tells me her mother knows full well what I do.

"I thought she might have," I say.

"Hey, get undressed," she says, flopping on her bed. "I've been waiting since you bought that suit to see you take it off."

"I've been waiting since I bought it to wear it." I take her hand. "Come on, let's go for a walk."

"Another one? No. It's almost dinner!"

"We won't be gone long."

Her neighborhood, Chevy Chase, is beautiful. Huge, distinct homes. A strip of nice little stores a few blocks away. People out walking, shopping, visiting. I love it. I wonder if the people here think the life they lead is just how life is.

"Do you know how lucky you are?" I ask Katrina outside.

She shrugs. "What am I supposed to do? Thank God every day I wasn't born poor? Be a nun, maybe, from gratitude?"

She takes my arm. "Besides," she says, "you're wearing two thousand dollars' worth of new clothes. Not exactly starving yourself."

153

"No," I say. "But it's not the same."

"I wonder how you would have turned out if you'd been raised here?" she asks.

"I wonder how you'd have been, raised in Forestville."

"Tell me."

"You'd have been a receptionist."

"Thanks."

"Maybe a schoolteacher, if you set your mind to it."

"And you, raised here, would have been an investment banker. Wheeling and dealing. Reading people's fears. Psyching them out. Making tons of money without actually producing anything."

I nod. "I read a book called *Liar's Poker*. Picked it up by accident, because of the title. I liked it, though. I think I would have been a great bond trader."

"A great trader, maybe. But a great asshole, too."

"Why?"

"You're a little arrogant. The only reason you haven't crossed the line to being an asshole is because you don't know how much better you are than everyone else."

I stop. Look at her.

"Then again," she goes on, "if you had been born here, you *would* be an asshole, in which case you *wouldn't* be better than anyone at all. Yet another Pinocchio Joe irony."

I scrunch my eyes to look confused. She laughs.

Christmas Day we go to my mom's. She's got a tree up. We drink some coffee. Talk. Exchange gifts, including some for Calvin, who's there.

We go out to a place in Waldorf for dinner. Calvin comes with us. He's doing well. My mom seems happy to have him around.

"What's Christmas like in prison?" Katrina asks Calvin.

He thinks a minute. Says, "Thanksgiving."

I laugh, almost get hysterical. My mom and Calvin join me. Katrina doesn't get it, but smiles along.

"He just means," I say to her, "that it's nothing special."

"Another turkey dinner," Calvin says. He's wearing the nice clothes he's gotten from us this morning. He's as stiff as the shirt collar, sitting as straight as the new-pants crease.

"Calvin is so cute," Katrina says later. "I don't mean physically, of course. But in the way he's so moved to be out with people doing normal things. It's really kind of touching, seeing a smile come over his face for no reason except that he's happy."

"He is happy."

"Childlike happiness."

"I guess."

"And your mom — the way she looks after him, protects him. That's not how I expected her to be."

"How'd you expect her to be?"

She shrugs.

Christmas night Katrina comes over to my place and we find Essay, Kevin, Old Charlie, K.C., Nug, and Fat Boy all there playing cards.

"Christmas night, and you guys are in action," I say. "What a fucking crew."

"Nice coat," Fat Boy says of my expensive new one. "Who owned it first?"

Katrina and I go on back to my room. I look around it and realize what a dump I live in. Compared to Katrina's apartment, or her room at her mother's. We go to sleep.

The next morning, the guys are still playing. The whole house has that stinking ashtray smell.

Katrina and I sit with them and watch. They all look like hell. Overnight poker sessions will do that. But they got money and time, so they're going to gamble.

I don't know what Kevin's deal is with Freddy, but I'm sure he's getting at least two dimes a week out of there. Essay's making eight hundred a week dealing; Fat Boy, too. Even Old Charlie Bad Back has cheese. He hit the five-dime lottery last week. Four years of playing every day. Finally hit it.

Katrina wants to play. She likes all these guys. They are a lively group, I guess. Noisy enough, anyway.

I go back to sleep. Wake up at eleven.

The poker game's over. Katrina's watching TV.

"I lost three hundred," she says.

"In a short-handed ten-twenty Hold 'em game with people who know how to play? That's not bad."

"I want to get it back, but they quit."

"You weren't going to get it back from them anyway."

"I still want to play. Let's go somewhere."

"What does it take to get a cup of coffee around here?" I say loudly. "Nug, when are you going to hire a real waitress?"

We'd gone to the Filipino casino and I'm playing ten-twenty high-low Omaha. Playing loose. Having fun. Losing, but not caring.

Nug comes over. Plays along. "This girl no good?" he says.

"Worst waitress I've ever seen."

Mary tries not to smile. "I'm going to give you some coffee real fast," she says, lifting the pot over my head.

"Hey, girl," I say.

"Hey, boy."

"I heard Allison was working here. I didn't know about you."

"She didn't want to drive down by herself every week, so she asked me to come, too."

"You make enough money to justify the trip?"

"Two hundred a day."

"The other waitresses are jealous."

"I can tell. I don't really know why."

"Because you have the poker room. And poker players are the best tippers."

"A dollar every time I bring them a cup of coffee! It's crazy. And all the guys in the business — Essay and Fat Boy, and K.C. especially — they give me at least two dollars. Sometimes five!"

"They're making up for me. I'm going to stiff you."

"That's fine, dear."

"I'm 'dear'? I like that."

"You do? How sweet. You going to put me on your list of girl-friends?"

"That's funny."

"How many do you have this week?"

"One. Her name's Katrina. She's sitting over there."

"Which one?"

I point her out. Mary looks her over.

"I heard about her. Also about Laura."

"It's not a secret."

"I vouched for you, by the way."

"With who?"

"Laura. She heard I was the girl you saw in Delaware. I told her you just came up for Nug's double date with Allison."

"It's true."

"Thank you."

"I just mean, you know . . ."

"I know."

"She's not my girlfriend, anyway."

"I know that, too."

I get some cards. Look at them. After I throw them away, I look up to see that Mary is gone; she's over talking to Nug at the dealer's hangout table. I join them.

"Laura getting big, man," Nug says.

"When is she due?" Mary asks.

"Early April," I say.

Nug goes off to take care of something. I sit down beside Mary.

"How do you feel about becoming a father?" she asks.

"I don't know. Wouldn't mind having had some choice in the matter."

"You going to take some responsibility?"

"We worked it out. Four hundred a month, plus major items like the crib and high chair. Plus medical expenses, including hers for the birth."

"That's pretty fair."

"I don't mind."

"Don't mind? No part of you is looking forward to it?"

"Looking forward to paying out four hundred a month for the next eighteen years?"

"How about looking forward to being a father?"

I make a waving off motion. "What do you care, anyway?"

"I've had some talks with Laura."

"Great."

"Her parents work here. She comes by. We've talked. No big deal."

"Her parents — what hypocrites. They hear how much money I'm making and suddenly they're all nicey-nice to me."

"It's natural. They're immigrants. They didn't come here for their daughter to be poor."

"You're not nicey-nice to me."

"I don't like you."

We both smile.

"If I bought a house would you like me?"

"Nope."

"If I took you traveling would you like me?"

"Traveling? What's that?"

"Something people do for fun."

"I don't have fun," she says. "I work. I commute. I watch my daughter. I run errands. I clean house."

She's actually getting a touch angry.

"Calm down," I say.

"I'm all right. I just don't need to have my life laughed at."

"I didn't laugh at you."

She looks at me. I can't help but smirk at her. She can't help but let a little smile come to her eyes.

"You're lucky, Joey," she says. "I wonder if you know just how much."

I laugh. "Lucky to be smart, maybe," I say.

"Uh-huh."

I take her hand. "Hey," I say seriously.

"What?" she answers, just as seriously.

We look at each other. "I'm glad I don't have to play poker against you," I finally say.

She shakes her head, disappointed. Goes back to work.

SEVENTEEN

Texas Hold 'em is a simple game. Each player receives two cards face down, after which is a round of betting. Then come three community cards placed face up in the table's center, and a second round of betting. Then another community card and another round of betting. And finally the last community card, and the last round of betting. Best five-card hand from the seven cards available to a player, wins. Simple. Along with seven-card stud, Hold 'em is America's most popular form of poker. But between seven-card and Hold 'em, among high-stakes players, and better players of every level, the latter is the choice. It is especially preferred for the greatest, most challenging form of poker — no-limit. No limit, that is, other than what you have before you, to the amount you can bet. (It is a Hollywood movie idiocy that people lose pots by running out of money. Poker could not be played intelligently if that were the case. Whoever had the most money, regardless of the cards, would win every time. The reality is that if a player cannot call a full bet, his hand plays for the fraction of the pot for which he does have money. From the point at which he ran out of chips, the other players begin a side pot.)

♣   ♣   ♣

New Year's Day, and it seems all of gambling Maryland is in Atlantic City. All the people associated with the charity casino, anyway. We're at a private club, a social club, having our own little party. And poker game.

There's a young guy, Philly, sitting across the table from me. A fast-talking, bossy, petulant guy dressed in designer sweats and wearing gold chains, rings, and a watch. He's got hair dark and straight and slicked back. Would-be stud, with big arms, but a fat stomach and butt. Probably thinks he's sexy because of those arms. Probably doesn't have too many women point out how unsexy the rest of his body is.

The game is no-limit Hold 'em, one thousand dollar buy-in.

"Freddy, I thought you said this guy was good," Philly says of me, turning over a nothing hand after bluffing me out of a small pot.

Freddy shrugs.

"Deal," I say to the scrawny, pimply-faced Italian kid in the box. He puts out the cards, two to a player, face down.

Philly bets a hundred. He bets often. He talks a lot, bets a lot, couldn't care less about the money, couldn't care less about the odds. He only has one speed — full out. First sign of weakness and he'll bet, putting the pressure on the other player. And because he truly doesn't seem to care about money, he's also hard to read.

I don't know where he gets his money, but it's hard to believe it comes from playing cards. Most people claiming to be professional are either unemployed or driving a cab or something else they don't want to admit to; have an illegal income they don't want to admit to; have only been at it a few months, and so should be saying they're *trying* to be a pro; or are bankroll hustlers, guys who win a few tournaments mostly on luck and then use their newly acquired reputation to borrow money the rest of their lives. (Many of the biggest names in poker are perpetually broke, perpetually borrowing: *Psst . . . hey bud, want in on a sure thing? I'm the greatest poker player in the world. Put me in this game and I'll split the profit with you.* One such player reportedly was asked what he would do if he won the World Series of Poker final event, with its one-million-dollar prize.

He said he'd pay off his debts. What about the rest, he was asked. The rest, he said, would have to wait.)

Philly won a major tournament last year. More than a hundred thousand. Lets us all know it.

Here, now, he bets. I look at my hole cards. An ace and a king of the same suit. Excellent. I raise four hundred.

Philly doesn't hesitate. When everyone else folds, he raises me back, fifteen hundred.

Goddamn, I think. What have I stepped into? I really don't want to be dealing with this.

The only hand he could have right now that's terrible for me is two aces. If he has two kings, he's a favorite, but I'm alive on an ace draw. If he has any other pair, we're basically flipping a coin. And if he has no pair, I'm the favorite.

I call. Even though we've only got two cards, and the five community cards are yet to be dealt, the betting is over. I turn over my ace-king. He turns over a pair of nines. Like I said, we're basically flipping a coin now. If one of the coming five community cards is an ace or a king but no nine, or if three of the coming cards are of my cards' suit, I win. If not, he wins.

The dealer puts out the five community cards. No ace, no king, no nothing for me. Philly wins.

He smiles and takes the pot.

"Why you call, man?" asks Nug, sitting next to me.

"It was the right play," I answer. "Fifteen hundred to call, to win twenty-five hundred in the pot. A five to three payoff on an almost even money draw. It was the right play."

He shakes his head.

I get up for a cup of coffee. This place has a bar where an old man pokes around, coming up with anything you order. They have an espresso machine, but I want regular coffee. He reaches under the counter and comes back up with a cup. I give him a dollar.

This "social club" is in a green-painted wood-frame rowhouse on a side street maybe half a mile from the casinos. The first floor is divided into two large rooms. The front is almost like a cafe, with little tables, a few couches, and an overhead TV. The backroom has the poker table and the bar. Looking through the door to the front room, I see Allison and Katrina and Freddy's blonde watching football on the TV. I bring my coffee in and stand by them.

"How's the game going?" Katrina asks.

"Okay."

"How's Nug doing?" Allison asks.

"Okay."

"If I lose this football bet," Katrina asks, "and I don't pay, will they beat me up?"

She's smiling. One of the old Italian men sitting at another table had said she could bet with him. She'd never bet on a football game before.

"You going to have her legs broken?" I ask the old guy.

He smiles. Says, "No, we don't hurt women. We'll have *your* legs broken."

Some of the other guys laugh. There's five or six of them sitting around, drinking wine or espresso. Freddy had introduced Nug, Fat, and me to them when we'd come in. They were a bunch of Frankies and Paulies and Luigis.

Coming over here was Freddy's idea. Nug and Allison and Katrina and I were staying at the Taj Mahal. All comped, of course. We'd gone out drinking and dancing and gambling until late last night, throwing money around, drinking champagne and kissing at midnight. We'd done the same the night before. Taken in some shows. Sat laughing and guzzling in lounges with pseudo Frank Sinatras and Henny Youngmans. Later, eaten flaming dinners with flaming desserts.

And now we're at this social club because Freddy Sorenson had sent Fat to invite us, and the girls had said they were too tired and hungover for another day like the last two anyway. Sitting around drinking coffee and nibbling at Italian food delivered from the neighboring restaurant was fine, they said. Allison, a football fan, wanted to watch the bowl games. Katrina said she'd survive an empty day.

163

I step outside for some air. It's cold, but I need a cigarette and a break. The sun is setting.

Katrina comes out. Takes my arm. Looks up at me, concerned.

"Losing?" she asks, tentatively.

"It happens," I say. "Poker's a long-run game."

I look down the street. A classic working-class New Jersey street.

"What's wrong?" Katrina asks.

"I don't know."

She hugs me. "Don't worry about it," she says softly.

I nod. "Yeah, it doesn't matter. They're catching some cards against me. This one guy, Philly, is lucky as hell."

"Well, don't worry about it."

"Know what's really bugging me? I don't know why we're here. Why we're invited to this private party."

"They invited Freddy. Freddy invited you. You brought me."

"No. It can't be that simple. They don't need anyone here just to have a crowd. These guys don't invite people for no reason. Freddy doesn't invite anyone for no reason."

"What do you think?"

"I don't know. We could play cards at the casino. There's something else."

The game's line-up is Philly, three other local Italian guys, me, Nug, Fat Boy, Kenny Jones, and Freddy Sorenson. Although Kevin and Larry Red were up here, staying at Bally's, Freddy had not invited them. He had taken them out to dinner, and seen that their rooms were comped. But he had not invited them, black as they were, to this house. I hate that kind of shit. That's bugging me, too.

I retake my seat.

"You want to play more, Joey baby?" Philly asks, laughing. "I thought maybe you'd had enough."

I don't say anything.

"I guess you're just not used to this format, huh?" Philly asks.

"No," I say. "We don't get to play much big-bet poker back home."

164

"There's a big difference, isn't there?" he says. "You play that pussy limit poker, don't you? No-limit's entirely different. No-limit's a balls game. Don't have no protection, like in limit poker."

Nug looks at me. Worried.

"What?" I ask him.

He doesn't say anything.

Twenty minutes later, I've got pocket kings. The best starting two cards except for aces.

Philly, ahead of me, bets one hundred. I raise three hundred. Everyone else folds. He calls.

The first community cards are dealt. There's an ace and two little cards.

Philly thinks half a second, then bets one thousand.

I take a deep breath, try to relax. When you have pocket kings, the last thing you want to see on the flop is an ace. If an opponent has an ace among his two hole cards, he has you beat. And in Hold 'em, someone raising early, as Philly has, often does so because he has an ace with a strong second card.

I shake my head. I know he has an ace. I know it.

Every time I've bet tonight, every card anyone's needed, they've gotten. And I'm tired of it. I'm not going to pay him off here. I'm not going to lose all my money by getting married to pocket kings, a rookie's habit.

"I fold," I say, throwing my cards away.

"Thank God," Philly says, turning over nothing.

Nug looks at me. Shakes his head.

"You knows what they say, Joey," Philly says. "Cards are good, but balls are better."

He's smiling. He's won five thousand off me and Nug and Fat tonight. Smiling and laughing. Talking shit. Playing aggressively, sure. But being very lucky, too. Four times he's bet with flush draws. Four times he's made his flush.

Grey Kenny Jones, sitting next to Philly and also winning, is also laughing, joking, smiling.

Thirty minutes later, Philly bets a hundred before the flop. I have pocket eights. A passable hand, but tricky to play. I decide to just call the hundred. I could raise, could fold. Do call.

The flop comes two, four, seven. That's a good flop for my hand. He checks.

I bet three hundred.

He raises twelve hundred, all I have.

I think about it, and call.

There are two cards coming, but the betting is over so we show our hands and let the other players enjoy the race. I've got eights, Philly has sixes.

The dealer puts out the next card. An eight. I have three of a kind. With one card left, Philly can only win with a five, for a backdoor straight (the six in his hand with the four, five, seven, and eight on the board).

The dealer puts out the last card — a five.

Nug winces. Fat winces. Freddy winces. I don't.

Philly laughs. Takes the pot, and laughs. Kenny Jones laughs, too.

I stand. "Think I'll let y'all off the hook," I say.

"No more play?" Nug asks.

"Nah."

"Good idea, Joey," Philly says. "Thanks for coming up, though."

He says that last line sincerely.

I nod.

Katrina has brought some cameras. Back in our hotel room, she's fiddling with them.

"What's up with all this?" I ask.

"I'm still thinking of doing that documentary," she says.

The subject hadn't come up for a while. I know some of her student friends had come out to the casino once. They'd taken some photographs, but had stopped when Larry Red told them to.

"What are you going to do this trip?" I ask.

"I want to get some shots of Atlantic City outside the casinos. It's such a beat-up area. I want to do some black-and-white stills."

"Sounds interesting."

"Oh yeah? Take some shots, too, then. I want to see what you'll focus on."

We drive up and down the streets, shooting all kinds of things. Shooting stills. Some video. It's fun. Katrina knows a lot about photography.

Then we gamble. She plays blackjack. I shoot dice. She spends some time with me. I spend some time with her. But mostly, she plays blackjack while I shoot dice. Five hours pass. I lose two thousand. She loses seven hundred. This is the first time she's ever lost, in about ten plays.

We stop to eat, dressed in jeans this time, not a suit or dress, like the past days.

We eat, kind of quietly. Katrina's not used to losing and is a little upset by it. She doesn't handle it well. I hate to see her hurt by it. I hate to see anyone hurt by gambling, but especially her.

We go back to the blackjack tables. I come with her. She doesn't play well. I learned how to play basic strategy and count cards a long time ago. I teach her some. But blackjack is mostly luck, and hers is bad. She loses another four hundred.

We go upstairs. I take a shower, to wash the smell off me. She takes a drink. Gets in bed. She's got that smell, but I hug her anyway, and kiss her goodnight.

She can't sleep. Watches television, I don't know how long, because after a while I doze off.

Sometime around dawn, she's shaking me awake.

"Joey, I'm going down to the boardwalk. I want to take some shots in the morning light."

I sit up. "I'm tired," I say.

"You can stay here. I'll be on the boardwalk somewhere. You won't have trouble finding me."

"Have you slept yet?"

"I'm okay. You stay in bed, baby."

She kisses me. I lie back down and immediately fall asleep.

♣   ♣   ♣

I wake at ten. She's not here. I get dressed — jeans, sneakers, sweatshirt, Orioles cap, and my leather jacket — and go downstairs.

For January, it's not so cold. The ocean air feels good. Walking along the boardwalk feels good.

I spot her out on the beach. She's the only one out there. I join her. She's happy to see me. We hug. Huddle together.

"I got some beautiful pictures," she says. "All kinds of people. So many old folks out on the boardwalk. And then this bus unloaded at one of the casinos and more old people got off. You just know they're all slot players. I took tons of shots of them. They were all so sad-looking. What kind of person has a life so empty, at their age, that they want to play slot machines?"

It's not so cold for January, but it's not *that* warm.

"Let's go in," I say.

As we walk, arm-in-arm, she says, "Wouldn't you hope that people their age would be more at peace with themselves? There's just something so sad to me about all these old people taking these dingy buses out to a dingy old city to play quarter slot machines."

I hug her tighter. "Come on, baby," I say. "It's cold."

Back on the highway, going home, Katrina lies down in the back of my van while I drink coffee and drive. I've got jazz playing. Cigarettes. Highway.

After a while, by about Delaware, she joins me up front. Kisses me. Sits down.

We find a diner. Eat meat loaf.

We don't want to go home. She tells me she wants to stay on the road forever.

We're sitting in a booth, looking out on the middle-class world of whatever suburb this is.

I take her hand.

We get back on the road. It's a long drive yet. She goes back to sleep.

I drink my coffee, smoke my cigarettes, listen to my music, and drive my van past all those same-as-the-last-one exits. I get in an analytical, philosophical mood, lost in my thoughts as I drive. I think about how I played last night. I wonder why, what it says about me that I played so poorly. Poorly for me, anyway. I wonder again what it meant that I was there at all.

The conspiracy of randomness is an illusion. I'm not going out on a limb saying those guys were mobsters. Italians in a social club, no jobs but lots of cash, not allowed to play in the casinos.

I think about Katrina. I don't know how I feel about her. She fills some need in me, but I think it's a wrong need. I'm with her a lot, but I know I'm not going to stay with her. There's no chance we'll get married. That's an unspoken truth to us. We have a knowingly temporary relationship. Is her social class what I like about her? The Chevy Chase home, the college? I don't know. She rejects her own class. Embraces mine.

Is it her drinking? That weakness, that my mom has too? No. I hate those weaknesses. When she acts smart, or slutty, it's bullshit. I like her sober and sweet. But she hates herself that way.

I drive by Mary's exit in Delaware. Remember kissing her in the woods that one day.

EIGHTEEN

Where would you expect me to be the night my son is born? Up three hundred in a 5-10-15 Omaha eight-or-better home game.

Two in the morning the phone rings. It's Old Charlie. Laura's mother called him, looking for me. Her father had just rushed Laura to Southern Maryland Hospital.

I jump and run. Don't bother to cash out my chips. K.C. will take care of them.

In my brand-new purple Camaro RS with every possible option — I hope the I.R.S. isn't watching — I fly up Kirby Hill Road to the Beltway to Branch Avenue South and try hard not to go *too* fast. The highway's empty. I go fast, but not *too* fast.

I park and run in and check the directory and find the floor and find the room and I'm about sixty seconds too late for the kid's grand entrance, but that's just as well, because I'm a little squeamish.

I see her. And him.

Wow.

He's so little. His face is all scrunched up. Looks like E.T.

Laura smiles at me. Her parents smile.

The nurse sniffs. Smells that gambling smell on me. Probably doesn't know what it's from, but knows I haven't been home.

I kiss Laura. Hug her.

"You okay?" I ask.

"Yeah."

"No problems? Everything's okay?"

"He's so beautiful, honey."

"I don't know. I guess. He's so small."

"Six pounds, four ounces," the nurse says.

"That's average for an Asian baby," Laura's father, Chito, says.

"It doesn't matter," I say. "He is what he is."

I run down the hall to the men's room and wash up. Come back. Stand over the incubator-type thing. Look at him.

"Can I kiss him?" I ask the nurse.

"Sure."

I do.

He smiles.

"He smiled!" I say.

The nurse looks at him.

I kiss him again.

His mouth curls at the corners.

"See?" I say.

Laura's parents come over.

"Babies don't smile until they're about one month," the nurse declares.

Right. Tell me what I didn't see.

Laura's parents go home. The nurse takes the baby away.

I sit with Laura until she falls asleep. Holding her hand. Laughing with her. All the problems we've had and will have are walking. They're not here now.

When she does fall asleep, I go down the hall to the nursery.

Find him.

Stare.

♣   ♣   ♣

171

I go outside and sit in my car.

The horizon is getting its first light. That dark, beautiful blue color spreads over the sky.

I roll my window down. Smell the early April freshness. Breathe it deep inside me.

I go back to the game. Get my money. Tell everyone, "It's a boy!"

The women hug me. The men shake my hand. Grizzly's there. K.C., of course. Essay. Nug and Fat Boy. Everyone asks how Laura is. How the baby is.

"Go see your mother," Grizzly says.

That's a good idea.

I go home and shower and change clothes.

I sit in the dining room. Have a cup of coffee. Think.

I'm kind of having trouble breathing. Like I have to remind myself to do it.

I think about money.

I'd written a check for four thousand for the down payment on the car, which I'd bought with Grizzly co-signing, because I don't have credit, so I've only got eighteen hundred in checking.

I had given Calvin my van when I bought the Camaro, and had taken out the ten dimes I'd stashed there. Lost it gambling on bullshit. I've been getting all this easy money from the poker room and I'm gambling like a sucker now. I've got to break that habit. I have put ten more dimes under the carpet of my new car, though.

I go in my room and count what I have there. I know what it is, but want to count it again. Another ten thousand, in hundred-dollar bills.

I've got about thirty-five hundred in my pocket.

Haven't touched my reserve ten thousand at my mom's house.

Essay owes me five hundred; Fat Boy owes me nine; Nug owes me fourteen. I'll collect from all them.

My mom owes me five because I covered her book at a north

county home game. But I won't let her pay me back. Not that she's likely to try.

Twenty different people owe me fifty to two hundred, from loans I've made to them up at the casino. Most won't pay. I've got to break that soft touch habit.

I go to my mom's house. The kitchen light is on. As I come up the walk, Calvin opens the door.

"Congratulations, man," he says, beaming.

We shake hands.

"How'd you hear already?" I ask.

"Grizzly just called. He's on his way over to pick me up for work. Come on in. I just made some coffee." My mother had turned him into a fan of good coffee.

We go in the kitchen.

"You wake up happy every day?" I ask him.

He smiles. Nods. "As you say — I am loving life!"

"Me, too, brother," I answer.

"Of course you are. Man. A baby!"

I laugh.

"It's pretty weird," I say.

"You feel different?"

I shrug. "I don't know how I feel."

I look out the window and see a battered old pickup truck pull in behind my car. Grizzly gets out.

I open the kitchen door for him.

"You play all night and work all day?" I ask.

"Hey, Dad," he says. "Congratulations again."

"Thanks, Griz."

He comes in the kitchen.

"Coffee chef got a cup for me?" he asks Calvin.

"Yeah, yeah. Sit down. How you play poker all night like you do, I don't know."

"Old guys don't need sleep," I say.

"Your mother up?" Grizzly asks me.

"I think I'll wake her," I say.

I go to her room, knock softly, and enter.

There's a mostly full bottle of bourbon by her bed. Full ashtray. Empty pack of cigarettes.

I shake her. "Wake up, Grandma," I say.

She comes to. Immediately figures out what my greeting means.

"Boy or girl?" she says in a voice deep even for her.

"Boy."

"Healthy?" she asks with trepidation.

"Seems to be."

She sighs relief.

"And Laura? Okay, too?"

"Yeah, she's okay. I'm going back to see her in a few hours."

She closes her eyes again. "Come get me when you're ready to go."

Back in the kitchen, Calvin cooks breakfast. Griz talks about his kids. And his grandkids. I listen up.

Calvin starts to clean, but I tell him to go on, I'll do it.

They leave for whatever construction site they've pulled a job at this day.

I do the dishes, sit and have another cup of coffee. Have that trouble breathing again. Scared.

About eleven, I wake my mom, and by the time she showers and dresses and we stop for flowers and finally get to the hospital, it's one o'clock.

We find Laura. She has the baby with her. Trying to breast-feed him, but not doing too well.

A half-hour later the nurse comes and takes the baby away.

"What are we going to call him?" I ask both the women.

"What's wrong with your name?" Laura asks.

"I want his middle name to be King. After Martin Luther King."

"So?"

"So, you want his name to be Joe King Moore? Sounds like an Indian name. Sitting Bull. Running Bear. Joking Moore."

Laura doesn't get it, but doesn't care.

"Then what?" she asks.

"John. After John Kennedy," I say.

Both women laugh. Nod. They don't care.

John King Moore it'll be.

I bring Laura and Baby J to her parents' house the next day. Drive slow as can be. Scared to death.

I carry the baby in. Walk slow as can be. Scared even more. I hold him right and all, but I'm just scared about handling him.

I'd already bought everything the baby could need. Bought everything new. A swing chair, a high chair, a crib. Clothes. Toys. A dresser. The best of everything.

Chito and I had put it all together. Put the crib in Laura's already crowded room. The baby would be staying there with her for a while.

I call Katrina. Tell her.

She's funny about it. Quiet. Bothered by it, I think.

I drive down to see her that night.

I have a million thoughts in my head, but she doesn't want to talk about it.

"I'm happy for you, Joey. But it's your child, not mine."

We're in her apartment. Her roommate is out. I wonder if there are any babies in this yuppie neighborhood. Well, of course there are. A few.

We sit on the couch. Don't speak for a minute.

I'm looking at her.

"Now that I think about it," I say, "every time I tried to talk about the pregnancy and all, you always changed the subject."

She's not looking at me. Her eyes are hard-set, her mouth frozen.

175

"I guess I didn't exactly press the matter, either," I say softly.

She pulls her lips in, lets them out. Breathes deeply. Lets that out. Closes her eyes.

"What are you so mad about?" I ask.

"How am I supposed to feel, Joey?" she says. Loudly. "Have you thought about how I might feel?"

"I barely know how I feel. I don't know what it all means, either. I don't know how it affects us. I don't know that it does affect us."

She gets up. Walks around. Raises her little fists like she wants to hit something. Puts them back down. Joins me back on the couch.

I take her hand.

"Are we still going to Las Vegas next month?" she asks me, harshly, suddenly.

What was I thinking when I made that commitment? I knew when the baby was due, but had still let Katrina make us reservations for a two-week stay at Binion's. She wanted me to show her the town. And I wanted to go out for the World Series of Poker tournaments.

"Yeah," I say, "of course we're still going."

She looks at me. Eyes full of hurt.

"You got off work, right?"

"Baby, we're going. I'm excited, believe me. I've been looking forward to it."

Which was true. The World Series of Poker, besides having the biggest tournaments in the world, also serves as a kind of annual card players' rendezvous. I don't play tournaments, but the side action is unbelievable. This would be my third Series. And the first one I'm going to with twenty dimes in my pocket.

Essay and Fat Boy will run the card room for me while I'm gone. I'm letting them split my cut. They're happy, and I don't mind, because the rest of our deal is that they'll use the money to pay off their debt to me.

I put my arms around Katrina.

"This boy — he's my son. But he's not a threat to you. I don't want you to resent him. I don't want you to resent me, either. It wasn't my idea to have the baby. And it wasn't the baby's idea to be had. But he's here, and I have a responsibility."

She nods.

"I'm sorry, Joey. I'm just — angry."

"I can tell."

"You used the right word before — threat. I do feel threatened. This baby is going to be a big part of your life, and I can't share it with you."

"Why not?" I say with an idiot's naïveté.

"I am nobody's mother!"

"Okay," I say, holding up my hands, "relax."

"It's not my baby. I'm not going to be its mother. You understand that?"

"Yes. No one is asking you to be a mother. Laura is the mother. I am the father. And you're my friend. Aunt Katrina, I guess."

"No. Not 'Aunt' Katrina. This is a part of your life you have to keep separate from me."

I let it go. I'm having such a rush of emotions I could easily do or say something rash. So I just make myself breathe deep, relax, and keep quiet. I certainly don't mention that anyone thinks the baby might be her half-brother.

She says of herself words I could voice, too —"I have got to calm down. I am feeling so much anxiety."

NINETEEN

Phone rings. "Hello?"

"Joey?"

"Yeah."

"Fat."

"What's up?"

"I need cheese."

"You always need cheese."

"I'm running bad."

"You got to play good to run bad. You don't play good."

"Thanks, Dad. You want to give me a lecture on responsible sex, too?"

"You don't get laid enough to need that talk. You are playing bad, though. Every damn time I see you, you're on tilt. Nose *wide* open."

"I was born with my nose open. You got the cheese?"

"Come on, Fat. You owe me enough."

"Yeah, and I never pay you back."

"You still owe me enough."

"I'll have it when you get back from Vegas. You still going?"

"Yeah. Don't fuck up the card room while I'm gone."

"Why you insulting me so much today?"

"I'm insulting you by asking you to do a good job while I'm gone?"

"I got to be asked?"

"I'm sorry. Who you owe money to?"

"Freddy."

"How much?"

"Thirty thousand."

I go quiet. That number's ten times bigger than any debt I've ever known any of us to have.

"But he only wants at least five dimes now," he says.

"Five dimes?"

"It's been building. Bowl games. Play-offs. I kept betting against the Redskins. Can you believe it?"

"Why'd he let you bet so much?"

"Because I was betting against the Redskins! I helped balance his action."

"But that was months ago."

"NCAA tournament. Duke fucked me."

"That was last month."

"I told him I'd have the money by this month."

"You're making fifteen hundred a week at least now, dealing for me and Nug."

"Twelve hundred. And I'm running bad."

"And you're playing so bad, you're *giving* the money away."

"Look who's talking about playing bad."

"What?"

"People are starting to call you Joey the Fish."

"Bullshit."

"Well, you ain't playing worth a shit."

"Am I calling up people to borrow money?"

He's silent a moment.

"What's your point?" he says.

"My point is, I'm not doing you no favor loaning you more

money. Especially not so you can pay back Freddy. Since when isn't he cool about things, anyway?"

"He needs the money."

"Bullshit. He's making ten dimes a week off the casino!"

Fat goes quiet.

"What?" I ask.

"That ain't his," he says.

"What?"

"The blacks are Freddy's front. Freddy is someone else's front. Where'd you think he got the hundred thousand to open the place?"

I go quiet. Fat keeps talking.

"Keep this under your hat — he owes his motherfucking ass."

"How did you hear about it?"

"His girlfriend? Old blonde? Big tits?"

"All his girlfriends are like that."

"The one he's had for a while now."

"Go on."

"She's my cousin."

"No shit."

"She told me she's heard a couple of conversations. She knows, man."

I'm quiet.

"Don't be telling no one," he says.

"Who'd believe me?"

"He wasn't sweating it early, because he had the wiseguys stalled on the payback, because he had all the money linked to the casino. I think he probably actually borrowed a couple hundred thousand from them. And I think — this is all from my cousin — that his juice is ten dimes a week. Plus I don't know how much he might owe from football. He booked bad in every way this year. Wrong side layoffs every week. Wrong side keeps. Every way he went was wrong."

"How'd he get in so deep, though? I thought he was Mister Careful."

"The Redskins. See, Freddy let me get oversize on my action against the Skins because I was helping balance everyone else betting *on* the Skins. But I hardly put a dent in his imbalance. What's my couple of dimes going to do, against the action pounding the Skins every week?"

"Why didn't he lay it off?"

"Did, some. But he got greedy. Or desperate. He was pumping the line up one or two points a game over the Vegas line, which was already inflated. He started holding the action, thinking the Skins would lose. They didn't. He got deeper and deeper into his players. Skins kept winning. He kept holding the imbalance. Every week his players kept betting more and more. Every week he kept holding it. The Skins win the Super Bowl, and he's done."

"The great Freddy Sorenson. Professional gambler."

"Fucked up like a punk."

"After all his talk to us."

"So, anyway, I need the money. Because he needs the money. Because they need the money."

"You want the whole five dimes?"

"Yeah."

"No, man. Laura just had the baby. I've got to cover all these medical bills and all. It's going to be at least a couple of dimes. And I'm going to Vegas. And I just bought that car. I'll do half of it. Get the rest from K.C."

"Yeah, well — here's something else you can't tell anyone."

"What?"

"Freddy's starting his poker game back up."

"So?"

"Monday nights."

K.C.'s Saturday night game was going so poorly he'd changed to Monday nights. Freddy's game will hurt K.C.'s by drawing customers away from it. Will probably close it down.

"Why Monday night?" I ask.

"Thursday and Friday the casino is open. Wednesday is the night before it's open, so none of us can stay up all night playing. Sunday and Tuesday is Sam's game. That leaves Saturday and Monday. Saturday is a bad night for home games because the casinos are open so late. So it's Monday."

"That's going to fuck K.C. That's going to fuck me and you, too. Freddy's not going to like us supporting K.C.'s game."

"We can't support it. Freddy's going to demand that everyone from the casino give him action."

"He's going to tell me I *have* to be there?"

"He won't put it like that. You know how he is. But yeah. Well actually, he's just going to want you to brush it up for him. You tell people Freddy's place is the action, they'll go."

"He could make a ton off this."

"Ten-twenty Hold 'em with a five-dollar cut? I'll kiss your ass if I don't chop a hundred and fifty an hour for him."

"You're dealing?"

"I got to! Freddy got me started in this business. And I owe him that money."

"Then why do I need to loan you the money to pay him back? You're just going to deal it off later."

"I'm just asking you to. Boulder is being a dick about things. Plus I said I'd have at least the five dimes for him by now."

"What's Boulder doing?"

"Calling my parents, asking for money. Shit like that."

"What an asshole."

"That's old news."

"Freddy's spreading ten-twenty with a five-dollar cut. Man. Greedy motherfucker."

"He gets two tables, five or six hours on one, fifteen or so on the other, twenty hours combined, one-fifty an hour — three dimes a night he makes."

"Almost all profit, too."

"He don't pay himself no rent. He don't pay the waitress no base. All he's got to cover is food and cigarettes. He'll make three dimes."

"This puts us bad with K.C. He's family, man. How can we fuck him like this? How can you fuck him? You work for him!"

K.C. hand-loaned Fat several thousand, and was letting him work it off.

"I got to quit him, that's all. It's business."

"Business, my ass."

"You going to buck Freddy? He gives the word and you're out at the casino. You want to buck Freddy on this? With that baby in the crib?"

"K.C.'s family, man. We've got to tell him. Work something out."

"It's his girlfriend that's fucking him."

"Why does Freddy not want to go up against Sam?"

"She owes him money."

"How much?"

"Enough. Plus she kisses his ass. And she's promised to be at his game with two dealers every night. K.C.'s fucked, Joey. He'll keep the Asians, but the yuppies will pretty much follow you. The pros will follow you. The rednecks will follow the Jones boys. And the blacks will follow Kevin and Larry."

"Kevin and Larry are going to help him?"

"Come on, man. Catch on!"

"I'm on, I'm on," I say reluctantly.

"What are you going to do?"

"When's he going to start?"

"Too many of the ten-twenty crowd's going to Vegas for the World Series. He'll wait until that's over and you all come back."

"He'll have a monster game, man."

"Monster."

"We got to tell K.C."

"You tell him."

"You tell him, motherfucker!"

"All right."

"And I ain't loaning you money so you can pay Freddy. Just dance him off until the game starts, and then deal him off."

"He's going to be pissed you wouldn't cover me on it."

"Don't tell him."

"All right."

"Don't tell him we talked. Tell him I was busy with the baby, and going downtown to see Katrina, and you didn't get hold of me before I went to Vegas."

"All right."

"And tell K.C."

"What good's it going to do him to know?"

"What harm's it going to do to tell him? He's not going to find out anyway?"

"All right."

"Tell him."

"Okay!"

"Fuck!"

"I know. The man's own girlfriend is backstabbing him."

"Who didn't know Sam was like that?"

"No shit."

"Freddy's broke, huh?"

"Yeah. The big shot's broke."

"It don't matter how much you make, does it? If you want to lose it, you can."

"Hey, you sure you don't want to float me the cheese? I just want to get Boulder off my back. You know he's the motherfucker I think pushed Mikey the Cop over the edge?"

"Yeah?"

"Him and Sam. She used to call Mikey's wife late at night. Wouldn't say anything. Just ask for Mikey. Hang up if she said he wasn't there."

"How you know?"

"Boulder brags about it. He likes Sam. That's part of why she's in with Freddy."

"What's she do for him?"

"Sucks him off, probably."

"They do share the same philosophy of life."

"I'm serious about the Mikey shit. Boulder was bragging about how persistent he and Sam could be."

"Why are they like that with you?"

"They like being like that."

"Just dance 'em off, Fat. If Freddy's starting his game, and you're dealing for him, you'll make four or five hundred a night."

"Thanks, brother. Tons. Really."

"Keep your cut of my percentage while I'm gone, okay? That should be twenty-five hundred, three dimes. That'll chill him."

"Yeah, okay. Yeah, actually, that'll be all right. I deal up eight hundred a week, two weeks, is sixteen. Twelve hundred from two weeks at Nug's. I could give him five thousand two weeks from now."

"See? Not so bad. But pull K.C.'s coat about all this."

"Yeah."

"I'm serious."

"I will. Oh hey, one other thing — remember that guy, Philly?"

"Yeah. From A.C., sure."

"I think he's the wiseguy Freddy's dealing with."

"Seemed like that kind."

"And the guys up there in that game, they thought you had a lot of money."

"What's that mean?"

"I don't know, man. Just that Philly was down here last week, and I was at Freddy's with him, and he was asking me about you. Thought you'd flashed a lot of cash. He didn't seem happy about it."

"I don't understand. You and Freddy were in the game, too."

"I'm just saying, he said you flashed a lot of cash. I'm wondering if Freddy's not telling this guy the casino's not doing well, and this guy's pissed to hear a casino employee has money to burn."

I'm quiet.

"Joey?"

"Yeah."

"Things are different now."

"Yeah."

"I'm scared, man."

I sigh. Tell him to chill.

TWENTY

I go to Laura's. Hold my munchkin boy. Kiss him. He smiles.

"He's got his papa's radar," I say. "His eyes are barely open, but he knows what I got."

Laura smiles. "What do you got?"

"A little munchkin boy. A little, baby, E.T. munchkin boy."

"You want to feed him?"

"You're not going to breast-feed?"

"No. It's not working."

"It's your call. Where's the bottle?"

I put the baby in his crib, and we go in the kitchen, where Laura shows me how to make his bottle.

We go back. I hold him. Feed him. She shows me how to change the diapers.

I put him in his crib. He naps. I sit on Laura's chair, staring at him.

"You happy, Joey?" she asks.

I turn around. She's in the bed behind me. I lie down with her. Hold her. Kiss her.

"Yeah. I'm happy. Thank you for having him."

"You're welcome."

"If you promise to be a good mommy, I promise to be a good daddy."

"Okay."

I roll back over to look in the crib.

"Hear that? *You* are the luckiest man alive."

We go into the kitchen. Let the baby sleep.

Laura's grandmother is there. Makes us lunch. Rice. Cold, oily fish. I can't eat it. Laura throws a frozen pizza in the oven for me. The grandmother gives me a dirty look.

I shrug.

"Joey?" Laura says.

"Yes?"

"Bobby Lotto wants to marry me."

"What do you want to do?"

She's silent a moment. Says, "I don't know."

I'm sitting at the kitchen table. Drinking a Coke. She's in her bathrobe, her hair a mess, standing by the sink. Facing me.

"He still thinks the baby might be his," she says.

"It's not."

"It might be."

"Do you want it to be?"

"No!"

"Then don't worry about it. First of all, I *know* he's mine. I feel it. Secondly, the timing is right. I told you, early April, he's mine."

"What if he's not?"

"He is! And I don't care if he isn't, really. I like him. He's cool. You know?"

"How do you know he's 'cool'?"

"I can tell. And since he's cool, how can he be Bobby's son?"

She shakes her head.

"You still going to Las Vegas?" she asks.

I nod.

"When?"

"Next week."

"I wish I was going."

"You're not a card player."

"No. I'm your son's mother. I'm going to stay here and take care of him while you go to Las Vegas and fuck some other woman."

I don't say anything.

I spend the afternoon with E.T. Change him and feed him when he wakes. Bathe him. Dress him. Get the hang of it all. I'm still scared about handling him, but I'm getting better.

Then I call K.C. He and Nug and Fat Boy are going to a strip joint downtown. They'd called me. Where had I been? I tell them I'll meet them there.

The place is in the business district, and it's happy hour, so it's packed.

I find the guys. Sit. Drink.

Nug has been coming here so long and pounding the girls with such big tips that most of them, and the waitresses, too, come by to talk. It's never been my thing to hang in places like this. I've never understood it — why look at something you're not going to get? Why torture yourself? But Nug likes these places. And Fat Boy. And me and K.C. — what do we care? And it's not like we're reading the paper in there.

Over the loud music, and in between visits from the girls (which the guys at the other tables don't understand, because they're all in business suits, and we're in jeans), we try to talk.

"Joey, know why we're here?" Nug asks.

"The reason changes?"

"He got an extra reason, today, brother."

"How you get drunk so fast?" I ask.

"He's little," Fat says.

"Know why we're here?" Nug says.

"Why, sucker?"

"I'm getting married."

"Get the fuck out of here!"

The guys laugh.

"I'm the last to hear?" I say.

"You ain't been around," K.C. says.

"Ain't that something?" Nug asks.

I jerk him off. "Who to?" I ask.

"Fuck you," he says, laughing. "Allison!"

The next-up dancer comes by. Sits on his lap while she waits her turn.

"I'm getting married, baby," Nug says to her.

She kisses him. "You going to stop coming in here?"

"One more time. Bachelor party."

She goes onstage. "Fat," I say, "you talk to K.C. about that thing yet?"

He shakes his head no.

"K.C.," I say, "Freddy's starting up a game on Monday nights."

"I heard," he says.

"You hear from Sam?" Fat asks.

K.C. nods.

"It looks bad, brother," I say.

K.C. looks down at his beer.

"Switch to another night," I say. "Move Monday to Tuesday."

"That's Sam's night," K.C. says.

"Tuesday. You could have a good game," Fat says.

"It best, I think," Nug chips in.

"I can't do that to Sam," K.C. says.

"Because she's your girlfriend?" Fat says. "She's fucking you out of your business, and you care about hers?"

"Be cool, guys," I say.

"You guys are always hurting her," K.C. says.

"K.C., she's the one who convinced Freddy to open on Mondays," Fat says. "We're just shipping her shit back at her."

"I gave her the dealing job like you asked," I say lamely. I was putting up with her at the casino, much as it irked me.

K.C. stands. Puts his jacket on. Walks out.

"What's going on, guys?" I say. "We just let him walk away, hurt like that?"

"What are we supposed to do?" Fat says.

I shake my head. I don't know.

I leave soon after. The guys are staying. I'm not.

I've only had one beer so I'm okay to drive.

I call Katrina. I'm not that far from her place.

She's home.

"Want to go to the video store? Pick out a couple of movies? Send out for pizza?" I ask.

"Sure."

I spend the night with her. In the morning I drive out to see Laura and Baby J.

I'd bought an expensive camera a few weeks ago and take a lot of pictures of my boy. Feed him. Bathe him. Change him.

It's a Thursday, so I go to work at noon.

Usual crowd. Except no K.C. And Sam's glaring at me.

"You got a problem?" I ask her.

"How come you tell K.C. to go against me?"

"How come you tell Freddy to go against him?"

She glares at me some more.

"Sam, this isn't like you," I say. "You usually smile in the face of the people you hate."

She explodes. "I get you, motherfucker! I fuck you so bad, you not believe it. You think I'm scared of you?"

"I don't think you're scared of anything except the mirror."

"Fuck you, asshole. I get you bad, motherfucker. You wait. I fuck you up! You think you something? You not shit, motherfucker. You not shit!"

She's raised her voice, so even though we're off to the side, heads turn.

Essay comes up.

"Quiet down, guys. Come on."

"Go home, Sam," I say steadily.

"What?"

"Go home. You're fired."

"You cannot fire me. I no work for you."

"Who do you think you work for?"

"I work for Freddy."

"Then go see him. But for now — go home."

"I fuck you bad, motherfucker. You wait. I get you."

She leaves.

"Damn, brother," Essay says, "what did you do to her?"

"She's been stealing the whole time she's been here. I was going to fire her soon anyway. But she's really pissed because I tried to talk K.C. into going against her on Tuesday nights."

"I heard about all that."

"Now she's going to go give Freddy an earful of shit."

"Call him yourself, man. First."

TWENTY-ONE

I'm upset.

Not particularly physically scared, although Sam has been known to be violent. She's hit one woman with a coffee cup, ripped a handful of hair out of another, and thrown a dealer's puck at a third. She carries a knife.

But then again, I'm not sure which side of five feet she's on, either. It's close.

I'm upset because she will cause trouble. And it's degrading to be dealing with her.

"Kevin," I say, alone with him in the casino office.

"Yeah, brother."

"Who's in charge of this place?" He just looks at me. "Who's in charge? Are you and Larry still in charge?"

"Sure."

"I just fired Sam. She's been stealing, and she cussed me out. So I fired her."

"No problem."

"She's going to bitch to Freddy."

He nods.

"And Freddy might bitch at me. Or you."

Kevin nods.

"So who's the boss?"

He throws up his hands in frustration. "What do you want me to tell you?" he says, with a touch of anger.

"How things stand."

"I don't know how they stand!"

I sigh.

"Does that answer your question?" he asks.

"Sure," I say.

"I get my money. Larry gets his. You get yours. What else matters? What difference does it make if we have to hire a few assholes? Look, Joey — things aren't going well around here. You don't know that because poker's holding its own. But there's so many people stealing so much that every week it's tougher and tougher to get Freddy his minimum. I got thieves for dealers, and thieves for bosses to watch them. Larry's stealing it faster than we can make it."

"Calm down, Kevin," I say.

"Calm down? You know how much pressure I'm under?"

"No, I don't."

"Tons! And *you* are complaining. You're making more money than anyone else here. Including me. Including Freddy. Maybe not including Larry, because he's stealing so much."

Sweat rolls down his forehead. He wipes it off. Looks away.

"Why didn't you talk to me?" I say calmly, to relax him.

"And say what? For you to do what? Your mother works in the pit. I'm going to come up to you and say I think your mother is stealing?"

He looks down. Uncomfortable. Then back up.

"Joey, you are the only one who's got anything squared away around here. I don't envy your money. You earn it. You're bringing in twice as much as we dared project for the poker room. But be cool about Freddy's people! What do you care if you have to deal with Sam? Take your money and be happy."

I'm not really thinking about what he's saying. I'm thinking about what he said. About my mom.

I tell Essay to watch things in the poker room, and I drive to a 7-11 and call Freddy.

Boulder answers the phone. I know he knows my voice, but he doesn't talk to me. Just says to hold on.

I do. Five minutes.

"Hello?"

That's Freddy. Mister Monotone. Mister Cool. "Hey, Freddy. You got a second?"

"Sure, Joe."

"I just fired Sam."

He's silent.

"She's been stealing, Freddy."

He's still silent.

I'm silent.

He speaks. "She's probably been stealing the whole time she's been there. Why all of a sudden does it bother you?"

I can't answer that.

"I heard you're going to open a game Monday nights," I say.

He's silent again. Letting me speak. Seeing if I hang myself. Seeing if I respond to his silence with babble. Revealing babble. I know the move.

"If you are having a game — great. You know I'll support you, one hundred percent. I'll be there. My dealers will be there. My poker brothers. All the yuppies who go where I go. But K.C. has a game Mondays, right? He and I and Nug talked it out. We know Monday is the best night for you. That's cool. Rather than have a conflict, we suggested K.C. move to Tuesday nights. Sam doesn't like that, of course. She started cussing me out today. I told her to go home."

Diplomatically told, I hope.

"You're the poker boss, Joe," Freddy says after a moment. "You've been doing a great job there."

He stops. Am I supposed to fill the silence?

"Thanks," I say, acknowledging the bone.

"You're going to Vegas next week?"

"Yeah."

"Let her work while you're gone. Two weeks notice. Severance pay."

Pause.

I give in. "All right. While I'm gone."

"I'll give her a dealing job here on Monday nights," he says. "That will be enough income to make up for what she loses dealing at the casino."

"What about the conflict with the other games?"

"I can't get involved in that, Joey. What you all want to do on Tuesday nights is your business."

He knows exactly what's going on. He knows exactly what impact his Monday night game will have. He knows exactly what pull he can exercise to ensure its success. He knows better than anyone the politics involved.

"She'll be calling you, Freddy. Tell her to come in the next two weeks, then. But when I'm back, she's gone."

"Okay."

"She steals. She's rude to the customers. She shows up when and if she wants to. And she gives me shit. I can't have her."

He's silent.

Look at this — I'm going to kiss his ass. I'm scared about my standing with the man, and so I'm going to kiss his ass.

"Thanks for talking with me, Freddy," I say. "I guess I just wanted to talk with someone more experienced about these things."

"Anytime, Joe."

"Okay. I'll see you when I get back from Vegas."

"Fine."

"That's when you'll be starting up Mondays, right?"

"Plan to, yes."

"You'll have a monster game, that's for sure. I'll see you then, then."

"Good-bye, Joe."

I hang up. Get in my car. Sit there. Feel like shit. What the FUCK is wrong with me? What has been wrong with me? Why'd I hire her to begin with? Why'd I not fire her the first time I had clear signs she was stealing? *Why am I going along with the bullshit?*

The money.

This ain't no mystery. The cows came home and I went to milk them. I am no different from anyone else. For three thousand a week I'll overlook the stealing.

I'm waking up when I'm tired, to be at work on time. I'm pretending to like customers who bore the shit out of me. To keep my job, I'm hiring thieves who steal from those customers.

What the *fuck* is wrong with me?

I sit in my car, there in front of the 7-11, for a full half-hour.

I'm not a person who gets depressed. You're on a skinny draw waiting for me to get sad.

But here I am. Pit-of-my-stomach down.

I take out a picture of John. Taken the day we brought him home. His face scrunched up.

I stare at it.

The magnitude of it all.

TWENTY-TWO

Vegas.

The jet drops into McCarran International at dusk. The city's lights sparkle up.

Katrina is looking out the window. First time here.

Me? I should have been born here, that's how at home I am.

We get off, get the bags, grab a cab, and unload at the Union Plaza. The rooms are dumpy, especially compared to what we'd had in A.C. But the action's at Binion's and this is the closest place to it I could find. Nice view of the railyards.

"Welcome to downtown Las Vegas," bellows Vegas Vic, the Pioneer's forty-two-foot-tall neon cowboy.

We walk around.

"This is the absolute tackiest place in the world," Katrina says.

"It's great, isn't it?"

She nods. She loves it.

We walk in the Horseshoe and I say hello to ten people from Maryland.

I see a hundred other faces I know. Few names remembered, but faces I know. "Hey, buddy, how you been?" from a few, to a few.

Faces. From all over.

From Artichoke Joe's, the Oaks, and Garden City, from the month I spent in the San Francisco area. From Sycuan and Barona and Oceanside, outside San Diego, from a three-week stay there last year. From Reno, where I spent a summer a few years back. Reno and Tahoe. From Foxwoods in Connecticut. From A.C.

And of course, a lot of people from L.A.

And of course, a lot of people from Vegas itself.

I'm jumping. I'm ready to jam. I got the itch. How could I not? During the World Series of Poker, everything you want to play is getting spread somewhere.

And I want to play pot-limit. I get my fill of limit poker the rest of the year. I want to play pot-limit. Twice the skill of regular poker, ten times the fun.

Katrina doesn't mind if I want to sit right down, but I know that's rude to her. I'll play later. I don't want to play cards with my itch bad as it is, anyway. I couldn't play with any kind of patience.

Katrina is amazed by it all. She's learned enough about poker to appreciate it. Recognizes the more famous poker faces. Tells me she's tempted to ask Johnny Moss for his autograph. Sees Amarillo Slim and wants one from him, too. Others. Just kidding, I know, but she's having fun.

We go up to the Strip. I show her Caesars and the Mirage.

Incredible, she says.

"Think of how much money these places have to make," I say.

"Can you imagine living here?"

In the Mirage, we play a little. Win a little. Blackjack. She's studied her book and knows how to count, and doesn't look like a card counter, and so wins a little but draws no heat. She's been lucky. Thinks she's skillful. Thinks it'll last. Won't listen when I tell her otherwise. Won't listen, or doesn't understand, when I tell her that if you win a jackpot the first time you pull a slot handle, you've got the devil on your shoulder, not an angel.

We go outside. It's two in the morning. Warm. Nice, compared to back home, where it's still a little cool.

We walk around. The neon glows on us.

How does neon work? How does it so effectively create the sensation of action? Because that's what Las Vegas is all about — action. That's what gambling is all about, and this city is about gambling. Twenty-four hours. A little bit of life, a little bit of death, in every roll, spin, and deal.

This is how gambling works — it fills the senses. Close your eyes and listen. In a casino, you'll hear the sounds of jingling, clinking, clanging, clicking. Open your eyes and you'll see the myriad colors of lighting and carpeting and walls and uniforms, shining and bright. Taste? Free drinks and meals to any decent-sized bettor. Free drinks and cheap meals to everyone. Touch, too, is thought of. Plush carpeting, brass rails, leather chairs, polished wood. And maybe in the air, with the smoke, is sweat.

But it is the sixth sense that casinos most seek to arouse. The sense of life itself. Of drama. Of story. Of passion. Of love and fear. Of power and sex. Of a moment frozen, of existence beyond the mundane, of escape from all other problems because right now your attention is focused on the money you have on the line. If time is money and life is time, then money is life. And you're gambling for it.

But it's a can't-win spot. Because if you win some, you'll want more, and if you lose some, you'll want it back. Casinos have learned to celebrate winners. Why not? The money ain't going nowhere.

Fat Boy and Essay came out here a few years ago. Stayed four days and three nights and never took the covers off their beds.

Old Charlie lived here a few years. Was asked to leave a place once, because he stood at a craps table so long and started to look so bad they were afraid he'd die on them.

A tournament-trail dealer I know tells me of a time he bought in for a hundred at a Stardust craps game, ran it up to forty-eight thousand, didn't quit because he'd set his sights on fifty thousand, and ended up broke. Thirty-seven hours later.

Over the next few days, Katrina plays blackjack, I play poker, and we make time to see a few shows, eat some good meals, and dance at a few non-casino nightclubs. We go hiking and picnicking at Red Rock, at Lake Mead, at Mt. Charleston.

I take her drinking a few times with some card players. She can talk the talk now, and likes listening to us. No bad beat stories, mind you (well, a few, maybe). Mostly talk of who's up to what, and where. How the action is at what card room in what town. Katrina likes it all.

She tells me she's really going to do the documentary. Says her father has given her twenty-five thousand dollars to make it with, which should be enough because she'll get a lot of help from class-mates. I tell her it's her business.

Our fifth day here, she tells me she's going up to the Strip. That's a good idea, I think. I want to play without worrying about where she is, or if she's bored. I've found a real sweet, relatively small (two-hundred-dollar buy-in) pot-limit Hold 'em game. I don't have much experience in pot-limit, so this is a good level to learn at. And I'm not such a big shot that a five- or six-hundred-dollar win won't put a smile on my face. I'm eyeing the big games, especially the thou-sand-dollar buy-in pot-limit Omaha. But I'm patient. I'll be there. Maybe not until next year. But if I spend the next two weeks camp-ing out in this smaller game, I'll be all the better prepared when I do step up.

Seven hours after sitting down and buying in for four hundred this night, I get up and cash out twenty-three hundred.

Nineteen hundred cheese.

Loving life.

Katrina's not in our room. I'm wired, but don't want to play. I want to party.

I cab up to the Strip. Check the Mirage. Check Caesars. Check the Flamingo Hilton and Bally's and the Barbary Coast. I don't mind the walk. It's a nice night. And a winner in Las Vegas loves the sight and feel and smell of the town.

I find her at the Dunes. Playing blackjack.

"Hey, baby," I say, coming up to her and kissing her cheek.

She just looks at me a brief moment, and then turns back to the cards.

It's two o'clock in the morning, and she's betting a hundred dollars on each of two hands. A week ago a single twenty-five-dollar bet made her nervous.

I don't have to ask if she's stuck. Her eyebrows are furrowed, her lips are tight, her shoulders are hunched. She's stuck.

I say gently, "Come on, baby. Let's eat."

"Not right now, Joey," she says, without looking at me.

This isn't the first time I've wanted to pull a woman off a table. I've wanted to do it with Laura more than a few times, with another gambling girlfriend I had before her. Standing, watching, waiting for a woman to quit a game.

I remember sitting at home as a boy. Waiting for my mom to come back. Putting Jack to bed. Waiting up in the living room. Falling asleep on the couch. Waking in the morning. Making breakfast for me and Jack, just cereal. Later, older — with quarters won from the neighborhood kids in real penny-ante games — I'd take Jack to the 7-11 and eat breakfast there. Give him money for lunch at school. Eat my own lunch at McDonald's. Come home in the afternoon. Maybe, but not always, find my mom sleeping.

I sit on the stool next to Katrina. It's late. She has the table to herself. Playing the dealer heads-up.

I order a drink. Down it. Get up. Walk around the casino.

Check the poker room.

The Dunes used to have legendary high-stakes action. Maybe the biggest games spread regularly in the world.

All long gone.

They have a single, one-three stud game going. Two off-duty dealers, a floorman, and three customers. Sad as can be.

I walk around some more. I stayed here once. For two weeks. Came out for a Gold Coast Open and stayed here because it was the closest available room, and cheap, too. Twenty-five a night, I think it was.

I rejoin Katrina. Sit with her. Order a coffee. Drink it slowly.

She bets her last chips. Loses. Gets up and walks quickly away.

I've been around enough losing gamblers to know there's nothing you can say to them.

She walks outside, and then down the Strip. Four A.M. and there are still people about. Still plenty of people out gambling.

She stops. Spins around.

"This," she says, pointing generally at the huge neon signs on all sides, "is hell. This is just the biggest trap in the world."

Her face is still hard — but I think I catch a slight glint of tear in her eye.

It breaks my heart.

I hug her.

"Let's eat, baby. Come on."

She's mush now. Wants someone to lead her away. I know the stages.

We go to a Denny's. I eat well. She nibbles.

"How did you do?" she asks.

"Good," I say. I don't elaborate.

She lets out a deep sigh.

"I don't know what happened to me," she says. Looks me in the eye. Says, "I'm sorry, Joey. I was rude to you."

"Nobody's going to understand better than me."

She looks away.

"I'm so embarrassed," she says, now unable to look at me. "I feel like such an idiot. I just can't believe I could be that unlucky."

I take her hand.

The waitress comes by. Pours some more coffee. Drops the check. Moves on.

"You want to get this one?" I say.

203

Katrina gives me a look. Then gets the joke. Smiles.

"The best time of day's coming up," I say. "Let's go get our cameras and get some pictures."

She nods.

"How much did you lose?" I finally ask.

"Sixteen hundred."

Wow.

"Won't happen again, though," she says.

I can't reply to that. I've said it and heard it too many times.

"Because I'm broke," she says, with affected nonchalance.

I'm not worried about her money. As far as I can tell, she's got a lifelong freeroll on her family's pocket.

"I just couldn't believe my luck could keep going so bad!" she says.

We cab back to our room, get the cameras, and head out.

We walk down Fremont. Past the jewelry shops and T-shirt shops and souvenir shops. Five-thirty in the morning.

Turn off on a side street. Past a cheap motel. Past another. Past another. Queen of Hearts. Apache. Beverly Palms. Weekly rentals. Monthly rates. Some boarded up. Some with hard-looking down-and-outs hanging on the corner. Past the blocks of derelict motels with the drunks and hard guys, past a parking lot full of old campers and trailers that never move on.

"People live here," I say.

Katrina clicks.

"They live in these motels. They live in these RVs. They live here."

She's nodding.

Up another block and into a residential neighborhood.

The sky is lightening, far in the distance. The mountains in silhouette. A breeze brings the desert air in.

"I lived there six months once," I say, pointing at a dilapidated wood-frame house with peeling green paint. "I came here, the first

204

time, on my first road trip, when I was twenty-one. Played three-six and four-eight every day, twelve hours a day."

She nods.

I lead her down an alley behind the house. The alley is wide enough for a car. Street, alley, street, alley — that's the layout.

A young bearded white man in dirty jeans comes toward us, but passes on, to a dumpster, through which he searches for cans.

Katrina takes his picture.

"I met a girl back here," I say. "I was walking to the grocery store, and she was sitting in her backyard, and she was staring at me. She was seventeen. She was staring at me a certain way. So I talked to her. American girl. Blond."

"Did you go out with her?"

"Yeah. She lived with her mother and son in that apartment there."

I pointed to the place. Took a photo.

"She had a son?"

"When she was fifteen. Rough. The three of them, sharing a furnished studio. Real rough. I was nice to her. She was so happy just to go to a movie or a restaurant or something. Kind of like Calvin is."

"What happened?"

"Nothing. I went on back to Maryland."

We walk on. Past Las Vegas High School.

"She was going to school there. A couple of times I brought her little boy to meet her when she got out. That little boy was crazy about me. Which I understood. I remember how quick I used to get attached to any man my mother had around for a while. Except for the two she married. And only until I got old enough, eight or nine or so, to realize that none were going to be around for good. I guess I didn't want to hurt that boy. That might be why I left."

"That's understandable."

I nod. I want to talk about my own boy, but know I can't with her. But I do think about him. As I think about that girl's boy, and what his life must be like, growing up without a father around.

♣   ♣   ♣

Back at Binion's, I sit in the pot-limit game. Katrina goes off to play 1-4 stud. We agree, first one tired gets the other and we both go to bed.

Two hours later she's tapping me on the shoulder. I'm up five hundred, so it's cool to sack, noon though it is.

Upstairs, we shower together. Make love in the shower. Get out, dry off, shut the drapes, go to bed.

With the overnight no-sleep and the gallons of coffee and my up day and her down one, we both toss and turn for an hour before I, at least, fall off.

I wake in the dark and someone's trying to break into the room. I jump up out of bed, frantically looking for the intruder. Then slowly, foggily, come to — I'm dreaming. No one's there.

I breathe heavily. Shake my head.

Katrina's up. Sleepily looking at me. This isn't the first time I've done this with her.

She rolls her eyes. "Crazy man," she says.

I nod. Get back in bed.

"Why do you do that?" she asks.

"Once, driving home from California, I stopped for the night at a motel. Route 40 I took that time. Might have been New Mexico. Maybe Arizona. Anyway, I checked in, and went to my room. It was set back from the court, at the end of a little hallway. The light in the hallway was out, but I didn't make anything of it. Forgot my street smarts. Just went in, undressed, and went to bed. About ten minutes later I heard someone trying the door handle. I called out, 'Who's there?' They left. I laid back down. About ten minutes later, I heard a big bang — the door was off the hinges. But the chain latch caught it. I jumped out of bed, grabbed the phone — the cord was cut."

"What did you do?"

"I kicked the door shut and yelled, 'Get the fuck out of here!' Whoever it was left. A few minutes later, I went out. Sitting on the hood of a car a few yards away were a couple of Indians with beers in their hands. Laughing. Pulling splinters out of their boots. About

206

a hundred yards away a police cruiser was pulling up behind a bar. I ran over to it. They were tribal police, and took the Indians away."

"Did you press charges?"

"I was on the road, baby. I just dressed and got back on the highway."

She's happy enough with that answer. I don't need to tell her I'd been waking up with that dream long before that incident.

I'm awake. It's late or early — two in the morning.

Katrina's gone back to sleep. People often want to sleep a long time after a loss.

I go to Binion's. Sit in the pot-limit Hold 'em again. Order a tomato juice, milk, and coffee. Play until five-thirty in the morning. Leaving my chips on the table, I go across the street and up to my room to see if Katrina's awake. I'm hungry and want to eat before the coffee shop gets busy with the morning rush.

The room is dark. I look for her in the bed. She's not there.

"I'm not looking for you this time," I say out loud to myself.

I go back to the game. Play. Lose some. Cash out. Eat. Go back to the room and nap. Wake up. Find she's not there. Go looking for her. It's not that hard to search a casino. Walk into it one way. Walk out another.

I search all downtown. Share a cab to the Mirage with a Marylander going that way.

Find her there.

I stand across the pit, looking at her. She doesn't see me. I watch her.

I don't want to say hello, because I don't want her to think I went looking for her.

I walk away. Step outside. Decide to get her.

"Hey, baby," I say as I come up to her.

"Hey!" she says.

"How's it going?" I ask, even though I know she's winning.

"Good. The law of averages is catching up with these guys. You want to eat or something?"

"I'll have a drink with you."

She's been playing one hundred dollars a pop, so we get comped. I'm not hungry, but it's nice to sit a while.

She wants to play more blackjack. She tells me she got some money off her credit cards at the machines all the casinos have for that, and she wants to keep playing.

I finally speak up.

"Baby, this is really hard for me to say, but I feel like I have to."

She beats me to it. "You think I'm becoming an addict?"

"I don't know about that. I don't know what an addict is. I just know I hated to see you lose last night. It hurt me to see you hurt."

"If I were one of your buddies you wouldn't care."

"Yes I would. I just might not say anything to them."

"I'm all right, Joey. I just want to see if I can beat this place."

"Why?"

"Look who's asking. Why do you gamble?"

"It's my living."

"You shoot dice for a living?"

"Of course not."

"Then why do you do it?"

"Because I'm an idiot."

"To shoot dice, yeah, you are an idiot. But to count the deck down in blackjack gives me an advantage on the house. I have a positive expectation. And I like the challenge. Besides — it's research for the documentary."

"Then play poker. It's the only form of gambling that's worth a damn."

"I have. Joey, I can't believe you, of all people, are nagging at me."

We finish eating. She goes back to the blackjack pit. I go to the card room.

I sit in the 20-40 Hold 'em game. Katrina and I had made our usual first-one-tired-makes-the-other-one-leave deal.

Eight hours later, I'm tired. I'm losing about six hundred, and the game has gotten bad.

I don't cash out, though. I just go to find her.

I see her. I can tell she's losing. The stress shows in her face.

I go back to my game. Play some more. Win some. Get up and this time do cash out. I'm done.

I find her.

"Ready to go?" I ask.

She shakes her head no.

"I'm going back to the room, then."

"Okay." She doesn't look up. Too busy counting the cards.

Back in our room, I try to nap. Can't. Dress again, cab back up to the Strip again, find her again.

"I'm going to shoot dice," I tell her. She nods. I take a deep breath and walk away. At the craps table, I pull out two hundred dollars. I'm not really looking to play big. I just want to pass some time. Buy in for two hundred and make it last.

Only it doesn't last. Doesn't last twenty minutes, because I'm placing the inside numbers and taking triple odds on the point.

So I buy another two hundred in chips.

That lasts another twenty minutes.

Now I'm pissed. I buy four hundred.

Seven out, line away.

Seven out, line away.

Seven out, line away.

I switch to a different table. Buy in five hundred. Lasts a half-hour.

Seven out, line away.

I can't believe it. Twelve straight rolls without making a single point. That's hard to do.

I take two hundred out of my pocket. Drop it on the Don't Pass bar and call out "money plays" as the dice roll.

Seven. Winner seven. Take the Don'ts and pay the line. I'm out two hundred.

I take out four hundred. Again drop it on the Don't Pass bar.

Comes a ten. That's a great number for a Don't bettor.

Next roll — ten.

I'm out four hundred more.

I'm having trouble breathing. I'm sweating. I'm scared. There's no such thing as the law of averages. You never have to win again.

I take everything out of my pocket. Six thousand. Drop two on the Pass line. One bet. Make a point of five. Take double odds.

Seven out, line away.

See ya.

I step back from the table. I go to my wallet. I have three hundred there.

What's the point in trying to play? in trying to hit a number? I'm stuck too deep. I can't get back slowly.

I throw the three hundred on the field.

Comes a nine. Winner.

I've got six hundred out there. I let it ride. Two more times, I'm thinking. Then I'll quit. Double up two more times and I'm out of here.

Five. No field, five.

I stagger away. I don't need a mirror to know what my face looks like.

I go outside. Ride the conveyor belt to the street.

As I pass over the fountains there, I take a dollar coin out of my pocket, swear to God on my son's life that I will never shoot dice again, and throw the dollar in the fountain.

I don't have cab fare. I don't deserve a cab ride anyway. Head down, hands in my pockets, sick to my stomach, I walk back downtown. Takes an hour or more, I don't know.

Up in the room, I shower. For a long time, I sit there with the water running over me.

I think about my son. It's his money I lost, really. His money. I just went and lost my boy's money, and for what? What did I get for it? *Nothing*. No fun. No challenge. Just waste. I wasted my time. Threw away my money. And made myself sick. No other word will do.

I step out, dry off, lie down. I want to cry, but tears don't come. I just lie there feeling stupid.

I wake. I don't know how long I slept because I don't know when I went to sleep. But it's morning, and I'm hungry, and I don't know where Katrina is so I go for a walk and end up at the Golden Gate, and have some pancakes.

I feel better. Last night was stupid. But it was last night. There's no getting the money back. I'm just never going to shoot dice again. I swore to God. I will never shoot dice again.

I had brought twenty thousand in cash with me on this trip. I'd deposited twelve thousand in the house cage, and then later added two more thousand to it. But after the dice fiasco last night, I have to take some money out. Two thousand. Been here six days and have nothing to show for it. Doesn't matter, though, I guess. Wait — what kind of attitude is that? Am I some fucking loser now?

Time to get back to work. Time to dance with the one who brung me — poker.

I get on the list for the five-hundred-dollar buy-in pot-limit Hold 'em game. Wait an hour and a half for a seat to come up. Spend the time talking with poker homeboys.

My name gets called and I take my seat and play for sixteen hours. When I play, I usually go to the bathroom about every hour, both to piss away the coffee I'm drinking and to wash the smoke off my face. But other than the piss breaks, I stay at the table for sixteen hours. And win twenty-four hundred dollars.

I'm tired, but I'm happy, too. I'm over the kick in the stomach of the craps tilt. I still feel stupid about it, but I've got my confidence back. I don't feel like such a loser.

Back in our room, I find Katrina sleeping. I shower and crawl in with her. Fall asleep. She's gone when I wake up.

I resist going to look for her. I go back to the card room instead. I've decided to take a shot at one of the tournaments. The one today. Pot-limit Hold 'em. Fifteen-hundred-dollar buy-in. I don't like tournaments, but I want to take a shot. Winner will make a hundred thousand.

Six hours later I'm out. Nothing to show for it. Moved all in with an ace-king against ace-queen, an ace on the board and only one card to come.

Came a queen.

See ya.

Back in the hotel room, Katrina is sitting on the bed, knees-up, watching television.

"You okay?" I ask her.

"Don't talk to me, Joey," she says.

"Why are you mad at me?"

She won't speak.

I leave. I've got nowhere I want to go, but I leave.

I end up in the sports book. Eeeny-meeny-miny-moe basketball games for four hundred apiece. Watch them. Lose.

I go back upstairs. She's gone. I look out the window. Nice view of the valley lights.

She comes back.

"We need to talk," she says.

"Okay."

"I don't think we can stay together."

I look at her.

She sits down. Looks down.

I look out the window. We're on the tenth floor.

"I just don't understand why we're with each other," she says. "We have nothing in common."

I'm still just looking out the window.

"You all right?" she asks.

I nod.

Face her.

"Sure," I say.

I am. Saddened. But okay. Because she's right. Why are we together?

"We've got this room for another week," I say.

"I want to stay. We can share it. No need to be enemies."

I nod again.

"I'm going out. You want to have some dinner with me?" she asks.

"No. I'm full."

She nods. Says fine. Leaves.

I feel real alone. I look out the window. Let myself be mesmerized by the twinkle.

When I snap out of it, I know I don't want to stay here with her.

I call the Dunes. Take a room there for the next week. Pack up, go downstairs, get my money, get a cab, go to the Dunes, check in, go to my room, go to sleep.

TWENTY-THREE

In the morning I eat, and then walk down the street to the Mirage. I play 30-60 Hold 'em fourteen hours. Lose my ass. Eat dinner somewhere. Go back to my room. Shower and sleep.

Wake up the next day and do it again. Same game. Same result. Win almost no pots.

Wake up the next day — same thing once more. Play all day. Win about three pots. Lose a dime.

The next day I take off. Rule of mine. Lose three days in a row, give poker a break. Luck is a description, not a prediction, but still, running bad can make you play bad in subtle, hidden, but costly ways, and if you can't shake the premonition, you've got to take a break.

I bet horses instead. At Bally's racebook.

Lose my ass.

How upset am I about Katrina?

I'm not sure. I know I don't mind breaking up with her. From the moment I saw her reaction to the news of my son being born, I knew I couldn't stay with her. Didn't know I knew, but knew, you know? But still, I'm sad. And worried.

A Marylander told me today he saw her at a blackjack table before he went to bed, and she was still there, in the same clothes, when he came down the next morning.

Next day I'm back at the Mirage. Same result. Limit poker, no pots. I'm not playing well. I'm not having any luck, but I'm also not playing well. Something's wrong. With me. I don't know what it is. I just don't feel like playing. I don't feel like concentrating. I resent the game.

Go back to the Dunes. Go to sleep.

In the morning, I wake when the sunlight comes through the window. I lie in bed. Not in a hurry.

I hear a popping sound. Another. Two more.

I sit up. I know it's gunfire.

I look out the window. Across the parking lot, a hundred yards or so, to the street.

Traffic has stopped.

I see a car pulled over. A body lies by the side. A man stands over it.

He moves his hand to his head. I hear another pop. He falls.

I stare.

People are running over.

I stay where I am. I decide not to do anything, because I can already hear the wail of sirens, and I know there are a lot of witnesses who saw more than me, and from closer.

I watch the ambulance pull up. I watch the detectives talk to people. I watch the bodies get taken away.

I watch a long time. Watch until everyone else has left. Then I go out. Stand over the site. Look at the bloodstains on the asphalt.

I'm more than a little shook up, but I go on. Go back to Binion's.

I sign up for the pot-limit game, but the list is long, and so I end up in a 30-60 Hold 'em.

Four hours later, having won all of two hands, I realize how little I want to be there. How little I've wanted to play these past days.

Because of Katrina?

Because of what she made me see?

The hours pass. The pots don't come.

I bet a baseball game. Lose.

I bet a fucking *dog* race. Two hundred. Picked a number and bet it. To win.

Lost. By a nose.

I eat. Go back to the Dunes. Sleep.

Next morning, over breakfast, I read in the paper that the shooting I'd seen had been a murder-suicide. A father had been fighting with his son. Had pulled a gun. Had shot the boy. Had shot himself.

My God.

I close my eyes. Remember to breathe. Can't eat. Can't drink. Remember to breathe.

I can't play cards. I just have no desire.

So I walk around some. Back to the Dunes. Get a room change. Move to the new one.

Go up front to the casino. What's there to do?

I buy in one hundred dollars at a dice table. I'm bored.

I want to pass the time.

Maybe I want to hurt myself.

Maybe I want to punish myself.

The hundred disappears as soon as I bet.

Seven out, line away.

I buy in five hundred.

A half-hour later, it's gone.

I'm steaming. I am so sick of running so bad. I can't hit a horse. I can't win a ball game. I can't drag a pot in limit poker.

And now I can't make a point in a craps game. I cannot make one fucking point.

I go to the cashier's cage. Get my money. What's left of it after the losing I've been doing this week. There's about seven thousand still.

I buy back in at the dice table.

Six hours later, I've got one hundred and fifty dollars left.

My hands are trembling. My whole *body* is trembling. I'm close to crying. I'm in shock. HOW IS IT POSSIBLE TO HAVE SUCH BAD LUCK?

Again, I don't need a mirror to know the look on my face. I can tell from the way the dealers don't look at me.

I dead-walk back to my room. Undress. Climb in the shower. Sit down and let the water flow over me for an hour.

I dry off, and step out on the balcony. I have a courtyard room. Second floor. Overlooking the swimming pool, which is closed for the night. Colored lights beam down on it.

There's a tree right by my balcony. Birds are flitting about in it. The beauty of the fresh, warm night air just makes me feel worse. Lonelier.

I go to sleep.

A bird flies into my room. A very tiny bird. A hummingbird.

I wake the next morning thinking I might have left the balcony door open. I hadn't. There's no bird in here. It was a dream.

I dress and leave the casino.

I feel very strange. Very weak. Anxious.

I sit down somewhere. My hands are trembling.

Then I remember something my mother had told me once — a dream of a bird in your room is a dream of death.

I had dreamed of a very, very tiny bird.

I had sworn to God on my son's life that I would never shoot dice again, and then I had shot dice.

I've never been so scared.

I don't believe in God. I've never been to a church except with a friend as a kid. I'm not at all religious.

I'm just scared.

My flight back to Maryland is scheduled for tomorrow, but that's not soon enough. I find a travel agent in one of the casinos and get my ticket changed for tonight. There's a charge, but I don't care. I have to get out of this town. I have to get back to my boy.

217

Meanwhile, I'm dancing. With God. I'm thinking maybe there is a God, and maybe he's pissed at me. How could I see what I saw, do what I did, dream what I dreamed, all to no end?

Psychology. Witnessing the murder-suicide was a fluke. Dreaming about the tiny bird was self-induced from seeing the birds outside my window before going to bed, and feeling guilty about leaving my boy to go gambling. The sick, weak feeling was from stress. From the losing, and the breaking up with Katrina, and the sight of the shooting.

But I still believe I have to go home.

And in whatever kind of capitulation to reason it may be, I feel a need for penance. For leaving John. For hurting myself with the gambling. And maybe for getting Katrina involved in gambling, too.

So I swear to God again. For the only thing I can think of — to quit smoking.

Then I pack and take a cab to the airport six hours before my flight leaves. I call home.

Old Charlie answers. I ask for Essay. He's not there.

I leave a message — my new arrival time and flight number.

"You're getting home just in time," Old Charlie says.

"Why?"

"Just better get back here is all I'm going to say."

"Don't jerk me off, Charlie. Is something up?"

"You just better get back."

"Listen, motherfucker, just tell me what's going on."

He hangs up.

I call Katrina at the Union Plaza. No answer.

TWENTY-FOUR

Eleven A.M. Essay is waiting for me at National Airport.

"What's up, man?" I ask. "Charlie was weird on the phone."

We shake hands.

"I don't know, Joey. But I think you might be out at the casino."

We walk along in silence. Go to baggage. Wait for my gear. Essay is more depressed about it than I am.

In the car, my Camaro, which I had let him use while I was gone, I say, "I'm not surprised."

"They asked me if I wanted your job," he says.

"You take it?"

"No, man"— he pauses —"Fat Boy did."

"No shit?"

"I think he owes them a lot of money."

"I know he does."

"Plus they don't have to pay him what they were paying you."

"They were paying me too much. But that was their own fault. Their own idea."

"I think they're going to pay Fat one dime a week. But he only gets four hundred of that. The rest goes to his debt."

"He tell you that?"

"Yeah. He feels bad."

"You should have taken it."

"I'm better off dealing. If I take the job, once I'm smooth with them, they'd cut me out. Give it to someone else who owes them money."

"Probably."

"You okay about it?"

"Sure," I say. And I am. "Never was my style to work for a living."

"You thought that was work?"

We laugh.

"How was Las Vegas?"

"Bad."

"How bad?"

"Twenty thousand bad."

"Ouch. Poker?"

"Nah. I made a bit playing pot-limit."

"What hurt?"

"Dice. Baseball. Horses. Everything."

"Get your nose opened?"

"Big-time."

"That's not like you. That's like us."

"I know, brother."

"How about Katrina? Where is she?"

"I got no idea."

"You guys break up?"

"Last week."

"She was a strange girl."

"Strange and getting stranger. But cool, in some ways. I'm glad I knew her. Feel bad, though. Got her into gambling."

"She liked it too much."

"She did. You should have seen her in Vegas. Bad as you."

"Wow!"

♣   ♣   ♣

We drive across the Wilson Bridge into Maryland.

"Let's go to Laura's," I say. "I want to see my boy."

He pulls off the Beltway onto Indian Head Highway south. To Fort Washington, to her parents' house.

"You seen this critter yet?" I ask him.

"Nah, man. I want to, though. See what a half-Filipino, half-Pinocchio looks like."

We walk up. Knock.

Laura answers.

Jumps in my arms. She's crying.

"Whoa — what's wrong?"

"Joey, my mom took the baby!"

"What?"

I rush past her.

Her parents are sitting in the living room. Chito won't look up. Her mother, Gloria, glares at me.

"Where's my son?" I ask, relatively calmly.

"He not your boy!" Gloria says. Hatefully.

"Bullshit!"

Essay puts his arm on my shoulder. "Calm down, brother. Let's figure this out."

"Where is he?" I ask again.

"He okay," she says.

"Where is he?" I ask Laura.

"I don't know, Joey," she says. Crying. Nearly hysterical.

"You no good!" her mother screams. She's getting hysterical, too. "They fire you at Churchville! We know. You think we don't know! We know. They fire you."

"Where's my boy, Gloria?"

I'm standing over her.

"You run off to Las Vegas. Don't tell anyone at your job. They fire you. We know. You no good. You no good father. We know!"

"You know what, you old bitch?"

"Hey!" Chito says.

221

"Don't fuck with me, Chito!" I yell. Very slowly, I ask again, "Where is my boy? Tell me or I'll fucking kill you."

"Joey," Laura says, taking my arm, "don't fight."

"Don't fight? Your own mother takes your baby, and you say 'don't fight'?"

"She baby!" Gloria says, pointing at Laura. "She baby. You fuck her. Leave her."

"Mom!" Laura screams.

"You go now or I call police!" Gloria screams.

"Call 'em," I say.

The old woman's trying to hide in her hysteria. I've seen it before. Intimidation through irrationality. It's a tactic.

She picks up the phone. Dials 9-1-1.

"Hurry!" she screams into the phone. "Man here try to kill us. Hurry!"

Chito goes down the hall. Comes back with a gun.

"Get out!" he says to me.

I cool-look him. "What's this, Chito? You an old woman, too? I don't have enough of them here?"

He looks sheepish. Lowers the gun.

I turn to Laura. Take her by the arm. Lead her outside. Essay follows.

"What is going on here," I say, steady-voiced, to calm her.

"My mom and Bobby got together. They have papers."

"What kind of papers?"

"Legal papers."

"What *kind* of legal papers?"

"Let me get them."

"Essay, go in with her."

They go inside. I reach for a cigarette, then remember my penance.

They come back out. Laura hands me two sheets of paper stapled together.

I toss my cigarettes to Essay. "Take these," I say.

I look at the papers. Read them quickly. It's a suit to determine John's paternity.

"This just says you have to bring the baby in to court for a blood test."

A squad car pulls up. A white man and a black woman, both pretty young, get out. Uniformed.

"What's going on?" the woman asks.

Before I can say anything, Gloria comes running out of the house.

"Arrest him!" she says in a high-pitched squeal.

"Calm down," the woman cop says.

"He say he going to kill us," she screams, bending at the waist. Then she starts bawling, like she's terrified.

I eye the cops. Read them for having been involved with about a million domestic disturbances. Read them for having dealt with a million bad actors. Figure there's nothing they're going to appreciate now more than a level-headed explanation.

I take out my driver's license. Hand it to the male cop.

"My name is Joseph Moore. This is my girlfriend, Laura. These people"—I point to Chito and Gloria—"are her parents. She lives here with them. I live at the address on my license. Laura had a baby a month ago. We believe I'm the father, but it's possible it's another man. That man has filed a paternity suit."

I hand the papers to the woman cop. Then continue: "The fight now is because Laura's parents have taken the baby from her. They won't tell her where he is. And when I heard about it, I got mad. And I did say I'd kill them if they didn't tell me where the boy is. But I didn't mean it for real, and they know it."

I decide to hold the fact of Chito's pointing the gun at me for reserve ammo.

The woman cop glances over the papers. Nods. Speaks to Laura.

"They took your baby?"

Laura has calmed down some. "Yes," she says.

"Without your permission?"

"Yes."

"Yes, they did not have your permission?"

"They did not have my permission."

"When did they take the baby?"

"Last night, I think."

"You don't know?"

"I put him to bed. When I woke up, he was gone."

"Why didn't you call the police?"

"They showed me the papers."

"These papers don't give them permission to take your son."

Laura nods. "I don't know stuff like that."

"And they're your parents. I understand." She turns to Gloria. "Where's the baby now?"

Gloria doesn't answer.

"Ma'am, you do not have a legal right to take the baby from its mother."

Gloria points at me. "He no good father."

"That's not the issue, Ma'am. Right now you are under suspicion of kidnapping, which is a very serious offense. Now either you get that baby back here to his mother pronto or we will arrest you."

"He at your cousin's," Gloria says to Laura.

"Where's that?" the male cop asks.

"I know," Laura says.

The woman cop says, "Let's go there and get the baby. Officer Remson will stay here with everyone else until we get back."

We all mill around for a few minutes. Officer Remson gets everyone's name and address and phone number.

When the woman cop and Laura return, Laura has the baby. I go to her. Take him. Hug and kiss him.

"Hey, munchkin," I say softly.

"Okay, everyone, listen up," the woman cop says. "This is how it's going to be."

She points to Laura's parents. "You two are going to mind your own business. Your daughter and I have had a little talk. She isn't going to press charges against you. But if you try this stunt again, I won't let her back down."

She's speaking very sternly. Gloria and Chito are pretty humbled. They nod.

"You," she says to me, "have a right to see your boy until it's proven he isn't your boy. But you cannot threaten these people."

I nod.

"Does everyone understand the rules now?"

Everyone nods. Except Laura. She says, to the cops, "Can he take the baby?"

"Me?" I say.

"Him?" her mother says.

"What?" the woman cop says.

Laura speaks to her. "I cannot say no to my mother. I have to do what she tells me. I'm afraid she'll tell me to keep the baby from him."

Gloria stares in disbelief. Then she says, "How he can take baby? He bum! He no can take baby."

"Take him, Joey," Laura says. "You can take care of him."

I know how frightened Laura is of her mother. How submissive she feels toward her, and how frightened she is of that submission.

Without thinking of what it means, I nod.

"You want him to take the baby?" the woman cop asks.

"Yes," Laura says, "it's better. Until we go to court and settle all this."

"It's your choice," the woman cop says.

"How he can take baby?" Gloria says.

"I am the boy's legal father until proven otherwise," I say, winging it. "If his mother and I agree that I should take him, how is it your business?"

"He's right," the male cop says. "He has more right to the baby than anyone except the mother. And if she agrees, then there's no problem."

The woman cop shrugs. "I guess that's true. This might be the best solution for a while."

She turns to me.

"Think you can handle it?"

I nod. I don't want to go back in the house, so I say to Essay, "Go in with Laura and get his stuff."

"Are you going to interfere?" the woman cop asks Laura's parents.

They shake their heads no.

"Then get to it," she says to Essay.

I'm holding the baby. Rocking him. His eyes are open. Staring up at me. I rub his nose with mine.

"Why you cause so much trouble, prune-face?"

He smiles. Stares up at me.

Essay and Chito break down the crib and put it in the back of the car. Laura brings a couple of bags of his clothes and diapers and bottles. We get the babyseat from her car and put it in mine.

I let her put the baby in it.

"Don't cry," I say to Laura. "We'll be fine."

"Where are you going to be?" she asks.

"I'm not sure. I'll call you."

"I'll come over every day."

I pull her to me. Hug her. I can imagine how much stress she's been under.

"We'll be fine," I say.

She nods. "I know," she says.

"Thank you, officers," I say.

"Take care of him," the woman cop says. I get in the back with the baby. Essay drives. We go home.

TWENTY-FIVE

I carry the baby in, and Essay follows with the baby's stuff.

"Old Charlie, what's up?" I say when I walk in.

He's sitting in the living room. Smoking. Drinking red wine. A half-eaten sandwich sits on a plate, on his lap.

"Who's that? Joey the deadbeat? Get a job, sucker."

"Shut up, man," I say, and sit on the couch.

"What's that?" he says, looking at the baby.

"My boy. John."

"What's he doing here? Ain't no baby staying here."

"He'll stay in my room with me," I say.

"Not in this house."

"Charlie, it's just for a while. I have to keep him for a while."

"Not here. That's not in your lease."

"What lease? When did we ever sign a lease?"

He taps his skull. "Your lease is written in here. And there's no baby allowed."

He's not joking.

I stare at him.

"You owe me money," I say. "Give me the rent I've got paid in advance, and I'm gone."

"What rent? Gambling losses are not collectible in a court of law. Now get out."

I stare at him.

Essay stands over him. "You're a piece of shit when you're drunk, you know that, Charlie?" he says.

"Fuck you. You can get out, too. I don't need neither of you."

He takes a swig from his wine bottle. Spills some down his neck and onto his T-shirt. It's just a fresher stain, and not a first one.

"You want to wait until he sobers up to talk to him?" Essay asks me.

I shake my head no. Lean back.

John is making sucking noises.

"Get me a bottle, will you, Essay?" I ask.

Laura had packed one ready, and Essay gets it from the bag and gives it to me.

I cradle John. Hold the bottle for him. He's pretty hungry.

"Ah. Look at Mr. Mom," Charlie says.

"Look at Mr. Boozer," Essay says.

"*Three Men and a Baby: The Hell Version*," I say.

"Goddamn right!" Charlie says.

Essay sits beside me on the couch.

"Where you going to go?" he asks. "Your mom's?"

"She's got no room. Calvin's in her second room."

Essay nods.

I get an idea.

"Charlie, how about if Calvin moves in here, so I can have his room at my mom's?"

"No! No fucking mass murderer's coming in this house."

"Probably too early for his parole reqs to be changed anyway," Essay says.

I nod.

Essay starts to light a cigarette.

"No smoking near the baby, man," I say.

He shakes the match out. Puts the cigarette away.

"You going to quit smoking?" he asks.

"Got to."

John is sucking the formula out of the bottle, but never takes his eyes off me.

"What?" I whisper.

He just keeps sucking down his formula. Staring up at me. My eyes water.

"Hey, Joey," Essay says, "know what you should do? Maybe?"

"What?"

"Call Mary. She needs a roommate."

"Is she living down here?"

"Yeah. She and Allison got a place together but now Allison has moved in with Nug."

"When did that happen?"

"Last week."

"I go away two weeks and the whole world changes."

"They're getting married."

"Nug and Allison? That I heard."

"I think she's pregnant."

"They should be happy. They get along."

"So Mary has the apartment to herself. Told me she was looking for a roommate. Asked me if I wanted to move in."

"You?"

"She needs help with the rent."

"You should have said yes. Get out of this hellhole."

"She said I couldn't smoke because she has the baby there. I got to have my smokes. But if you're quitting anyway, maybe you should call her."

I look at Charlie. He's slurping his wine. I know after he sobers up he'll apologize. But he's right, too. I can't keep John here.

"You got her number?" I ask Essay.

He picks up the phone. Dials. Says, "Mary? It's Essay. Joey's back from Vegas. Wants to talk to you."

He hands me the phone. I hand him the baby.

229

"Mary?"

"Mr. Pinocchio. How can I help you, sir?"

"You need a roommate?"

"Yes."

"I need a place to stay."

Pause.

"Why?" she asks.

"I got my little boy now."

"*You* have him?"

"Yeah. And the old fart won't let me keep him here."

She's silent.

"It's just for a while, Mary. And believe me, I just want to be your roommate. I hope you know I'm not a pig. I'm not going to bother you."

Pause.

"Are you home?" she asks.

"Yeah."

"Maybe you should come over and see the place before we talk anymore."

"Where is it?" She tells me. "I know it. Those condos there."

"Yeah."

She gives me the building and apartment number.

"I'm going to check out her place," I say to Essay. "You okay with the baby?"

"Sure."

"Hey," Charlie babbles. "They cut you out at the casino, huh?"

"Yeah, Charlie," I say.

"Not such a big shot now, are you?"

"Know what else, Charlie?"

"What?"

"Katrina dumped me in Vegas."

"Hah!"

He bangs his knee so hard his plate falls off and his wine spills.

"He's happy now," Essay says.

"I thought that would make his day."

♣   ♣   ♣

I find Mary's building easily enough. In high school I had friends who lived in this complex. Mostly middle-class blacks. Some whites. Safer than most of the rest of the area. Owning the apartments instead of just renting them makes a difference.

I knock. Mary answers. Holding her baby.

"Hey, Melissa," I say to the baby. "Is she talking yet?" I ask Mary.

"Some."

"How old is she now?"

"Eighteen months."

I follow Mary in.

There is very little furniture. An old couch. An old easychair. An old dining table. Other old stuff. Toys scattered about.

"Let me put her to bed," Mary says, and disappears down the hall.

I sit on the couch.

She returns a moment later. Sits in the easychair across from me.

"I heard you lost your job," she says.

"I guess."

"I'm sorry, Joey."

"It's okay. How did you hear?"

"Working in the poker room. I hear everything. People love to gossip."

I nod. I know how fast word of something like this would spread.

"Where's your baby?" she asks.

"With Essay."

"I saw him last week. The baby, I mean."

"The baby? Really?"

"Allison and I brought some clothes over. Visited Laura. And I was curious, too, sure. Beautiful boy, Joey. Honestly."

"I guess. Looks funny to me."

Pause.

"Mary . . ."

I can't finish. I suddenly get overwhelmed by it all. Put my hands over my eyes. Try to shut out the world.

She doesn't speak.

I take a deep breath.

Still with my hands over my eyes, speaking into the darkness, I say, "Mary, I need some help for a little while."

I rub my temples. Breathe deeply.

She moves to my side. Puts her hand on my shoulder.

I drop my hands from my face.

"I'm all right," I say. "I'm just getting rushed with stuff."

She nods.

"Maybe we can be a good team," I say. "We both have kids to take care of."

She nods again.

"You want to try?" I ask.

"Yes," she says softly.

"How do you want to work it out?"

"I don't know."

"What days are you working?"

"Saturdays and Mondays for Nug."

"What are you doing with Melissa on those days?"

"There's a woman in the next building who watches her."

"She okay?"

"Yeah. She has a bunch of other kids to watch, though. Too many. I don't really like it."

"You want to maybe do this? Have me watch the kids while you work, and then two days a week you watch them and let me go out? And we tag-team the other three days?"

"Joey — you really think you can do this? Have you ever watched a baby before? Do you have any idea how hard it is?"

I get up to leave.

"Joey!" she says.

"What?"

"I'm just asking. Calm down."

I sit back down.

"I'll do the best I can," I say. "You never took care of a baby before you took care of a baby, either."

She smiles. "Okay."

"Okay."

I stand up, go over, look down the hall.

"You have three bedrooms here?"

"Yes."

"I know these places' layout. The back room's got a bathroom, right?"

"Yes."

"You want to take that room, and I'll take this one closest to the front and use the hallway bathroom. We'll put the kids in the middle room, so we can both hear them cry if they do?"

"Okay."

"How much are you paying for this place?"

"Seven hundred a month plus phone and electric."

"Want to split it?"

"Sure. Food, too?"

"Yeah." I'm standing in the middle of the room. Looking around. I look at her. She looks at me.

I smile, tired.

"What?" she asks.

"I just wish the world would stop for a minute. I feel like it's moving a lot faster than I am."

"What are you going to do for work?"

"What do you mean?"

"You lost your job."

"I lost my job? No. I lost my freeroll. My *job* is playing cards. And as long as I got a bankroll, I'm okay."

She shrugs.

"What?" I ask her.

"Nothing."

"You want me to drive a cab? Flip a burger? Dig a ditch?"

"It's not my business."

"That's right." She looks at me. Looks at me like she always has. Makes me smile. "Always know when I'm dancing, don't you?" I say.

She nods.

We look at each other a long moment. Why does she see what she sees in me?

I call my mom. Calvin answers. Says she's not home. I ask him if he can come over with my van and help me move.

He says of course.

We bring my little bit of furniture over, and my clothes, and John's crib and stuff. Move Mary's stuff to the back room. Set up the kid's nursery. Then I bring John over.

That night, Mary goes over some things with me about caring for the babies. I listen carefully. To show her I can, I feed and change Melissa and John both, and put them to bed.

She and I stay up a bit, talking. I call Laura and tell her where I am. Tell her not to tell her parents.

In the middle of the night, I hear crying. I stagger into the hall and open the babies' door.

They're both up. John's crying. Not loud, but he's making his point. Melissa's peeking over the side of her crib.

"Ooog baa baby?" she says.

"Probably," I say.

I pick John up. He's wet. I change him.

He's hungry. I put him down. Make a bottle. Come back and sit in the rocker Mary's put in their room, and feed him.

Melissa looks at me. Repeats her earlier statement.

"I guess, hon."

I hear Mary's door open. She comes in.

"Yes?" I ask her.

"Everything okay?"

"Yes. Why are you up?"

Mary takes care of the babies in the morning while I sleep. I sleep a long time. Until three in the afternoon. Jet-lag. Stress. Everything.

"Call Nug," Mary says when I come out.

I shower, dress, and feed John. Change Melissa. Then call. I

234

have to get his new number from Mary. Allison answers. She and I talk a minute. Then she gets Nug.

"What's up, man?" I say.

"You lose job, sucker. Bad beat."

"It's all right."

"What you do now?"

"Go back to playing."

"You got baby now?"

"How did you hear?"

"Allison and Mary talk all day."

"Figures."

"You cannot play poker and take care of baby."

"I'm only taking the baby for a while. Laura's taking him back."

"Essay say might not be your kid."

"It's my kid."

"He say Bobby Lotto take you to court."

"It's my kid."

"How you know?"

"I know, that's all. And Lotto's a dick. Fuck him."

"He sleep with Laura?"

"Yeah."

"Why she do that?"

"It was when K.C. and I were road-tripping to Colorado. We'd broke up. Her mom fixed her up with Lotto."

"Filipina mother always try to make daughter marry rich man."

"*All* mothers do that."

"Asian mothers serious about it."

"I guess."

"How you take baby?"

I told him what had happened the day before. Told him about Las Vegas, too.

"You stay with Mary?"

"We're going to try."

"You can take care of baby might not be yours?"

"I can do it for a while."

"Okay. Me and Allison come over some night. Watch you change diapers."

"Cool."

"Hey! Call Fat Boy. He at Branchville."

"He say to?"

"I see him there. He say something like your mother in trouble."

"What?"

"I don't know. He tell me. I call you. You call him."

"Why he didn't call me?" Nug's got me talking like him now.

"Need your new number."

Branchville is a charity casino in the north part of the county. I call up there. Wait a minute while someone who knows me gets on the line, and then another minute while that person gets Fat.

"What's up, sucker?" I say when he picks up.

"Joey, you back?"

"You quick?"

"We got to talk, brother."

"I think so. Hold on."

I turn to Mary.

"I have to meet Fat Boy. See what's up. I know you've been watching John all day, and I'm not going to make this a habit —"

She interrupts. "Go, Joey. I understand."

"Thanks."

Half-hour later I'm at Branchville. It's a two-story redbrick fire station. The casino is on the second floor.

I go in. See some people I know. See Fat. Wave him over.

Couple of people say hi to me. Ask me if I "got 'em" in Las Vegas.

Fat hurries over and we go downstairs.

We stand in the entrance because it's drizzling outside. Cold, drizzling evening. Fat's shaking his head.

"Boulder fucked you, man. He kept saying you were making too much money. And he was pissed you fired Sam."

"Why is it Boulder's say-so?"

"Just Jones's boy shit."

"You got my job now?" He can't look at me. Turns away.

I notice his cheek is bruised.

"Who hit you?"

"I hit myself. On a door."

"Boulder fucking with you?"

He looks down again. Brushes his red hair off his face. Big, soft-bellied guy. Younger than he should be.

"I got to do what I got to do," he says.

"I ain't mad."

"I didn't do nothing to you."

"I said I wasn't mad."

He still can't look at me.

"Nug said something about my mom being in trouble."

"They think she stole a bunch of money, Joey. They think she got mad when she heard you got fired and stole a bunch of money."

"Who is 'they'?"

"Kenny and Boulder. Freddy. Philly."

"Did she have access to anything?"

"I don't know, man."

"Lot of schemers up there. Quick thinkers. Hear I get fired, see her get mad, figure they can steal a bunch and get her blamed for it. More than a few people in this world think that way."

"I ain't saying anything about her, Joey. I'm just saying she went home early last week. Right after she heard about you. And then supposedly it was discovered a lot of money was missing."

I shake my head. "I'm glad I'm done with that place," I say. "It wasn't what it could have been."

"You going to hurt the card room?"

"Why?"

"Kevin and Larry were afraid you'd tell people not to go there anymore."

"Tell them to relax. They might lose the fifteen-thirty crowd, but they'll keep the two-five."

He reaches in his pocket. Pulls out some money.

"Six hundred on what I owe you," he says, handing it to me.

"Good. I need it."

"You lose out there?"

"Shot bad bones."

"You hurting for money?"

"Nah."

"I'm sorry about this, Joey."

I nod. "Me, too."

Pause.

"That guy Philly is back down here, huh?" I ask.

"Yeah. Scary guy."

"Watch your ass, Fat." He goes back upstairs to the smoke and noise and heat. I go outside into the cool and the drizzle. The sun is down.

I stop at a 7-11 for coffee and ask the clerk for a pack of cigarettes before I remember I don't do that anymore. I get a roll of Wint-o-Green Lifesavers instead. I haven't been missing the cigarettes that much. Surprise myself with how little I miss them. Too scared to smoke them to miss them, maybe. True penance. Literally the fear of God.

TWENTY-SIX

I go see my mom. She and Calvin are eating. Sitting down, having cooked, and eating. Like normal people.

We all quickly say hi, and then I tell her, and ask her, about what all happened while I was gone. About the money. My mom can't lie to me. Can try. Can't do it.

So when she says she didn't take it, I know she's telling the truth.

And the rest of the time she was there?

She smokes. Drinks from her glass of wine. Says, yes, she'd been stealing. Not much, really, she says. Not as much — or no more than — everyone else. But she'd been there watching it all happen, and so, sure, she got her share. A couple of hundred a week. No big deal. No big score. No big problem. Compared to what everyone else was taking, nothing special at all.

She's not proud, but I don't know how ashamed she is. All I can do is accept it.

She eyes me. Am I going to get mad at her? Get holier-than-thou about this?

To what end would I do that, Mom? I think.

I ask her again about the accusation that she stole a lot the day she quit. I mean, Mom, how much trouble are you in?

None, she says confidently. Boulder and Kenny aren't going to press her.

Had they yet?

They'd called. Told her they "knew" she had taken it. But she'd told them to fuck off.

"And how much are we talking about?"

"Seventeen thousand."

"What did Kenny say?"

"Yeah, what did he say?" Calvin asks.

She rubs out her cigarette.

"He tried to be tough. Said friendship wasn't going to help me here. Said they 'knew' I took it, and were going to get it back, one way or the other. Said there were other people involved now. People who don't care about me like he does. New York people. Some guy named Philly."

A frightful look of fear and worry comes over Calvin's face. His huge arms flex. His eyes go razor thin.

I know how he feels about my mom. Like she's his mom. The one he never had. He's told me how she's been to him. Putting him up. Helping him with his reading. Walking him step-by-step back into the regular world. Patiently. Sincerely. Gently.

My mom laughs. "I've known them boys my whole life. Don't y'all worry none. They won't do nothing."

"I'm going to go see them," I say.

"If you want."

"Need me?" Calvin asks.

"Nah. Thanks, brother, but I'm just going to square them out."

I call Freddy. Sure, he says. We can talk.

Rainy and cold, my collar's up and my Orioles cap is pulled low.

I knock, and as usual it's the blonde who answers and leads me downstairs.

Boulder, Kenny Jones, Freddy, and Philly are sitting around the dining table. Big, fat, greasy, dark-haired Boulder in his designer sweats; grey-haired, grey-skinned, fish-eyed Kenny Jones in his Redskins T-shirt and hat; white-haired, soft-bellied old Freddy in his golfer's plaids; and Italian, slick, polyester-wearing Philly. Eating, drinking, smoking.

"How you doing, Joey?" Philly asks. He's smiling. He's got a grimacing smile. Great hair.

"How you been?" I say, coming up to them all.

"You got your mother's money?" Boulder asks.

"Fuck you," I say.

He starts to stand up. Freddy puts a hand on him.

"Sit down, Joe," Freddy says.

I do, and say, "My mom didn't take your money. If there's money missing, ask someone else. She didn't take it."

"Bullshit," Boulder says.

"Fuck you," I say.

Kenny Jones stands up now, quickly, and comes around the table.

"You little punk," he says.

I stand. I'm pissed off and there's no hiding it. "What the fuck are you going to do, you old, ugly, fag-assed motherfucker?"

We're nose-to-nose.

"Calm down!" Freddy commands.

We stay nose-to-nose. The bills of our caps brush.

"Sit down," Freddy says.

After a moment, Kenny moves away.

I sit. Relax.

Philly laughs. Thinks it's all funny.

"We don't have much to talk about," I say. "I already heard you cut me out."

"You were making too much money," Kenny says. "And for doing what?"

"I built that card room."

"You didn't deserve that much," he says.

"So you fired me because you were jealous?"

241

"No," Boulder says, "we fired you for being such a pussy-faced punk."

I shake my head in disdain. "So like I said, we don't have much to talk about. If you think you can make more money without me, give it your best shot. Personally I think you'll lose half your customers. But it's your business."

"You threatening us?" Kenny says.

"About what?"

"You going to queer our action?"

"You don't think people are going to hear? You don't think half the players in this county already know?"

"I don't think they'll care," Kenny says. "You aren't always the most popular person in the poker world."

"Not always. But I am respected. And known. And that's what you need in a poker boss."

"No one respects you."

I shrug. "Then why are you nervous?"

"You are such a punk," Boulder says, with true disgust. "You're nobody. You think you're something? You're nobody, let me tell you."

"He's been thinking he's a big shot because he's been allowed to hire and fire a few people," Kenny says. "Thinking he's on his way up."

Boulder laughs.

"Thought you were something, didn't you?" Kenny says. "Punk kid making all that money. Buying himself a new car. Really thought you were something."

Boulder and Kenny sit back, looking smug. Philly is studying me.

"K.C.'s game is done for. And Nug's out at Oxon Hill," Kenny Jones says.

I think of Nug and Allison, and her being pregnant. Now I am shook.

"Why?" I say, and don't catch the hurt in my voice.

"Oh, isn't that sweet?" Boulder says. "He cares about his buddy."

"Fuck you," I say to him once more. I'm not being original, but I am being consistent.

Now a different look comes over Boulder's face. Hate comes over his face. This time when he stands, Freddy doesn't hold him down.

Boulder walks around the table. I stand, scared, because I don't think I can take him in a fight.

From a pocket he makes a quick move with one hand while flicking out and grabbing my hair with the other, and the next thing I know I have a gun in my face. Pressed into my cheek. My hat's knocked off, I've got a gun in my face, and Boulder's got a wicked frown and hateful look and says, deeply, slowly, "What did you say?"

I keep my mouth shut. I've got my hands gripping his collar, but I keep my mouth shut.

"What you want to say, boy?"

A moment passes. I let go of his collar.

He drops his hand. Lets go of my hair. Moves unhurriedly back to his chair.

I take a deep breath. See, out of the corner of my eye, Kenny smiling, Philly looking amused, Freddy looking ashamed, and Boulder looking pleased.

I reach down and pick up my hat. Take another deep breath.

"My mother didn't take your money," I say, with I don't know how much shake in my voice.

"Then she's got nothing to worry about," Freddy says. "Now get out."

I stare at him. He still can't look at me. He used to be my hero. I almost say that now. I almost say how much I used to respect him. But I don't. I just start to walk away.

I hear Boulder say, "Hey!"

I turn back.

He's pointing the gun at me. "Don't let us hear you asked anyone to stop giving us action."

I start off again, and once again he bellows, "Hey!"

"What?" I say, turning around once more.

243

He looks me in the eye and says, "If I told you to suck my dick or I'd kill you, would you do it?"

He's pointing the gun at me. Smiling. As is Kenny, who has always hated me. As is Philly, for whom I'm just some local specimen subject for entertainment. And Freddy just sits there looking down, sadly. *Still* unable to look me in the eye. Still going along with the other men. I wonder if I'm the only one who's been cut out at the casino. I wonder what Boulder and Kenny's new show toward me is about. Who are they acting tough for? Putting on a show for a new boss, maybe? Trying to impress upon Philly that they're big leaguers?

"If I seriously thought you'd do it?" I ask Boulder.

"You punk-ass motherfucker," he says angrily. "If I say I'll shoot you, I'll shoot you!"

I know I'm not getting shot. I've got enough radar left for that. I'm calm. And I answer his pig's question with the last thing he'd expect — the truth.

"Would I suck your dick if my life depended on it?" Pause. "I hope so."

Philly's eyebrows rise. Liking the answer. Boulder looks stupid. Doesn't get it. Kenny gets it, but won't let himself show it.

And old Freddy, still not looking up, smiles. A small, but true, smile.

TWENTY-SEVEN

I go home. My new one. No lights on, no coffee on, no TV on. No one sleeping on the couch. No beer in the fridge.

I get a glass of tap water, sit in the living room, in the dark, and think.

I hear John cry, and go get him.

Mary pokes her sleepy-eyed, messy-haired head out her door. She looks good in that way some women do when they think they look their worst.

"I got him," I say.

She comes out anyway.

"When did you get home?"

"Just now. You sleep, hon. I'll take care of him."

"Let me get a drink of water."

She follows me to the kitchen. I turn the light on. She looks at my face.

"What happened?" she asks.

"What?"

"That bruise." With my free hand I touch my face. Feel the

swelling. She looks at me just the right way. No fooling her. "Boulder," I say. "But don't worry, it's settled."

"You're okay?"

"Yeah."

She helps me get John's bottle. Sits with me while I feed him. Waits while I put him back to bed.

When I come back out, she's on the living room couch.

"Can we talk a second?" she asks.

I sit with her.

"You have to get out, Joey."

"I am out."

"No, I mean all the way out."

"Of poker? And do what?"

"Whatever you want! You are so smart. I would kill to have your brains. Don't you know how people talk about you? I mean, there's lawyers and doctors just plain in awe of you."

"I play good cards."

"You're the best around here, sure. But so what?"

"What do you mean, 'so what?' You're the one giving the lecture. What's your point?"

"That you are wasting your life. That you could be something better. That you could give to people, instead of just taking."

"Hey — I don't have to kiss anyone's ass. I've got money. And I don't have to pretend to be something I'm not."

I look at her harshly. She big-eyes me back. I give in. Smile.

"How come you like me so much?" I ask, very softly.

"Because from the moment we met, you knew I liked you, but never took advantage of it."

"Thought about it," I say, smiling.

She smiles, too.

We sit there a long while after that, there in the dark, talking. She tells me she wants to go to the community college. Says maybe I should take a class, too. One class. Probably wouldn't kill me, she says. *Probably* wouldn't.

She tells me she's done a lot of thinking about this "getting ahead" stuff. Says she doesn't want things just to have things. She wants a house in a safe neighborhood, a job she doesn't have to hate going to or worry about losing. And, sure, a man to be nice to her, to help her, one that she can be nice to and help. It's not so much, but it's everything, she says. And it seems so impossible, but what can she do? *Not* try for it? No.

Leaving me to wonder if she hasn't been playing me perfectly the whole time after all.

In the morning, I sleep a little late while Mary takes care of the babies. Then she goes to work and I take care of them. It's hard. Exhausting. But I do it. And well, I think.

Mary gets in just before midnight, which frees me to go out. The kids are sleeping, so it's no hardship for her. She just goes to sleep herself.

I'd been on the phone with my mom an hour or so earlier when she'd had to hang up because Kenny and Boulder had pulled into her driveway. Now she isn't answering the phone, so I want to go over and make sure everything is all right. They've probably just all gone out drinking somewhere, like they've done a thousand times. But I want to check. They were trying to act so tough last night. Like maybe it's only ever been Freddy keeping them in line?

It's a two-minute drive. Real close by.

Kenny Jones's Lincoln is in the driveway, behind my old van.

I park on the street and walk up the driveway to the side door. And stop. Get stopped. Get frozen. By what I see in the kitchen.

Calvin is sitting back against the refrigerator. My mom is by his side, holding his head to her chest. She's crying; he's staring blankly ahead.

Boulder is on his stomach, his face turned toward me. Blood seeping from his skull into a growing pool on the floor. Kenny Jones is on his back, his eyes rolled up. Fish-eyed forever, now. Grey-man for real.

I go in, stepping over the bodies, and lean down to my mom. I take her in my arms, help her up, and lead her into the living room.

Her nose is bleeding, her left eye darkening. She's wearing a sweater and jeans. The sweater is torn. One of her breasts is exposed.

I sit her on the couch and pull a blanket over her. She lets me.

I go back in the kitchen. Kneel beside Calvin.

He turns. Looks at me with the saddest eyes.

"It's okay, brother," I whisper.

"They called her *whore!*" he says. Tears roll down his face.

"It's all right, man."

"They said, 'Suck my dick, bitch.' I heard them. They didn't know I was here, but I heard them. And then they hit her. They hit her, Joey!"

I put my arms around him. Help him up, much as I can, big as he is. Lead him, too, into the living room. To a chair.

I call 9-1-1. I think about not calling. Think about just taking the bodies somewhere. But I also pretty quickly think better of it. The harder thing to do is the call.

The police and the ambulance come. Neither Calvin nor my mom are in much shape to talk. My mom keeps saying only that Boulder and Kenny had been trying to kill her.

Calvin is taken out in handcuffs. I watch him hold his arms out, get braced, get taken to a patrol car. Get his head pushed down as he gets in the backseat. Watch him sit there as the scene is photographed. As the bodies are taken off in the ambulances. As my mom is photographed and then patched up by the paramedics.

The police take my mom to the station. Take Calvin to jail. Take the bodies to the morgue.

I go in my mom's room. Pack a bag for her. Figure she'll want to stay somewhere else for a while.

I leave, through the front door because the side door is taped shut. A cop has been following me around. I give him a set of house keys, and then watch as he tapes the front door shut behind us.

The neighbors are out. Cold and wet as it is, they're out. Looking.

I was going to follow my mom to the station. But first I drive four blocks down to the house we'd lived in the longest around here.

I park out front. Reach in my jacket pocket. Pull out my Lifesavers. Remember what it was like to have them as a kid. What a treat candy was then. What a simple joy.

Remember running around these streets as a teenager. Remember my high school girlfriend. Necking with her over by the basketball court.

I sit outside that house twenty minutes or so. I'm not crying. I'm too confused for that. Not confused about what has happened. That isn't difficult to figure. Confused about how things work. I mean, how life works. I can't see a pattern to it. Just luck. Happenstance. A huge conspiracy of people and places and time. It is a conspiracy of randomness after all. Who's where when.

I go on to the station. Give my statement again. Wait an hour. When my mom is finished she comes out and we leave.

"You okay?" I ask her in the car.

She nods. "I'm just tired," she says.

"I packed a bag for you, Mom. Why don't you stay in my room tonight."

"Where are you staying now?"

"I moved in with a friend. Nice girl. Has a baby, too. Helps me with John."

"You have your son?"

"Yeah. I guess I haven't even had a chance to tell you. Wow. How could I not have told you? Laura doesn't trust her parents with him, so I've got him. For a while."

She leans back in the car seat. "You're a good boy, Joey. I've always been proud of you."

At the apartment, I help her out of the car, get her bag, and bring her in. Three A.M. though it is, Mary's up. Changing my son's diapers.

"Mary," I say, "this is my mom."

They nod.

Mary instantly knows something is wrong, but doesn't press.

"She's going to stay here tonight, okay?" I ask.

"Of course."

249

"You sleep in my room, Mom," I say, opening that door.

"Okay," she says. I've never seen her so easy. So lost.

"Nice to meet you, Mary," she says, absentmindedly.

"Nice to meet you, too," Mary says tenderly.

My mom shuts the door behind her. I pick up John.

"He woke you, huh?"

"Yes," Mary says. "Just now. What's going on?"

I blow onto John's stomach. Tickle him. He smiles.

Mary waits. Never rushes me.

"You know Kenny and Boulder?" I ask.

"I know Kenny."

"They were the ones who got me fired. And my mom worked there. When they fired me, she quit. But someone set her up. She was accused of stealing seventeen thousand from the backroom before she left. So Boulder and Kenny Jones went to get it from her."

"And they hit her?"

"They're dead, Mary."

"What?"

"There's a guy, Calvin, who lives with my mom. He was in his room. They didn't know about him. Or didn't think about him. Or didn't worry about him. I don't know."

Mary's stunned. I go on. Getting it out.

"They went over to her house, and she let them in, because she's known them all her life. They asked her for the money. She said she didn't take it. They started calling her names. Slapping her. Hitting her. Apparently started to rape her, because they ripped her sweater, and Boulder's pants were unbuckled and his zipper was down."

"And then Calvin came out?"

I nod. "You have to understand, Mary — my mom was the first person in Calvin's whole life to care for him! He spent his childhood in one foster home after another. One juvenile hall after another. And then at twenty was sent to prison. Where he'd be now if my mom hadn't helped him with his parole. So to him, she was the world. She got him his job with Grizzly. Helped him with his reading. Went shopping with him. Took him to restaurants and the movies. All the stuff that's so normal to us, was so special to him. Can you imagine how he would react to someone threatening her? With his jailyard code?"

Mary nods. I think she does understand.

"Fucking Boulder," I say. "Thought he was so big and bad. He didn't know what bad was. Compared to a hard-timed con, he was a softie. Compared to a man who's spent the last thirteen years of his life lifting weights, he was a weakling." I shift the baby in my arms. Go on.

"Calvin took Boulder's head and cracked it back on the edge of the kitchen counter. Cracked it back so hard Boulder's skull split open. And then Calvin hit Kenny. Just one time. One time, on the jaw. But too hard. Kenny Jones was getting old. One punch in the jaw. Gone."

"My God," Mary says softly.

John is falling asleep on my chest. I stand and quietly tread into the babies' room. Manage to put him to bed without waking Melissa.

"What happens now?" Mary asks when I return.

"Probably Calvin goes back to prison."

"Why? If he was defending your mother?"

"Unreasonable force. They'll say he didn't need to kill them to stop them. Say he didn't give any notice. That Boulder and Kenny had no weapons. Something like that. And he's an ex-con still on parole. They'll say he's unable to keep from extreme behavior. Unable to refrain from violent overreaction to perceived threats."

"Whose words are those?"

"The detective who took my statement. I got done fast, because I didn't have much to say. So we talked a while. He was cool." (No gun in Boulder's pockets? I'd asked him. No, he'd said. No gun.)

We sit in silence.

I've got my head in my hands. Eyes shut. Closing out the world. Rubbing my temples. Wide awake and tired.

My mom comes out. Wearing one of my T-shirts as a night-gown. She's still got the legs to get away with that.

"I can't sleep," she says, and sits across from us.

"Joey told me what happened," Mary says. "It must have been so horrible."

My mom nods. Breathes deep. Lets the breath out.

The three of us sit there. Nothing to say. Sit there in the dimly lit, poorly furnished living room of a rented condo, in the dead quiet of the middle of the night.

A baby cries. Mine again.

I get up. Get him. Come back to find Mary's already working on his bottle.

"Give me my grandson," my mom says.

I hand him over. She cradles him. Rocks him.

Mary brings the bottle out. My mom feeds him.

"You been playing his birthday number?" she asks me.

"Mom, you know how I feel about the lottery. My mom believes in the numbers," I say to Mary. "Lives for them."

"Don't get smart with me, Joey. You know why I believe in them."

"You believed in them before that, Mom."

"You tell her why," my mom says.

"What?" Mary asks.

I shake my head. "Supposedly —"

"Not supposedly," my mom interrupts. "This is a true story."

"Okay, okay. It's a true story. Anyway, when I was a boy — this was during a real hard time for us, I know, because me and Mom and my brother Jack were all sleeping in the same room," my mom looks down at John when I say that, "I was having some kind of nightmare. I dreamt that a man had come in the room and was hiding under the bed. And my mom says to me, 'Ask him the number.' Which I, still sleeping, still dreaming, did. And apparently the man in my dream tells me three numbers. The next day she goes to the store to put five dollars on that number I said the man told me."

"That was my dead-last five dollars, too," my mom says. "And would you believe that number came home? Three-digit number came straight up that very night!"

"My mom. Bets her last five dollars on a little boy's mumbles."

252

"It won! Saved us, too. That was during the hardest time in my life. Won us twenty-five hundred cash, which got us out of that room and into a house. That's when I knew you were a lucky boy, Joey."

She kisses little John. "Just like this one's going to be lucky, too," she whispers.

I can see the tears falling down her face. John's looking up at her with his big baby eyes, and she can't help it, I guess.

I take the baby from her. "Come on, Mom," I say gently. "Get some sleep."

She doesn't argue. Gets up, goes in my room.

I hold John's bottle for him until he won't take anymore, and then put him in his crib. I go back to the living room.

"What a night," Mary says.

I nod.

"Go on to sleep, Mary. I'll be up all night. Till tomorrow morning, probably. Sleep as late as you want. Because then I'm going to sleep. For a long time."

TWENTY-EIGHT

I do sleep a long time. I don't wake until four A.M. the following day.

John's crying gets me up. I take him into the darkened living room. Make him a bottle. Feed him. Change him. Put him to sleep.

I've got a few hours before Melissa gets up. Mary doesn't have cable TV, so there's nothing to watch. I make a pot of coffee. Crave a cigarette real bad, but don't go out for some.

The apartment is on the third floor and has a balcony. I pull a sweatshirt over the T-shirt I'm wearing, and take my coffee outside. Sit in the cool, fresh dark. Wait for the sun to rise.

At five-thirty, the phone rings. I jump to answer it because I don't want it to wake the babies.

"Hello?" I say.

Silence.

"Hello?" I say again.

"I tell you I fuck you, asshole. Now you know!"

Click.

I recognize her voice. Cambo Sam.

Melissa wakes a little later. I feed her. Change her.

Play with her. Watch *Sesame Street* and *Barney* with her.

I hear John cry a slight sound. He's never yet let out with a full-fledged crying job. Just makes enough noise to get attention, and then goes quiet. Natural cool.

I hear doors open. Then my mom comes out, holding John.

"Where's Mary?" I ask.

"Right behind me. I slept in her room last night. You got good coffee on?"

"Yeah. And there's a bottle cooling on the counter. Check it's not too hot."

"You need to tell me that?"

She hands John to me. I kiss him good morning. Mom brings me the bottle and I feed him.

Mary comes out.

"Good morning, Dad," she says.

"Want coffee, Mary?" my mom calls out from the kitchen.

"Yes. Joey, can you watch the kids for a while?"

"Sure."

"Me and your mother are going over to her house to clean up."

"That ought to be fun."

"The police said it was okay. Said we shouldn't wait, because it'll start to smell."

"My mom okay about going?"

Mary nods.

"Joey?" my mom says when she comes out of the kitchen with Mary's coffee. "Would you call Grizzly for me? Tell him what happened?"

"You didn't tell him yesterday?"

"I haven't told anyone yet."

"Were he and Calvin going to work today?"

"I think so."

I give her John, and pick up the phone. Call Grizzly. Tell him all about it. He doesn't understand. I have to tell him again. He goes silent.

"Mom," I say, "You talk to him."

255

She trades me the baby for the phone, and talks to Grizzly for a few minutes. He says he's going to meet them over at her house.

They leave. I watch the kids, who need nonstop attention. Who'd have guessed?

Grizzly comes back with Mary and my mom.

"All cleaned up?" I ask.

They nod.

Grizzly takes John from my arms. He and Mom sit on the couch and play with him.

"Mary, you're working tomorrow?" I ask.

"No. Next day. Saturday."

"Today's only Thursday? Okay. Listen — I'll watch the kids tomorrow, and the next day when you're back at work again. But I need to go out today."

It's fine by her.

I go first to my mom's house. Use the key under the mat to get in.

The kitchen is clean. The rest of the house, too. Must have been Mary's doing. My mom's never exactly been a neat freak.

I check in the heating ducts for my stash — still there. Ten thousand. That's what I'd been worried about. I put it in my jacket pocket.

I've got another ten thousand in my car. Twenty-five hundred in the bank. Five hundred in my pocket. I'm okay.

I go to Charlie's to see Essay. He's sleeping. I wake him. Ask him for cheese. He's got three hundred he can spare. I tell him the bank's closing. Meaning I'm not going to be loaning money anymore. He calls K.C. K.C. agrees to loan him what he needs to smooth me out.

Essay and I meet K.C. at a Ranch House diner in Oxon Hill. I wait until we're there together to tell them about Boulder and Kenny Jones. They're shocked. It is kind of unbelievable.

"There's going to be about a hundred people partying when they hear this," Essay says. "Everyone who owes them is off the hook."

"I'm going to call Nug," K.C. says. "You tell him yet?" he asks me.

I shake my head no.

K.C. comes back after phoning. "He's coming over. I called Fat Boy, too. He's supposed to drive you to work, isn't he, Essay?"

Essay nods. "I'm not going in today, though. There's going to be a lot of questions asked. The cops might be there. No way I'm going in today."

"What the cops going to want up at the casino?" I ask. "There's not that much of a connection."

We eat, drink coffee, while we wait for Nug and Fat. I manage not to smoke. It's hard, but I manage.

Nug gets there first. I tell him what happened at my mom's. Tell him also about Freddy's threat to fire him.

Twenty minutes later Fat pulls up in his pickup truck. I get the story out to him real quick, too.

No one knows how to react. Except for Essay, none of them knew Calvin, and so don't feel for him.

I tell everyone I want to be smoothed out. Nug has a roll on him, and pays me off what he owes me, and loans to Fat so he can do the same. K.C. pays me what Essay owes. Now no one I think would ever pay me back anyway owes me.

"Why you need money, sucker?" Nug asks.

"You taking off?" K.C. asks.

They all look at me. They've known me to several times have hit the road, usually for California, when I've gotten tired of this area. They know that such a taking off is usually preceded by a collecting of debts.

"And leave all this?" I say. We're in a booth by the window. I look out at the grey day, the wet asphalt, the half-empty shopping center across the parking lot.

"You deal for me if you want," Nug says. "Make good money. Freddy no got pull with Filipinos. He no can fire me."

"But Laura's mom ain't going to let you hire Joey," Fat Boy says.

257

Nug nods. Frowns. Admits it might be a problem.

"Open your own game," Essay says. "With the following you've got, you have to make money."

"No," I say. "No nothing for a while. I'm just staying home with the baby."

"Sure," they all say, and laugh.

We talk more. Try to make sense of it. I think we all feel like the killings are a big deal, but don't really know in what way. Death larger than life.

At eleven-thirty we leave, in different cars, for Churchville. Fat Boy and Essay are going to work. Nug and K.C. are going to play. I'm going to talk to Kevin and Larry Red.

At the casino, I get put off. Kevin is uncomfortable; Larry busy. Tell me they have to get things set up. So I sit in a card game and wait.

Sam's there. Sees me. Smiles real big. And it's not a pretty smile.

Nobody had heard about Kenny Jones and Boulder's deaths yet. But Fat and Essay talk about it, and the word spreads like blood on a floor. Kevin comes up to me, taps my shoulder, asks me back into his office.

"What's up, Kev?" I ask once we're back there. Borrowing Freddy's monotone.

"I'm sorry about all this," he says.

"About what, exactly?"

"It wasn't my idea to move Fat into the poker boss spot."

"I know." I let a little understanding creep in my voice. Letting him off the hook a bit.

"Did that guy really kill Boulder and Kenny Jones?"

"'That guy'? His name is Calvin. And yes, he killed them. Because they were hitting my mom. They were going to rape her. So, yeah, he killed them."

Kevin is nervous. Feels awkward.

"Listen, Joey — I never thought your mother took that money."

"That's what I'm here to find out."

"Did you talk to her about it?"

258

"Yeah. And she said no. Said she never had the opportunity."

He nods his head. Takes his glasses off. Sits down.

He's sweating.

"Who had access to it?" I ask.

"Anyone in the cage. It was back there, in a strongbox. Unlocked, maybe, because we were always going in it. The cashiers and all. And there were always people around it."

"What people? Who?"

"That day?" He shakes his head. "Everyone," he says sadly. "Larry. Me. Essay. The three cashiers. And Boulder was back there a while."

"Sam with him?" I ask.

He thinks about it. Nods.

"Remember her saying she was going to fuck me?" I say.

"Everyone in the casino heard her say that."

"She and Boulder were tight. She worked on him to work on Kenny Jones to get me gone. I'll bet she ripped off your money."

"I was thinking Larry was a more likely suspect."

"It doesn't really matter, Kevin. Not to me. Except for one thing."

"What?"

"I want you to tell everyone that it could *not* have been my mom. I want you to tell everyone that she never had access to it. I want her name cleared."

He nods his head. Looks down at some papers on his desk.

"You're not getting much to the charity, are you?" I ask.

"Nothing. And I really wanted to. I wanted the money for myself, too. But I did want to have a real charity."

"Is Freddy getting enough?"

"Maybe there's a bright side to these deaths. There isn't anything written down. Kenny's gone — now I just have to deal with Freddy."

"You know who Freddy has to deal with?"

"Don't tell me he's not him?"

"Nope. He's honest-to-God mob affiliated."

He bangs his hand on the table, says, Jesus Christ. Like the news is a final straw.

"News to you?"

"I never knew what those motherfuckers were about. Never understood it all. Just knew I had to come up with money for Boulder every week."

I nod.

"Kevin," I say after a moment.

"Huh?" he says, looking distracted.

"Do me that thing for my mom's rep, will you?"

"I will, Joey."

We shake hands.

I go back to the card room.

Sam and K.C. are there. She's sitting on his lap while he plays. K.C. can't look me in the eye. What does he know?

Sam doesn't talk to me. But she says loudly enough for me and everyone else to hear, "That killer — he know she do it. He know she take money. He in on it. Why else they kill Boulder and Kenny? They get caught. She tell him to kill them."

I don't get a chance to say anything. K.C. beats me to it.

"Shut up!" he screams, standing up and dropping her off his lap and onto the floor as he does. "Shut up!"

He reeks of humiliation. One of the proudest guys I know, reeks of humiliation. He runs out of the building.

Sam gets up. Shrugs. Takes K.C.'s chips. Cashes them out. Leaves.

The games stop. But only for a moment.

Nug and Fat and I look at each other.

"Remember when she first started going out with him?" Fat says.

I nod.

"And I said maybe we should have her killed?"

I nod again.

"I think I was right."

I nod once more. Maybe he had been.

260

Nug hits my shoulder and points to the entrance. Philly is coming in. Coming right over to us.

"Fat Boy," Philly says, "Nug nuts, and Pinochle Joe. All my Maryland buddies are here."

Fat says hello to him. Nug and I are silent.

"Joey," Philly says, "Freddy is in the parking lot. He's afraid to come in, but he wants you to go see him. Fat — set me up a meeting in a few hours with these African-Americans who think they own this place. In the meantime, get me a poker game."

I go out and see Freddy sitting on a car hood.

"What's up, old man?" I ask.

He smiles. "How you doing, Joe?"

"Okay."

"I wanted to explain some things to you."

"Go ahead."

"I'm the one who recommended you lose the poker boss spot."

I'm silent.

He hesitates. Eyes me. "Joe, is your word still good?"

"What are you talking about?"

"You've been through some shit, in a lot of different ways. Your word still good?"

"Yeah," I say, a little peeved by the suggestion that it ever wouldn't be. But then I think about it. Understand what he means. And say a second time, calmly now, "Sure."

"I ask because I have to hear your promise that what I tell you next, you tell no one else."

"What?"

"Joey, you're going to want to tell this to some people, because it involves your friends. But you can't. If you can't keep a secret that would help them, walk away now."

I hesitate. Think a second. Dive in. "What is it?" I ask.

"The casino's going to be raided some time in the next few months."

"Goddammit! Why?"

261

"Remember that officer who killed himself?"

"Mikey the Cop?"

"That required an Internal Affairs inquiry. Got them on a mission to look into gambling around here. Bobby Lotto gave them a short list of names to check into, including yours. Yours, and Kenny Jones's. And then Mikey's wife told them about Sam's and Boulder's constant threats. Including, apparently, pushing Mikey around, slapping him around, right in front of the wife just hours before Mikey killed himself. I heard about all this, and knew where it would lead. So when Boulder and Kenny started their usual bitching about how much you were making, I used that as an excuse to get you out. I also was getting your mom out. She didn't quit that day because you had been fired. We just used that as an excuse so no one would get suspicious."

I shake my head, thinking about it.

Freddy continues. "And now, to top it off, your convict friend and your mother, not to rat or anything, just to explain what happened the other night, have talked to the police about the casino. So things have taken on a more serious tone. Not to mention that with Philly down here to run things, everything's also more serious from our side, too."

"How's it add up?"

"The place goes down, real soon."

"Why can't we tell the guys?"

"Philly owns the place now. I gave it to him to clear my debt. But the casino's value comes from being open. If people start deserting, and the place gets raided, he'll know I had advance word. He knows there's some risk, but he doesn't know he won't last the summer. He can't ever know that I knew when I sold it to him."

I stand there a moment. Organizing what he's told me.

"Goddamn, Freddy," I say, because when I look at him I realize it, "you're half a century older than me."

He laughs.

A moment passes.

"Why did you tell me this now?" I ask.

"Your mother knows it all. I had to tell her, and then we worked out what we thought was the best way to handle it. She agreed you had to get out, but didn't think you could leave peaceably without telling your buddies, so we came up with the bit about firing you and having her quit in anger."

"Why'd you have to tell her?"

"She's the closest thing I have to family."

I nod. Maybe I've always sensed a feeling like that in him, for her. And by extension, to me, some.

"Larry Red I don't care about," I say. "But Fat, Essay, and Kevin — it's hard for me not to warn them."

"You can't, Joe. You gave your word."

I nod. I had given it.

"But if it makes you feel better," he says, "neither Essay or Fat will get in any real trouble. Six months suspended is typical. Kevin couldn't escape trouble now even if he did quit, because he's the charity's official head. But even he won't go to jail. The county's got too big a drug and violent crime problem. They don't have the prison space. And of course, as you know, no customers get in trouble. They aren't breaking the law."

"Can I get in trouble for having worked here in the past?"

"No. Only people physically present at the time of the raid get hurt. Evidentiary problems arise for anyone else. Prosecutorial time investment problems."

I nod. Understand. Accept. Everything.

"Personally, Joe, I'd just as soon not tell you all this. You don't really need to know. But your mother asked me to fill you in. So I have."

"All right, Freddy. I'll keep my promise. Might have trouble looking the guys in the eye for a while, but I'll be okay."

We shake hands. He gets back in his car and drives off.

The day has turned pretty. Bright sun, blue sky, fresh air. And I feel free. Content, even.

Then I remember that I have a son at home, and I might be all

263

he's got. Which means I'm not at all free. How all those people trying to raise kids do it, I don't know. Especially the ones having to do
it alone. Like Mary. Like me, too, I guess. I don't know how they do
it, but I do know it's got to be done. And I'll be all right. Maybe I'm
the last person in the world anyone might think would make a good
father, but I know better. I know I won't run. I know I love my boy.

I've stupidly left my jacket inside and go back for it. I see and
hear Philly noising up the place.

"This all you play down here?" he yells so that everyone can hear
him. "Fifteen-thirty is as big as you guys play? That's not even worth
my time."

What a kid he is, I think. He's supposed to have business here,
and all he does is strut around like a big shot.

He sees me. "Well, it's Pinochle Joe," he says, deliberately mis-
stating my name again. "Hey, Joey, these guys all tell me you're the
best. But we played before, didn't we? Tell them how it went up in
A.C. Tell them how Maryland's best did up there."

I ignore him. Walk over to my jacket, pick it up, and sling it
over my shoulder.

"Come on, anybody," he says loudly, laughing.

"Your name's Philly, right?" someone says to him. "I heard
of you."

"Yeah, me too," someone else says. "Heard you're good as shit."

"Last thing we need here," a third person says, "another professional."

"Philly," Fat Boy bellows, "no one here wants to play you. Your
rep's too big."

I can't tell if Fat means what he says, or is just kissing the man's
ass. But it doesn't matter. Because when I look around the card room
and I see people looking at Philly the way they used to look at me,
something inside me rises like a demon and speaks before I even know
what I'm doing. "Philly," that part of me says, "I'll play you."

He stares at me. I stare back. I smile. I almost cry, because the
part of me that issued that challenge is an old friend I haven't seen
for a while, and I miss his arrogant little ass.

"Ten-thousand-dollar buy-in no-limit Texas Hold 'em," I say, picking the figure because that's how much I've got in my pocket.

Philly's still staring at me. Fat Boy is staring. Nug is staring. Kevin and Larry Red and Essay and fifty other people are staring.

And I smile. Sit down. Take out the ten thousand and set it on the table.

I laugh. Everyone must think I'm crazy, but I laugh. I don't know why I feel this good. I don't know how the sight and sound of a pompous braggart like Philly could give rise to this feeling in me. Maybe by reminding me what I'm not. Maybe by reminding me of how lucky I am. Maybe just by being an insult to the game I love. But however he did it, he did it.

He sits across from me. Pulls money from his pockets. Fat gets us a dealer and cards, and we get started. A crowd gathers. People make phone calls to friends, spreading the word.

The best poker I've ever played has always entailed peace. A relaxed comfort. Eyes open, ears open, radar up. Absorbing my opponent's every message. Taking them as they come. Not mixing what those messages are with what I want them to be. It's like an aerial view. A view from above the myriad luck-dependent reactions of those many people who never gain such a peace.

And when you gain that view, that peace — when you'd rather have the truth, no matter how disappointing, over a false hope, no matter how desirable — then you're a player. The hand you're on slips into a stream of thousands of other hands, no one of which, because of your lofty view, seems unduly important. And because no particular hand seems unduly important, no false, fearful emotions rise within you.

When you gain the peace of lofty perspective, you're a player, and when you're a player, you're free. You can't be fired or laid off. You have no promotions to hustle for, no resumés to submit, no job interviews to undergo, no office politics to play. No lies to tell, no rules to bend, no indignities to suffer. The life, I suppose, isn't for everyone. Maybe not even for me anymore. But the spirit? I'd lost it,

I think. Lost it in the panic of my son's birth and that ambush of rushing emotions. Lost it in the easy money of a fraudulent charity. Lost it in the arms of a woman I was with for the wrong reasons.

But now have found. Because I remember something. Something unimportant in the universe at large, I know, but huge to myself, because for a long time it was all I had. I remember, now, small though it may be, of what world I am king.

Philly, to his credit, plays his best game. Asshole though he may be, he isn't stupid, and he isn't a coward. But he lacks patience. He goes after every pot, and though I let him take many very small ones, when I do step out he's caught dancing.

We both avoid showdowns. This is too much money to lose on one hand. But three times he comes out on the wrong end of one-to two-thousand-dollar pots. All three were close, but each time I had the ever so slightly better hand, and bet him. It's scary to be in his shoes — calling a man unafraid to press even a slender margin.

Philly's looking at the crowd. Running his fingers through his hair. Straightening his sweatsuit. Affecting cool.

The end comes suddenly. And on an innocuous hand. When the last card hits, I check, where before I'd been betting. He thinks, and, surprisingly, shoves in all his money.

His fingers tap, and his eyes focus on the pot. I sit back. Watch him. He stares at me.

I look away. Think.

The community cards consist of four diamonds and an unimportant fifth card. With four diamonds on the table, anyone with one diamond among their two hole cards has a flush.

I don't have a diamond. A jack is the highest card on the board, and I have an ace and a jack in my hand. If it weren't for the possible flush, I'd have a good hand for heads-up play. But with an easy-way flush out there, calling now seems crazy.

I turn over my cards. Watching Philly's face as I do.

Someone says, "Bad beat, Joey."

"You fold?" asks the dealer.

I ignore him. Keep looking at Philly. As is his way, he stares right back at me.

There are better hands to move in on. If he's got a single diamond, even a deuce of diamonds, he wins. I don't need to worry about his having two pair or something, which would also beat me, because if he did he couldn't bet into that board, because he'd have to worry that I had the diamond. In fact, he probably doesn't have a low diamond, either, because if he did, he'd be happy to just take the pot, and wouldn't be betting into what might easily be a higher diamond in my hand. No, either he has a very good diamond in his hand, or nothing.

I don't fear a bluff. I fear he's got a diamond. I fear how stupid I'm going to look if I call here with only one pair. Calling four thousand dollars with only one pair. With the whole county looking on, with my money now belonging to my son, with no job backing me up, with the Vegas drop still on my mind, I fear Philly has backdoored a flush.

Poker is life. Human interaction. The interaction of desires. All of life, except love, can be found in the game. And not all of life can or should be about love. Poker is what life can be apart from love: rewarding of honesty and courage; punishing of childishness and egotism; creating of an understanding of the nature of randomness; developing of qualities that lead to love, of self and others, of friend and foe.

I smile. "Good try, Philly," I say.

And when I say that, his face pales, his lips turn down in the slightest bit in worry, his eyes flicker the slightest bit in fear — and I shove in my money.

The room is silent. People shake their heads, confused, disbelieving. Nobody moves. Until Philly does.

He nods. Says very quietly, but steadily, "That's good, Joey."

"Thank you," I say.

The crowd breaks out into a chorus of "Wow!" and "Did you see that?" and "What a call!" and "What a bluff!"

I let myself breathe. I think I've forgotten to do that for a few minutes. I let myself smile, too.

Philly and I look at each other. Stand. People are sticking their hands out for a shake. But I wait. And then Philly nods, once, and puts his hand out. We shake. He's all right. Give him credit.

He lets out a deep sigh and says, "I didn't think you had that much sand."

"I know," I say.

Nug and I make eye contact.

I pick up the money and turn to leave. I hear a voice call out. Loudly. Getting everyone's attention.

"Joey!"

It's Kevin.

"Yeah?" I call back.

He's halfway across the room, but not coming closer. Yells back, loud enough for the whole place to hear, "Don't forget to tell your mom to call me, man. Everything's been cleared up about that misplaced stuff, and she can come back to work any time she's ready."

I nod. It's okay.

EPILOGUE

As a boy I played cards for lunch money, and by high school I was
playing at a home game my mom was running in our basement, where
I used her money. Having been lucky there, I hit the southern
Maryland home game circuit, until I was twenty-one and, old enough
to play in the legal joints, made that first road trip to Vegas and became a true pro.

When I came back from that trip, I met the guys. Brother
gamblers. Nug, K.C., and Essay; and Fat Boy, who had always been
around.

We were a family. We even said that sometimes. Said things like
"We got to take care of him, he's family." But fraternity, too. Because
we partied. We traveled. We played. We kept all hours. We chased
girls, went through falling in and out of love.

And we learned about gambling. When other people were off
in college or starting careers, we were in our own college, starting our
own careers. In our own way.

I loved the times we had together. The great camaraderie. Late
night, long night, all night, every night camaraderie. What a life.

But still, even with all that, I had always liked being alone. I liked driving across America by myself in my van. Playing poker everywhere it was legal, as much for the excuse to see a place as anything else. Meeting people, and moving on. Achieving that fresh coffee, open road, endless miles, no-place-you-got-to-be peace. Never missing my buddies, or my mom, or whatever girlfriend I might have left behind. Missing them, sure. But not *missing* them.

Not like I missed my boy. One year after beating Philly for that ten thousand dollars, I made another road trip. Hadn't played much in the intervening year, and when Nug and K.C. had talked about driving out to Vegas for the World Series of Poker, I'd felt an old itch. But it was a false one. This time, the endless miles became pointless miles. Torturous, every one of them. Because a hollow feeling inside me just grew and grew with every passing exit sign, with every emptying coffee cup. I had never known it was possible to miss someone like I missed my son.

I sometimes said to people that from the day my boy was born, except for that redeeming game against Philly, I couldn't win at cards. That my luck turned sour. That my luck was bad when it was bad, and worse when it wasn't. And there's some truth to that, too. I did run bad. In the long run there's no luck in poker, but the short run is longer than most people know.

The greater truth is that I could no longer play with my old fearlessness. Because I wasn't fearless. I was fearful. Not always as much as when I'd first held him, newborn and small in my arms. But not much less scared than that, either.

Good poker is patience; great poker is courage. And after John was born, I lacked them both. No — earlier, even, than his birth. From the moment I heard about Mikey the Cop, I lost something.

But it was also my son's birth that got me out of non-poker gambling. And hadn't I been cursing my luck at having had him forced upon me? Sometimes good luck is bad luck, and bad luck good. I knew a girl who met what she thought was a great guy, so great she couldn't believe her luck in landing him, because he had looks and money and glamour. He turned out to be a wife-beating adulterer whose business went under. I know a guy who'd been pining away for months about this new job he wanted, finally got it, gave up his current job to take it, and half a year later was laid off. I know a woman who backed out of plans to open a clothing store with her sister because she was scared to give up her job shuffling papers for the government. Her sister opened up anyway, expanded to a chain, and made millions. Sometimes good luck is bad, and bad luck good. That sister who went ahead and opened that clothing store only did so after suffering the "misfortune" of being fired from her job and being unable to get a new one. And a guy who I think is probably happier in his marriage than anyone I've ever met, spent his high school prom drunk and miserable because the girl he'd been planning to date changed her mind on him. He'd had to settle for this somewhat plain girl I fixed him up with at the last minute, the girl with whom he ended up so happily married. Sometimes good luck is bad, and bad luck good. You just don't always know. There's no such thing as not gambling.

Late May, and K.C. and Nug and I are hauling out of Las Vegas in K.C.'s bright yellow Trans Am. We've got the windows down and the radio up and we're flying. Down to Kingman, Arizona, and then Route 40 up the mountains to Flagstaff. Find a bar, sack out in a dive motel, and hit the highway again in the morning. Miles and miles of it. Route 40 goes a long way. All the way. Winslow, Gallup, Albuquerque. Another bar, another drink, another sack out in another dive motel. Another morning of coffee for breakfast, and then more miles. Oklahoma comes and goes, and then we get off 40 around Amarillo and meander south through Nothingvilles to Dallas and overnight it to New Orleans.

"What a town, brothers," I yell as we walk and bar-hop and eat well for two days and nights. "What a town."

Then we go across the bayous one sunny morning in late May to find the casino in the Gulf Coast town of Biloxi.

I haven't told the guys what I'm looking for. Who I'm looking for. I just told them I was curious to see what the action down here was like. They were curious, too, so it was an easy sell.

But I've got a strong, anxious premonition about this place. Biloxi Billy Long Hair — where else should I expect to find him?

We take a motel at the beach. Go swimming. Charter a boat and go fishing. Great days. Beautiful weather. Beautiful area.

We play cards. At least I do. Nug and K.C. don't want to sit in the games here because they're small stakes. They shoot dice instead. I can't join them, of course, because of my vow. Don't want to wake up thinking there's a little bird in my room again. Besides, I'm here to play poker.

So I do. At Bay St. Louis and Gulfport and the Biloxi riverboats. Play and play. Changing card rooms, changing tables in the card rooms. I'm not sure I'll recognize my father. I'm not sure I'll talk to him if I do recognize him, or let him know who I am if we talk. But I keep playing and looking.

We're there two days and, waking up on the third, K.C. and Nug want to head home. I stall. Tell them I've been winning and just want to play out my heater. They say pick up the motel tab, then. I say that goes without saying.

This day I sit in the biggest game in town. Twenty-forty Hold 'em on a riverboat in Gulfport. I play two hours. And then see a man, older but not old, white-haired but not long-haired, handsome for his age and sharp-eyed for any, take a seat, buy his chips, look around the table — and set his sight on me. On me staring back at him.

"You want a hand, Billy?" the dealer asks the man.

So now I smile. Smirk like I do, actually.

And so he smirks like I do.

Or maybe it's me smirking like he does.

The game goes on. I hardly play a hand. Not concentrating. Not wanting to get involved in anything.

I don't know if he knows me or not. I don't know if he ever thinks about the fact that he has a son somewhere. I don't know if the possibility that I or anyone else might be his boy could ever enter his mind without someone screaming it in his ear.

He plays well. Makes moves. Shows a few bluffs and rattles some of the other players. Plays a little cute, maybe. Flashy. But it works well enough with this crowd. He talks a lot, too. Everyone knows him. Has known him for a while, I gather. He's the main noise.

Nug and K.C. come up behind me.

"Pinocchio, what's this?" K.C. asks, meaning the game.

"Twenty-forty."

"You Pinocchio Joe?" someone asks in that great local accent. I nod.

"I heard of you. Hear tell you play a fair hand."

"He's the best," Nug says.

Another of the locals says, "I heard that name, too. Pinocchio Joe? Met some kids out in L.A. they was talking about who the best players were, and they said that back where they was from, this boy named Pinocchio Joe was as good as they got. And now here you are. Ain't that something? I know I heard that name. Stuck in my mind."

"What their names? The guys who tell you about him?" Nug asks.

"Oh, I don't know. I was there for the Diamond Jim Brady last summer. Mexican kid. And a black kid."

"Essay and Kevin," K.C. says. "They went out there after Churchville got raided."

A few hands' play. K.C. and Nug look over my shoulder, and finally, say, "Come on, man, let's go!"

I pick up my chips. Make eye contact with Billy Long Hair. Leave.

Outside the sun is setting. I look out at the town's lights coming up. Hear the water lapping away. Smell and feel a warm salty breeze.

Back in Maryland I tell my mom I was pretty sure I'd seen my father. She asked me if I'd talked to him and I said no. She asked me why not, and I told her I didn't know how. I just wanted to see him, I said. One time. Don't know why.

She was interested, though, and called the card room down there for a few nights, having him paged until she got hold of him. They had a good talk, she told me later. He asked about me. She filled him in.

"Did he know who I was when he saw me down there?"

"No. He said, 'That was my boy? Damn fine player.'"

I laugh. "I guess he wouldn't know what I look like."

"Yeah, he would. Admitted himself you look a lot like him."

"Maybe."

"It's been a long time since he's seen you."

"My whole life."

"Well no. Not that long. Since you were six, I guess."

"What do you mean?"

She's quiet a minute. We're in her kitchen. The baby's with Laura, at my place. Laura comes over and baby-sits a lot. Loves him a ton. She actually gives me some child support, too. We've worked things out, and she and Mary get along. I've looked for cattiness between them. Haven't found it.

My mom says, "He came up once. Here."

"My father? When?"

"You were about six."

"I met him?"

"No. But he saw you."

"What was I doing?"

"Sleeping. He came by, late one night, passing through. Said he wanted to see you. I told him I didn't think it was a good idea. He said he just wanted to see you. I told him your step-daddy at the time was home, and wouldn't let him in. He said he'd just climb in the window, then. Just wanted to see you. That's what he did, too. But he woke you, and you started screaming. I was just outside in the hall and knew what was happening, of course, but when your step-daddy came out, we went in. You said a man had come in the window and touched you. Scared you. I said it was just a burglar. You asked what that was. I said it was someone who came at night to take your money." She laughs. "You were so afraid." She laughs again. "And your step-daddy called the police! God."

She pauses. "I called your father at the motel he was staying at that night. Told him. He asked me not to tell you it had been him. Said he didn't want your only memory of him to be a scary one."

I smile. "What did you talk about with him? Last night, was it?"

"I told him how I was. How you were. Told him he was a grandfather."

"Oh, yeah? What did he say?"

"He was happy. Asked for a photo of the baby. And one of you, too. What do you think?"

I sit a moment. Say, "Okay."

"Let me send him that one of me holding the baby, so he can see how good I still look after all these years. You know the one I mean?"

I know, and later at home I dig into the closet looking for it, into a box full of pictures and important papers, and as I do I find a sheaf of photos Katrina had developed and mailed to me after we broke up. Great shots, some of them. Taken during our trip to Atlantic City, and during our walk in Las Vegas.

But looking through them, I see one I don't remember. One of her, which she must have taken herself. She's on the bed in this shot, shoulders hunched, hair strung out and limp, her eyes to the camera with that look of inexpressible bewilderment losers get after a really bad run. I hadn't noticed this shot before, so I turn it over for the date and see writing on the back. She'd written, "Remember I told you my father gave me money to shoot the documentary? I lost it. I lost it all, Joey. Twenty-five thousand. So here's the documentary. This one photo. The Picture of Gambling."

I'm kneeling there, holding in one hand that picture, and in the other hand John's birth certificate and the blood test result saying I was indeed his father, and pictures of him as a newborn, and I read again, on the back of the photo of Katrina in her sadness, "The Picture of Gambling."

And I think, one of many.

One of many.

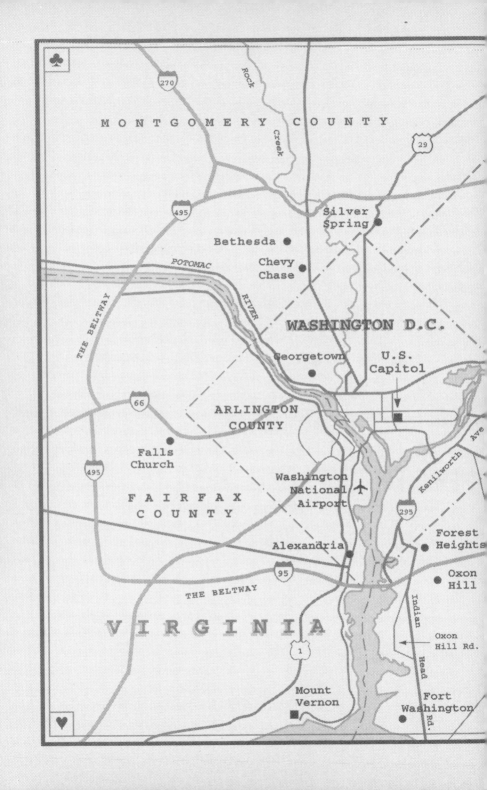

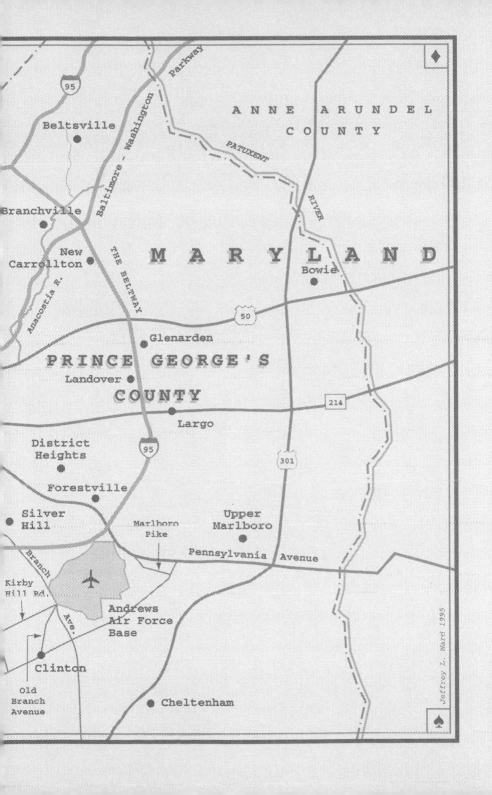